HER
PERFECT
DISAPPEARANCE

A.K. SMITH

This tense tale will keep readers on edge until its surprising finale.
- Kirkus Reviews

A.K. SMITH

Her Perfect Disappearance

An absolutely addictive tale of fate and second chances.

Bookswithsoul.com
Press

First published by Books With Soul® Press 2024

Previously published as Pseudocide by A.K. Smith

Second edition

ISBN (paperback): 978-1-949325-58-4
ISBN (hardcover): 978-1-949325-63-8

Editing by Jessica Lee Anderson

This book was professionally typeset on Reedsy.
Find out more at reedsy.com

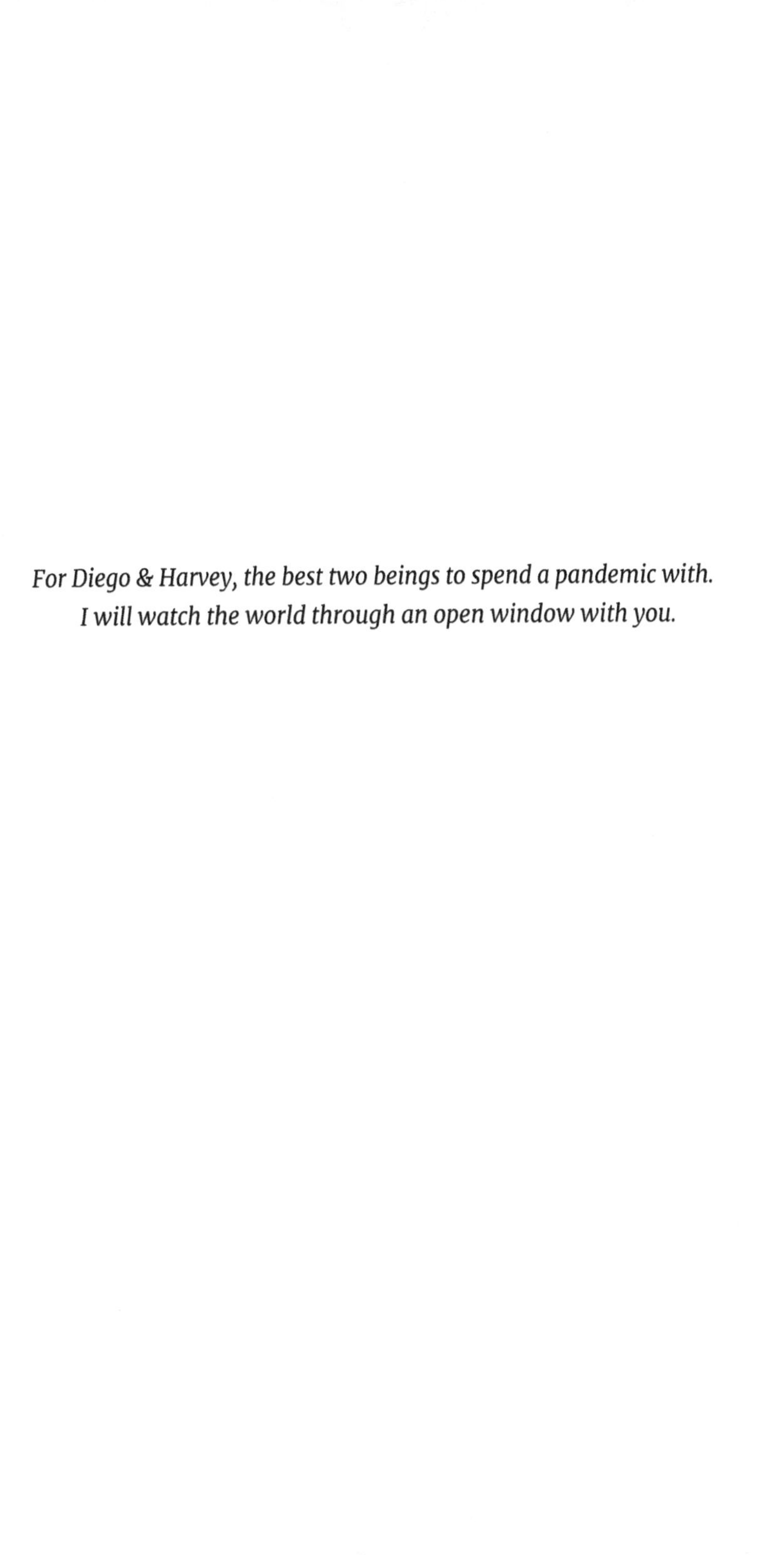

For Diego & Harvey, the best two beings to spend a pandemic with. I will watch the world through an open window with you.

A.K. SMITH

Her Perfect Disappearance

An absolutely addictive tale of fate and second chances.

Bookswithsoul.com
Press

First published by Books With Soul® Press 2024

Previously published as Pseudocide by A.K. Smith

Second edition

ISBN (paperback): 978-1-949325-58-4
ISBN (hardcover): 978-1-949325-63-8

Editing by Jessica Lee Anderson

This book was professionally typeset on Reedsy.
Find out more at reedsy.com

*For Diego & Harvey, the best two beings to spend a pandemic with.
I will watch the world through an open window with you.*

*For Diego & Harvey, the best two beings to spend a pandemic with.
I will watch the world through an open window with you.*

Contents

Praise for Her Perfect Disappearance

This tense tale will keep readers on edge until its surprising finale.
  -Kirkus Reviews

Fast-paced with unexpected twists, *Her Perfect Disappearance* intrigues and satisfies yet leaves you thinking about the characters long after the conclusion."
  –Jessica Lee Anderson, author of **Border Crossing**

"Maybe that's what tragedy does to you: it wakes you up and gives you a second chance at life." Her Perfect Disappearance exploration of this process and how Sunday discovers her own strengths and abilities to survive makes for a **thoroughly engrossing story that's hard to put down**.
  -D. Donovan, Senior Reviewer, Midwest Book Review.

"Either you will need to put it down a few times or you will keep reading until daylight."
  -Katie Did It Book Reviews

Other books by A. K. Smith

A Deep Thing

Pseudocide (soodo-syd):
the act of someone faking a death in attempt to start a new life,
often due to extreme circumstances.

Chapter 1

Raised by the Internet, HE and SHE, THE PLAN

This is happening. I am here and soon I will not be, but in this moment, I am safe. I put my pen in my mouth and bite down hard. My hand caresses the worn whiskey-colored leather of my journal, the words on the page echoing like a mantra in my head to the beat of the rushing water in the creek below.

April 17, 2017

Sunday Foster will be dead next week. I know this to be true because I am Sunday Foster. One day soon I will disappear, and all evidence will point to my death. Everyone wants to escape something. I want to escape my life. No, I'm not going to kill myself—pseudocide, not suicide.

The water provides white noise, blocking out my reality for at least a minute. My safe spot, my refuge, is a small patch of dirt under a low hanging tree by the creek below the house I live in. When I was younger it hid my body in its entirety. Sheltered me from all eyes except for the tiny silvery fish travelers who always swam below me in the stream. Now, my 5'5" frame can curl up cross-legged. But between my new height and my uncontrollable mane of blonde hair halfway down my back, it's impossible to hide.

There are other ways to hide. I love my journal, full of my thoughts and ideas. It belongs to me. A rare item paid for with cash, not an overcharged plastic card from the people I call HE and SHE. Thinking of them as anything but HE and SHE is impossible. They don't deserve the names Dad and Mom. Mothers and fathers are supposed to love their children. Not mine. I've been raised by the internet, silence, and anger.

I remember forcing myself to hand over fifty-five dollars of my hard-earned money three years ago in a shop down by the wharf in Baltimore, an eclectic place with a musty scent. I had imagined Shakespeare lounging against the old walls with cracks and peeling wallpaper, books stacked three feet high around clusters of bound words from the past and rows and rows of bookshelves almost touching the ceiling. A leather journal, filled with creamy white empty pages, beckoned to me, begging for the touch of ink. My companion now bears the stains of my tears and holds the secrets of my heart. A tight brown cord wraps around it three times to keep the truth hidden inside. No one will ever read my words—but somehow, the inked words on the paper make what I'm planning a reality.

Does leather burn?

If not, the pages will. Again, I rub my hand over the cover. I know I can't take my comrade with me—it's my witness to the truth.

Truth–what a concept. Faking my death will make my whole existence as a human being a lie. THE PLAN didn't start this way, but if I learned one thing in sixteen years, even the best-laid plans change.

Chapter 2

Two Weeks Earlier

I clear my throat, and with my right hand, hold my nose as I pick up the overflowing ashtray of cigarettes. The black ash clings to my fingers as I dump the dozens of crimped, pink-tinged sticks into a plastic bag. At 6:00 a.m., the pungent odor trapped inside is held hostage by the plugged holes of filth on the screened-in porch. The clogged squares in the screen and the line of trees declaring the woods' edge remind me of an edited photo with a pixelated filter.

SHE is still asleep. HE left the house five minutes ago.

I have sixty minutes before SHE wakes, and I head to school. This is my hour. I finish cleaning the bathroom and the living room and move to the kitchen. As I wipe the table and place the dishes in the dishwasher without making any noise, I imagine a happy family living here. I pour a glass of orange juice and lean back against the counter, visualizing a cheerful conversation between a mother and daughter, a scene from a television sitcom I watched as I child. Fictional stories of parents called Mommy and Daddy, who loved and supported their children. The fairy tale plays before me.

"*Sunday, you're running late for school. Come on down and eat, Honey.*"

"*Coming,*" *I answer back with a smile.*

"*I made your favorite eggs and extra crispy bacon.*" *A smiling mother kisses the side of my head as she squeezes me in a loving hug.*

"*Thanks, Mom. Ummm... I'm starving. You're the best!*"

Poof. The fairy tale scene vanishes, and I see HE, smashing the glass in the see-through kitchen cupboard doors followed by the sound of SHE screaming, "It's all your fault that he's so angry! Clean up your mess." The ear-piercing shatter, hammer pounded against glass, still vivid in my memory. My thumb rubs the scar of embedded glass on the palm of my hand. One of the many visible scars. Thinking of them as anything but HE and SHE is impossible.

I open the refrigerator door to put the juice back inside, staring at the empty shelves with two bottles of wine and some dried-up piece of crud.

I can't help myself and pick up the unknown squishy particle. I sniff, then hurl the disgusting clump into the garbage. My backpack and dress for work in one hand, I lift the trash bag, keeping my nose as far away from the opening as possible.

I'm out of here. I'm careful.

Timing is everything. My schedule is orchestrated for the minimum interaction with HE and SHE.

"Your parents must be proud. That's quite an impressive SAT score."

"Thank you, Mrs. Clark, they are ecstatic." The lie slips out with ease. HE and SHE have no idea I even took the SATs.

Vanilla lotion fills the air in the small office. That's one thing about me: I have an extraordinary power of smell. Maybe it's a freak talent. I can smell if a teacher had a drink the night before, and I can smell bad breath from Mason Hicks, even three rows away. Most times my superhero power of smell is a curse. Right now, even though it's pungent, Mrs. Clark's odor matches her pleasant personality. Sweet. Safe. Kind. I like my Guidance Counselor. I've decided if I had a grandmother, she would resemble Mrs. Clark. Behind the thick black glasses, I sense she sees a glimmer of the truth behind my façade, but she doesn't pry. I like that even more.

"I'm certain that with your perfect G.P.A. and these scores, a scholarship to some university out west is imminent. Are you positive you want to go so far away from your friends and family? University of Maryland is always looking for bright students just like you, Sunday."

I like the word 'imminent'. The scholarship is part of THE PLAN.

"California is my first choice. My parents are looking forward to warm winter trips in the sunshine." Another lie. If my parents tanned their white pasty bodies, it might interfere with their zombie tendencies. Zombies are unemotional with no mercy toward their victims, and with all the booze and pills they absorb, they are definitely in a decaying state. Just like the dead, they don't speak, they howl cruel words.

She smiles. "Sunday, you realize you're way ahead of the game. Your junior year isn't over. You might want to wait in case you change your mind over the summer." I keep eye contact, my eyelids blinking rapidly. She hesitates, studying me. "But, as you requested, here are the eight scholarship applications we discussed, and my letter of recommendation. I'll email you the letters with a stamp on it. Complete the forms, register online and gather your other letters, and start thinking about writing the college essay. You shouldn't rush it, so give yourself time to prepare your best words."

"Oh, I won't. I'm just excited. Thanks, Mrs. Clark." I push the corners of my mouth up, thinking of THE PLAN.

THE PLAN, a five-year project designed with precision and calculation. My way out. Away from HE and SHE.

Jack's electric smile chases the darkness from my thoughts as I walk out into the sunlit courtyard of Sunset Park High School.

"How'd it go?" he asks as he slings his arm around my shoulder.

"Great." I hold up the thick pile of applications.

"And your score?"

"Not too bad, I guess. 2250, 780 on Math." I can't suppress the smile; I studied assiduously for the SATs.

"Outstanding, Foster. Who wouldn't want you? Amazing!" He places his smooth lips on my cheek, his hands on both sides of my face. "I'm so proud of you. All your dreams are going to come true."

"I hope so." I kiss him on the mouth and linger, our electric current circling my stomach. I breathe in his unique scent, a mix of soap, coffee, and spearmint. I pull away with a whisper, "Miss you already. I'm off to catch the bus for work."

"Miss you already. See you later?"

"Not sure. I'll text you," I shout, running toward the bus stop to make the 389.

The heavy door of the courthouse slams with a thud in the echoing quiet of the vast space, and the few chins in the lobby lift and point in my direction. Taking a deep breath, I fix my coat and hair. Smile. Shoulders back. Eyes forward. Time to adjust my attitude and demeanor to match the clothes and make-up I've donned. I hand my key card to the uniformed security guard without hesitation. I belong here. I like the rules, strict procedures, and calmness. I can breathe and relax.

Until I see him.

Tyler Glass. Even with his back to me, he's unmistakable. His bleached-by-the-sun, wavy blond hair curls perfectly above his collar. And he's always dressed in the lightest of blues or grays to capture his unique eye color, which seems to make direct contact with whatever audience is under his spell. Blue-eyed god, or devil? Staring at the back of his crisp whisper of a blue shirt, I close my eyes and inhale. He invades my mind at work.

I follow his swagger down the pathway between the cubicles, his head only a few feet from the low ceilings. Tyler is four years older, enrolled at Towson University, and an intern at the courthouse where I work part-time. He oozes sex as he flirts with the women in the office. The real truth, which would never be spoken aloud: I'm in a constant state of anticipation of a chance encounter during my part-time shifts. He is one of the hottest older guys I've actually talked to, and he doesn't disappoint me when he whispers, "Did you know hot fudge sundaes are my favorite?" or "If Sunday's here, it's a weekend, let's go home!" and the one he sings under his breath, "Yeah, I'm easy, easy like Sunday morning." I laugh or roll my eyes, I've heard that joke from Jack. I want to act unaffected by his sultry breath next to my ear. When he is in close proximity, my heart beats faster, the hairs on my arms seem to be charged, pulling toward him, and I can smell an unknown earthy clove-like smell. It drives me crazy. I love Jack. What is wrong with me?

My body betrays me. Sweet, kind, and loving Jack has put up with me for almost a year and a half of not having sex, and I'm thinking about the courthouse hottie Tyler at work. I block Tyler from my mind and focus on Jack. Even if I didn't have Jack, Tyler would never be interested in a high school girl like me.

Jack wishes I did more than kiss, but he doesn't pressure me. Even when we get carried away and my shirt is unbuttoned, he's usually the one who stops and pulls away. I credit his parents. Good parents. They passed down wisdom mixed with love and they taught him strong morals and beliefs. Graduating from high school a virgin is important to me, it's one thing I can control that no one else can take from me. I know mistakes can happen because I don't think I'd be here otherwise because clearly HE and SHE didn't plan for me. In my mind, unless you are ready to be a good parent and ready for the responsibility of loving a child, wait. Jack agrees.

He gets that from his parents. They are the real deal. If you looked up "good mother" in the dictionary, there would be a picture of Jack's mother, Marcia (she insists on me using her first name). She is a kind, loving woman with gentle arms that hug you for no reason. She dresses trendy and doesn't act old. She gets us. She cares. She's had the sex talk with Jack and his sister Tara—more than once. I think it's cool.

Marcia's "do as I say, not as I did" speech is pretty effective. We were fourteen when Jack and I figured it out. His older sister Tara had just turned eighteen. Sitting in my special place down by the creek, all we could think about was how incredible it would be to be her age. After taking a stick and marking in the dirt Tara's age and his parent's anniversary, we computed that his mom gave birth to his sister when she was eighteen, only five months after their wedding date.

We worked up the courage to ask Marcia, and she answered, "I wondered when you would figure it out. Yes, we were young, broke, with a new baby, and we struggled." Her voice increased in volume. "That's what happens when you make love before you're ready." Marcia and Ed both dropped out of college. Ed quit to get a job selling copiers, and Marcia gave up her dream of ivy halls to give birth.

"Be whatever or whoever you want, but dream big," Marcia likes to recite, along with, "Make a plan."

I agree.

That's kind of where my plan comes from.

Ed and Marcia have plans for their kids. Plans full of lessons and love. They are offering Jack and Tara $1,000 if they never smoke cigarettes or try drugs by the time they reach their twenty first birthdays. No drug test needed to verify the truth, just love and trust. Jack honors his mother and father. It's part of what makes him so special. Because of how he was raised, I know he loves me and will wait for me as long as it takes.

I believe him. He will wait.

I'm lucky, when it comes to Jack.

And that brings me back to handsome college boy Tyler. Why does he affect me? I hate that he makes my body disagree with my brain. Today is his birthday. We both clock out of work, ready to walk out the doors of the courthouse at 5:30 p.m. when a few of the secretaries start singing Happy Birthday and present Tyler a round, carrot cake with thick icing and a big candy 20 on top.

"Oh, to only be twenty years old!" an older secretary says. "Your twenties will be the best years of your life."

I watch them flirt without shame.

"Oh, I'm living my best life right now with you great ladies.

I'm a pretty lucky guy, right? Surrounded all day by beauty. Now, is this Miss Julie's special carrot cake? Can't say I've ever tasted anything so delicious. Thank you." Tyler actually winks, and their faces turn rosy.

Birthdays and celebrations make everyone laugh and smile. Yes, "being twenty" would be a wonderful life, I agree. At twenty, I'll be far away, in college, doing something with purpose.

I stand there holding my piece of cake, lost in good thoughts.

Tyler's breath tickles my ear as he whispers, "Sunday, come out to dinner with me."

His scent and his hot breath give me a shiver. His blonde hair is an adorable mess from the secretary's hugs, and he flashes his gorgeous sexy smile, waiting for my reply.

He is asking me, a sixteen-year-old with a crooked nose and eyes too big for my face, out to dinner.

He knows my name.

He is asking ME out.

Every inch of me wants to say yes.

"I can't. My science project's due, and I don't think my boyfriend would be too happy." I smile back at him, knowing my words rush out like an idiot, wishing I could say yes.

"Really? It's my birthday. I'm going to eat dinner all alone. Just sayin'." He bites his lip in such a way that warmth rises on my cheeks. "My roommates are away at a basketball game. Doesn't that sound lonely? Poor, abandoned Tyler, all alone, eating ramen noodles... unless you come eat a birthday meal with me? Come on, it's only dinner for my birthday, not a date."

Okay, he said the words that push me.

It's not a date. This is research.

Tyler came here from California, and UCLA is one of my top picks for schools out west.

"Okay." The word spills out in front of me before I have any control to snatch it back.

"Great."

Tyler doesn't register surprise as he casts a winning grin. "I'm driving. I know where to go."

I wish I hadn't worn my blue dress, a wrap dress from H&M that ties in the front. It was an impulse buy, part of a shopping spree for my job at the courthouse. I would never wear the business dresses and suits to school, but putting them on and going to work seemed like dress-up. An adult costume. Now I wonder if the top reveals too much. My boobs fill out the blue lacey Victoria's Secret bra underneath, which makes me worry about my secret tattoo: the words "live free" printed in a tiny circle, about the size of a dime. I can see the edge of the tattoo if I look straight down—a consequence of one of the ugly rampages with HE and SHE.

It happened a night SHE had passed out after drinking two bottles of wine, and HE had punched the fridge, smashed the plates, and thrown spaghetti sauce all over the kitchen. HE left to wherever it is HE goes and I had snuck out and drove to a tattoo shop near University Park. The brown-eyed tattoo artist, Max, blew me off as soon as I walked in the door because I didn't have any ID. But when he saw my rendering, the size of the tattoo and the two simple words, he paused, studied my face, and said, "I'm sorry, can't do it. Come back when you're really 18."

Pain is a childhood friend I loathe but sometimes need. A video and a home tattoo kit taught me how to ink my own skin. Jack is the only other witness to my hidden impulse. And now, after the slow healing, Jack likes the tiny tattoo, often tracing the circle with his finger. I think he likes it because he's the only one who knows it exists.

Tyler's eyes focus on the cleavage in my flushed chest. With confidence, he orders a dirty martini. The dark-haired, pretty waitress turns to me. "IDs, please."

"The martini is for me. Young Sunday is helping a lonely twenty-one-year-old enjoy a decent dinner, before I hit the party with my buddies." He holds out his bogus license. His eyelashes never flicker as his lips slide into a smooth smile.

The waitress turns her scrutiny off me and focuses on Tyler, eyeing him up and down like a delicious cupcake she wants to lick. Within minutes, she brings the staff over to the table to sing Happy Birthday. As their voices rise higher, my cheeks flush red. The attention adds a centralized energy in the room. Everyone is looking RIGHT AT US.

Us. Together. I still can't wrap my head around what I am doing. What am I doing?

The first martini is on the house.

"Taste it." Tyler slides the delicate martini glass across the white tablecloth.

"No thanks."

"Oh, come on. Have you ever tasted a dirty martini?"

"No."

"Try it."

It tastes like earth mixed in with bitter olives, a man's drink. When he ordered the second one, I smiled, but my gut constricted. HE's blood-shot eyes flashed in my mind. I heard my father's cruel words that came with sucking down alcohol. "You are stupid. If I didn't have to take care of you, I could have a better life. You and your worthless mother." Alcohol loves a cruel vocabulary.

"Have you been on the UCLA campus?" I ask, focusing on the task at hand.

"Of course, I've been to the Bruin Bash, it's an annual festival that kicks ass. Maybe you come out when I'm home visiting, and I'll give you a tour?"

"I would love to visit next year, though I'm not sure it will happen, but thanks for the offer." He is handsome and kind.

"Well, let me know, because I have lots of frequent flyer miles, I can probably score you a free ticket."

When the waitress brings him the third martini, Tyler continues to be electric, milking the twenty-first birthday story for the entire staff, and recounting stories of UCLA, sharing tips with me. His voice increasing in volume and charisma.

Biting my lip, I check my phone. Jack's texted me twice. Sweat forms under my arms and on the back of my neck.

"Sunny California is a place where you can be whoever you dream of. You can create your own path, exactly the way you want it. I might have to start calling you Sunny. You'll love UCLA, it's like going to another country compared to here. Palm trees, new clubs, young people everywhere, free thinkers." Tyler leans in close, our heads almost touching from across the table. "The beaches, the people and the weather, you'll fit right in as a summer girl." A slow sexy smile lit up his face. "You might never come back, just turn into a California Girl."

Tyler paints a picture of a place I imagine in my dreams. As much as I was enjoying the dinner, my stomach feels queasy when I think of Jack. At 7:00 p.m., he texts. again. **You on your way home?**

ALMOST, I text back, adding a frustrated smiley face. What am I doing here? My throat feels thick with guilt.

The restaurant in Fells Point, a nostalgic waterfront area, has a vibe of a time-gone-by atmosphere, the streets lined with soft lights reflected on cobblestones and old warehouses turned into pubs and shops. It would be at least another twenty-five minutes to get home.

"I like your name." Tyler squints his eyes and runs his hand through his wavy rock star hair, his square jaw jutting out. "Are you always so serious, Sunday?"

"Am I serious?"

He laughs and touches my hand. His long warm fingers linger on my clasped hands on the table. He lowers his chin and studies me.

Those eyes, maybe too pretty for a man, but mixed in with his other strong features paint an interesting portrait.

"Excuse me." As I push my chair back, a loud scraping screech echoes through the intimate dining area. My face is on fire, like the spot on my hand where he touched me. Tyler stands when I leave the table.

This is an innocent dinner. Why am I so nervous? I inhale deeply and let my breath out slowly as I study myself in the bathroom mirror. Flushed face, shiny eyes. I haven't even been drinking.

He stood up when I left. His manners are classy. From the few conversations in the office, I know he came from the country club set. I heard the law clerk whisper a joke about old money and Tyler. Not that I've ever known someone else with old money before, but I get the idea—although I pictured a dusty, dark attic with boxes teeming full of cash, untouched and forgotten. It's hard to imagine Tyler untouched and forgotten. His father, a judge in Berkeley, knew Judge Henderson in the Baltimore Superior Court, where we worked. By the time he started interning, his reputation had preceded him: the office gossip was that, besides his looks and his swagger, he had ultra-rich connections.

When I return to the table, Tyler smiles at me. Deep breath in. Deep breath out. This is just dinner. Rich lobster soup, grilled salmon, spinach, and truffle risotto, like nothing I've ever tasted. No wonder why I fumble over which fork to use.

Tyler picks up the closed leather folder with the check and slides a silver credit card in it. "You can take me out someday to lunch in California."

The brunette waitress flashes her long fake eyelashes, bumping into Tyler as he stands to leave, and for a minute I was sure she slipped him a little white folded-up piece of paper. I wonder if I could ever be so bold. Was it that easy to snag a guy like Tyler?

Everyone in the dining room wishes him Happy Birthday when we leave, yelling things like, "You're only twenty-one once! Live it up!"

Tyler slings his arm around my shoulders as we walk to his car. I shouldn't allow his triceps to rest on my skin, with his hand dangling close to my beating heart—but I am not sure I exactly want him to move. Where he touches me, I pulsate. I glance around to see if anyone notices my intoxication, his special smell all consuming.

He comes around to open my door. "My lady."

I laugh as he remote control starts his black Land Rover, and the rock bass vibrates the car. The music pulses louder as Tyler maneuvers through the side streets and jerks the vehicle onto the expressway, flying by other cars on the highway. He crosses two lanes and yanks the car to the next exit. I dig my nails into the armrest.

"Tyler, what are you doing?"

The empty exit is dark, a turnoff to an old county back street leading to a historical lookout point. Speeding, he flies down the tree-lined road.

"The martini's going right through me. I need to pee. it'll just take a minute."

He makes a sharp turn and pulls over at the Civil War monument. The moon hides behind the clouds, making the large stone monument hard to see.

I wait in the car for what seems like an eternity. Glancing through the rear window, I see Tyler leaning against the back of the Land Rover. What's he doing? Finally, I open the door and walk to the back.

He opens the tailgate.

"What are you doing? Are you okay?"

He pulls me into his arms and kisses me hard and long. I can't help but kiss him back. I pull away, breathing fast. The tang of olives lingers in my mouth.

"Tyler, I have a boyfriend. I think you are great, really great, but I have a boyfriend." My voice feels raspy, lacking conviction.

He grabs my shoulder and his other hand cups my face. He kisses me again, this time slow and gentle. It feels good. I know it's wrong. Sexy. Almost grown-up. He's a great kisser and his strong cologne smells mysterious and dreamy. He pauses, studying my face, smiles, and goes in for another kiss. He holds my face gently in both hands.

He kisses me with intensity. Lost in the moment, my heart races in a new rhythm. I want to forget everything about my life for a minute and focus on how this hot man is into me, Sunday Foster. Placing his hand on my chest, he kisses me again. I wonder if the vibration of my heart thumping is detectable to his hand. My phone dings. Jack. *What am I doing? This is so wrong.*

I attempt to nudge him away, but we are too close. He doesn't budge. A new bitter body odor permeates the air, and I'm not sure if it is from him or me.

I push him back a second time with no result. His heat and weight crush against me.

I push harder, to no avail. I drive my elbow into his chest, my heart racing, this time in alarm. "Tyler."

His fist pushes into my back, his biceps holding me in place.

"Are you kidding me, Sunday? You're a tease? I know you want me. I can feel you." His other hand slides under my dress and his fingers slip under my panties. I gasp.

Lightning fast, he strikes. One pull of the wraparound tie and my dress falls open, exposing my bra. He pushes me backwards into the rear of the Land Rover. I lose my balance as my hands try to tie my dress. He unzips his pants before grabbing my two hands with one of his, shoving me with force, my dress gaping open. He kisses my breasts.

"Tyler, stop! I can't do this."

The more I struggle, the tighter he holds both my hands to the side. Bent in an awkward position, half-lying in the Land Rover, I can't stand up. The pain on my spine is excruciating. Panic knocks my breath away.

I whimper, gulping air. "Tyler, you're hurting me. Stop, please. No, Tyler, no—please stop." The tears spill down my face.

My voice fails me. In disbelief, I don't scream. I don't yell for help at the top of my lungs. I push weakly with my two hands caught in his left hand, trying to lift my head up. "Stop, stop, please stop." Is this really happening?

It's over in minutes. Tyler kisses the side of my face. He lets go of my wrists. Still in an awkward, slanted position, gasping, shaking, and in shock, I try to stand up and fall, hitting the ground, losing control of my legs.

Something wet trickles down my legs. He helps me up and then tries to kiss my lips. I turn away, sobbing. Speechless.

"Jesus, Sunday. Don't cry now that you changed your mind. I did you a favor—you had to get it over with sometime. Get yourself together."

Chapter 3

Rain, Poker, and The Plan

Sour milk. Why do the fumes of rain at a bus stop smell like spoiled milk? My shoes are sopping wet, and I don't care. I know I have to get up and walk to Jack's house. A futuristic looking homeless man wrapped in plastic bags watches me. I'm sure he's puzzled why I don't move. Half of me is covered, half is getting soaked. He has a dirty tarp tied to three tree branches above him, the tree about 100 ft away. I wonder if my sadness is as noticeable, as the pain on his face?

I sit, not even flinching but blinking the rain away. Can I face Jack? Could he possibly know I'm no longer a virgin when he sees me? I feel different inside, violated, angry, and mad. The last two days, I skipped school, work, and spent the day hidden in my room sleeping. SHE never even noticed, I didn't go to school. I told Jack I didn't feel well. Bad cramps. Which is funny because I should be getting cramps today. I have painful periods. Not that I'm not in pain now.

I want to erase Tyler from my memory.

The rain is like spittle, just misty spits in the air as I force myself to walk to Jack's house.

I need to pretend like this never happened. Move on and focus on THE PLAN.

THE PLAN has evolved over the years, and with thoughtful strategizing, I will escape. I'm at the top of the list to receive a full ride college scholarship. Far, far away I'll go. I'll never have to think about HE or SHE again, and now I can add Tyler to the list.

Money is a big part of THE PLAN. It has to be. I have to get out and survive. I've been saving for the last four years, babysitting, tutoring, and selling items online. I've sold just about everything—outdated electronics, smart devices, and even vintage clothing I pick up at garage sales and trash bins. Basically, any way I can make cold hard cash, I pounce on it. Before HE and SHE were so overextended, I used to charge clothes, take them back, and get the cash. Those days are over. My nest egg is up to $3,235.00. I wanted to double that, but I can't go back to work at the courthouse. Not with Tyler there.

I have back-ups. I've researched every student loan, grant and partial scholarship out there. If I have to, I will get emancipated. Whatever it takes, I am escaping.

Jack knows about THE PLAN and somewhat supports me. He understands that *I want to get away*, but he doesn't understand that *I need to get away*. Jack knows most of the ugly truth about HE and SHE, because I can't keep anything from him, UNTIL NOW.

God, I don't know how to tell Jack about Tyler.

Over the years, I minimized the viciousness of HE and SHE, and Jack knows the less time I spend at home, the better it is. He knows how much it upsets me to talk about them, so he doesn't press me on the subject. I can't imagine trying to tell him about

Tyler. I'm focused on the goal ahead.

Jack is the closest thing to family that I've got. I've kept naïve classmates and wannabe friends at a distance.

I shuffle on the sidewalk, the rain is falling heavier now, as I see Jack's house up the street. Warm light radiates from inside. Jack is inside with his mom and dad. I'm sure it smells like heaven in there. We've been friends since sixth grade, the day I stuck up for him when the bullies in the lunchroom were making fun of the fresh pink scar on his cheek.

I stand in the rain, remembering that day like yesterday. That day changed everything for me. Plopping myself beside him in the empty seat at his table, I noticed a repulsive, pink, jagged line of healing skin and bruises on his cheek. "What happened to your face?" I believed if you couldn't stop looking at something, you should acknowledge it instead of pretending it doesn't exist. The pus-filled scab was hard to ignore. I wondered for a moment if he had a home life like mine.

"I tripped on the ice and hit my sister's skate blade." He shrunk in his seat.

The bullies were having a field day coming up with nicknames to describe the cut on his face.

"Does anyone know how it happened?" I whispered.

He shrugged his shoulders, not looking me in the eyes.

"Don't worry, we are going to make up the best story about how you cut your face. You'll be a hero."

He looked at me, I mean really looked at me, and right in the eyes. I liked that because in his eyes I saw something different, something kind, and something unexpected that I couldn't describe. He invited me to his house for an after-school snack that day and I concocted a story of how he walked across Briars Lake and he saved a dog from drowning. I was a good liar even back then. The dog's name was Harvey and the owners called Jack a hero. By the time we were done, I couldn't look at his cheek without seeing Jack rescuing a black soaking-wet shivering dog named Harvey.

Going to Jack's house after school is the best part of my life. He is my hero. I find the courage to make the rest of the way there now. As I raise my hand to knock, the door of his cookie cutter home opens and that Grant family smell makes me want to cry and release my shame and sorrow of the other night. Cinnamon, mixed in with onions with a splash of fabric softener invades my nose. I'm addicted to the smell, the Grant family, and their happiness. For a split second I want to tell them what happened, but the words don't surface. I can't. Impossible. I blink back the tears and thank the rain for making my face wet.

"Where's your umbrella? Sunday, you're soaking wet." Jack's mom goes to hug me but then pushes me inside and grabs a towel to help me dry off.

I need the hug.

"The boys are playing poker, in the dining room."

"Jack? Hello, Jack, are you in or out?" Jack's Dad, Ed looks as irritated as I feel.

"Call." Jack slides another poker chip in the kitty and flashes his adorable smile.

Ed has laser eyes on Jack, talking to me without looking. "Hi Sunday. No umbrella?"

"I forgot it."

"What? It's raining out?" Jack starts to get up to give me a hug.

"Wait, Jack. Sunday, Jack will be with you in a minute. All in." Ed pushes his large stack of poker chips in.

Jack is biting his lip and shrugging his shoulders.

"If you lose, you're mowing the lawn Saturday." Ed winks at me.

"I got nothin', and I don't feel like playin', but maybe you're bluffin' again." Jack pushes his chips in.

"And you're going to tip over backwards if you keep leaning on the back of the chair like that."

"Three Queens." Ed scoops the chips to his side.

"It's your tell, Jack," Ed says, grinning, scooping up the pile of chips with an annoying chuckle.

"Stop it, Dad, why are you laughing at me?"

Jack tries to catch himself at the last second, as his chair loses control and he flips backward.

Ed shakes his head and with an exaggerated loud whisper, "Jack, it's your tell!"

"What are you talking about?"

"Figure it out, son, or don't play poker with real money. Ever. And next time, don't play cards and leave Sunday waiting for you."

The words roll through my mind. *It's your tell.*

Chapter 4

Geek Shoes, Birthday Presents, and Bullies

The trickling stream usually gives me clarity, but not today. My focus is stuck on the black and blue bruises on my wrist. Images of Tyler crushing my wrists together with his left hand flash like a blinking light behind my closed eyes. I couldn't tell Jack what I'd let Tyler do. Last night, I ended up fake sleeping during an entire movie. Finally, when Jack fell asleep, I snuck out. I didn't want to wake him.

I won't ever be ready to tell him. I can't. I am ashamed. I'm mortified and infuriated. How, how did I let this happen?

I throw the flat matte stone in the creek with a vengeance, and then I wipe my tears with my sleeve. I'm out of my mind, blaming myself for going out to dinner with Tyler and then kissing him. I definitely kissed him.

Oh yes. I clench my teeth and close my eyes. I remember what he said, what he called me. Maybe he was right: I asked for it, I was a tease. Sick to my stomach, I try to push it out of my mind.

I hear a branch snap and a rustle. I jump, but I don't turn. It's my next-door neighbor Amir. I'm certain as he always shows up when I need to be alone. I'm used to it. Somehow, he feels when I'm in trouble.

Amir slowly enters my side vision. He positions his chunky body on the rock nearest the water, about twenty feet from me, his shoes slowing turning darker with water and mud below his dress pants. Does he know they're getting wet? It's ridiculous, his father never lets him buy jeans. I feel sorry for him, being controlled by his father, but I understand putting up with things that are nonsensical. Somehow, our proximity as neighbors and the fact that both our parents are freaks have created a weird friendship.

We sit in silence, Amir staring at the water through his old-fashioned black frame glasses and thick lenses. Hidden under the square glasses are kind eyes. His left pant leg continues to become wet with water splashes, and I can't stop staring at the dark stain. It makes me think of everything I don't want to think about it.

"Everything okay, Sunday?"

I lift my eyes and notice a cut on his cheek. The raw wound makes me flash to Jack, who still bears the scar on his right cheek from the so-called saving the dog story. How many times have I kissed Jack's scar? My stomach pangs sharply. I swallow my grief and turn my focus on Amir.

"What happened to your face?"

Amir adjusts his glasses, focusing on the running water. He glances down at his pants, the spots growing darker. He is clearly getting wet, but he doesn't move.

"HLB," he grumbles.

HLB stands for Hard Liquor Boys. The two cliques at Sunset Park High School, the Hard Liquor Boys (HLB) and the Dream Team (respectively, six spray-tanned wannabe models and a clan of seven guys, mostly from the wrestling and football teams) run the school.

Even though Amir and I are both high-scoring academic nerds, Amir, with his Muslim mother and militant father, enthralls the HLBs. His body is a magnet pulling the bullies toward him. They're drawn to him to knock him down on a daily basis.

It's been tough for Amir for as long as I can remember. Amir moved in next door when I turned ten. I remember it clearly because, just like today, I was crying in my backyard, hiding on the side of the house so SHE would not see me from her smoking porch. HE and SHE had missed my birthday again. Even though I expected it, at ten, it hurt like hell. Amir gently spoke to me behind the broken slat on his side of the fence, introducing himself as the new neighbor.

Casting quick glances through the barrier, he sat in silence, pretending not to see the wet tears on my face or the discolored swollen pattern of blue, purple and yellow welts on my arm. I'm not sure why but I told him the truth: that my parents forgot my birthday. He never asked about the bruises.

Every year since that day, Amir has always given me some sort of present on my birthday. He never forgets. Sometimes it's a candy bar or a used book, but this year, for my sixteenth, it was a little pair of blue amethyst earrings. His face was bright red when he handed me a little wrapped box. "It's your birthstone." It was sweet, but the expression on his face for some reason made me uncomfortable.

He hasn't changed much from back then: he still wears the dress shoes and out-of-style slacks forced on him by his father. Amir's thick black hair is cut so short that when it grows in, it surrounds his head unevenly giving him an oversized head. His brown skin is dotted with acne sores and his braces seem to crack his lips. He's not helping his cause as he has a bad habit of continuously chewing on his bottom lip. But, for what he lacks in outward appearances, his kindness to me is transparent.

His father, an ex-soldier, met his mother during Desert Storm. They fell in love, got married and came back to the States, where Amir James Carter was born. Now retired, his father's full attention is on Amir. He wants him to be the doctor he never was.

Amir loves technology and computers and envisions himself as the next Mark Zuckerberg—being a doctor isn't even on his radar—but he never voices this to his father. He lies, too.

His father calls him Dr. AJ, a nickname Amir hates, but it's better than what the bullies call him: terrorist, towelhead, or Amir the Queer.

Amir doesn't have many friends, except for Eric Beck and me. Our covert friendship exists only outside the school boundaries, and Eric, another neglected, nerdy soul who is a senior like Amir, barely utters a word at school. He comes over occasionally to surf Amir's computer and play some crazy zombie killing video game in Amir's basement. I'm not into video games. The game they play is an exceptionally dark and disturbing game, and when I ask Amir why he likes it, he shrugs his shoulders.

Amir watches me through the trees—he's done it for years. He follows me when I escape to the clearing by the creek, my special place. Most days I know he's sitting back in the tree line before he approaches me. Sometimes we sit in silence and throw rocks. Some days, we quietly complain about our parents.

Amir is aware that my family situation sucks. He witnesses the yelling from HE and watches SHE, the medicated smoker who never speaks or touches her daughter, sit on the porch. Amir is smart. He observes and remembers everything, filing it away in the computer of his brain. In the last six years, Amir has witnessed a lot of what happens next door to his house. He has heard the crashes, thumps and my cries. Jack only knows what I tell him, but Amir witnesses the reality. He hears the truth. Just like Jack, Amir knows about THE PLAN.

Jack also doesn't know how much Amir and I whisper our dreams of escape. Amir has his own plan, and it does not include medical school. We talk about the day we will be uncontrolled. Jack would have a hard time identifying with the overwhelming desire that compels Amir and me.

I don't have issues with the bullies like Amir and Eric do. Not anymore. I think they finally figured out I just don't care. I mean, I really don't. I've been bullied by my parents my whole life. What these high school kids think they have on me when they call me names doesn't begin to touch the cruelty of not being loved my entire life. HE has called me awful names so many times, their words roll right off me.

The late afternoon is a perfect early spring temperature with a blue sky and soft breeze. I try to remember how a wonderful day used to make me happy.

"Are you going on the Spring Fling whitewater trip?" Amir says quietly as he tosses another stone in the creek. Amir must be in another growing spurt, even his sleeve doesn't seem to reach his wrist.

"I don't know. I know Jack..." My voice quivers as I say Jack's name. I can't go over to his house tonight. Last night was tough enough. "He would like to go. He loves whitewater rafting." I put on my fake face, a gesture I have mastered. Like a classic actress winning an award, I can speak and mask my emotions. "It's a couple weeks from now, so we'll see. Should be fun. You going?" I think about Jack again and then Tyler. I want to throw up.

"Not sure. I don't know... it's a junior-senior thing, I've never gone before, but thought maybe I should go because I'm a senior. Eric mentioned he might be going."

"Eric Beck, whitewater rafting? Now that's a funny picture." I snort, only because it seems weird to picture Eric Beck out in the water.

Amir's face darkens and he turns away, his other pant leg starts getting wet. I know Amir will not go on this trip. Why is he acting so strange? He never participates in anything in school. His father is probably on him to attend, since the permission slips and all the parental forms were sent through email and mail. Mine are oblivious to any school activity. If I wanted to go, I could sign the consent form, like I have for the past five years.

"You should go, maybe like a last thing to do before you graduate." I try to sound convincing, supportive.

Amir told me before that his father was elated over his acceptance into the pre-med program at MIT, so perhaps they were getting on him about participation in school functions before he graduated. I couldn't imagine declaring a major that I had no intention of staying in. Once Amir graduated and turned 18, his father was going to be surprised. I knew Amir would not become a doctor. Nausea hits me again.

"You sure you're all right? Are you sick?" Amir asks.

The word pregnant slithers in the back of my mind like an evil snake. My period was due three days ago, and it didn't happen. I'm never late. My stomach hurts just thinking about it. I bow my head...tucking my grief under my skin. I know what I have to do.

"Sunday, is everything okay?"

I look at him, this gentle techie oddity, and the words I want to say are stuck behind my teeth. I want them to spill out of my mouth. I need to talk to someone about what happened. If I could just tell someone. Someone. Anyone. A squirrel runs down the edge of the bank, knocking rocks, stones rolling, breaking the silence. The confessional moment is over.

I close my eyes, digging my nails into the palm of my hand so they stop shaking.

I get up, brush the dirt off my jeans, and look back in the direction of my house. "Everything is fine. I gotta run to the store."

Chapter 5

THE DARK, Lies, and Loss

"Can I help you?" a worker asks.

Really? I want to shout. Never have I been asked if I needed help in a dollar store. Do I have 'I'm buying a pregnancy test' written on my face?' I just want to get it and go. God, I wish I had somewhere to go. It's Sunday, ha, my day of the week, and I lied to Jack, again. I've lied to him all week about work. I can't go back to work, ever. I called in sick for five days. They will fire me. It doesn't matter.

Jack matters, but I can't face him right now.

Now there is a line at checkout and everyone can see my purchase. I want to run.

"Did you find everything okay?" the old woman asks and then looks at what I'm buying. Silence.

She quickly bags it as I pay for the test, and run out the door to get on the bus. When I finally look out the window, there's a billboard for Clarks Pharmacy.

A sign. Clark. I know where I want to go.

Sandy Beach State Park.

After an hour on the bus. I arrive. It's crowded. Sunday, family day. Walking away from the crowds, I need to think, alone. I can't believe what could actually be happening right now. I'm late. Only five days now, but I'm late. As I perch upon a rock, I know this could change everything.

The sand escapes through my closed fist. As it runs through, I scoop another fistful. The unknown is definitely better than the known—it has to be. What I know is that sick, awful guys are wrapped up in handsome packages. What I know is that I habitually lie to everyone; no one knows the truth about the incident with Tyler, not even Jack. What I know is that HE and SHE are self-absorbed, materialistic, addictive, hateful freaks who couldn't care less about their only child.

Well, let me clarify: I'm not their only child. I'm the only living child.

Laughter, yelling and music. The soundtrack of families creates a melody. The distant shimmer of the bay is constantly changing, I search the horizon for answers. I can think here. I can think about Clark and remember.

Once, there was Clark. Clark was the first. I am the last. Clark died before I was born. HE and SHE do not have any photos of Clark hanging on the wall, or in a frame, or at the office. Clark is not spoken of. Ever. I know that if my big brother was alive, he would let me cry on his shoulder about Tyler. He would probably beat him up to teach him a lesson.

My discovery of Clark was an accident.

I was seven and remember sneaking into SHE's room when I was left home alone, yet again. SHE has a separate bedroom from HE. Perching myself on her enormous window seat covered with pretty pink flowers, I played dolls. Playing with my dolls in her room—was off limits to me. This particular day, the window seat offered a warm place to create a tri-level house for my dolls. Designing their new home with my treasure trove of small objects—jewelry boxes, cardboard containers, coins, tiny plastic furniture, and a few pieces of carpet and fabric—I began building a lovely habitat. The creak of the front door opening and closing struck me like a shrill fire alarm, spreading a pounding panic. I demolished my newly-built real estate. Rushing to gather my pieces of plastic furniture and little boxes, I cringed as one of my little blue marbles (used as the bath water in the miniature doll tub), rolled, dropped, and hit the floor, rolling again under the bed. In my hurry to retrieve it, my elbow hit the Bible on the night stand, and it went flying. Three pictures stuck inside the pages, fluttered to the floor. A cute boy sporting a goofy smile, wearing a striped navy blue and green shirt, smiled out at me.

I forgot about the marble.

The boy, two or three years old, sat behind a red and yellow Big Wheel. His smiling face captivated me. As I picked the picture up, the larger photo underneath, froze me in place. SHE was actually smiling, and HE was suppressing a laugh as they sat in the sand with the boy. All three dressed in white shirts and khaki shorts with black flip-flops. Their white teeth glowed against golden skin. Who were they? Imposters? Not my parents—khaki and white did not exist in their closet.

A sharp pain in my gut, startled me. Who was this kid, this cute boy who made them laugh and smile? HE and SHE had never been happy with me. Never.

Now that I know he is my brother, I can see the resemblance. Clark was beautiful. He had the same blonde wavy hair as me, but with startling green eyes and large lips. My eyes are blue, sometimes blue-green in sunlight, but way too large for my face.

His were perfectly sized, sea-green. It was hard to remember my thought process at such a young age, but I remember entering the kitchen, gently carrying the Bible like a platter with the pictures on top. I asked something simple like, "Who is this?"

SHE, getting a red plate out of one of the upper cabinets, glanced at the Bible in my hand with the pictures lying on top. Her face contorted and she dropped the plate. Just like that. It hit the granite countertop with a crack and shattered into little red pieces. Transfixed, not bothering to pick up the broken shards, her eyes lingered on the photographs.

Silence.

My mother stepped on the sharp broken fragments of the ceramic red plate to rip the Bible and the pictures from my little hands. She walked out to the screened-in porch. Blood oozed from the cut in her foot, leaving little smudges on the white tile floor. Gripping the black book and photos, frozen, in her hand, she stood locked in place. Minutes passed.

Finally, she moved, opening the Bible and placing the photos back inside. The click of the lighter was deafening. Smoke filled the air. I crept back to my room.

Her hideout, her screened-in smoking porch, was another place off-limits. I had been warned not to bother her when she was out there. SHE was out there a lot. I knew the consequences. No, SHE wasn't one to rip the cabinets off the door or scream nasty insults like HE, but SHE used *THE DARK*.

I obeyed.

I waited forever for her to come inside. She smoked cigarette after cigarette, staring at the trees. As the sun sank lower behind the trees, and the long-tailed shadows engulfed the porch, SHE left her hideaway. I kept my distance for the next few hours and then I cautiously approached her. Like a fly, landing close then backing off, I would work up my nerve and move a little closer, waiting for her to look my way. Always invisible to her, this time I was certain if I stepped in her angry circle, she would throw me across the room.

THE DARK was my punishment for years. It seemed like every few months, I did something to make her mad, something where she could no longer look at me. Sitting alone, in silence, lights off. I hated *THE DARK*. SHE put in special blackout shades and curtains on the only glass block window in the empty spare bedroom. When they were closed (and they were always drawn), I wished my eyes would adjust, but it was lightproof. Tense and anxious, I loathed not knowing or seeing, and it smelled like cleaner fluid. After five hours, anything could be sitting beside me. I hated *THE DARK*.

So, I played my fly game, getting close, then scurrying away. I tiptoed, as if walking over hot red coals, worried about my words. After hours of circling, I snuck up. I didn't touch her. I knew better. I waited in silence beside her, afraid to form a word, and finally, in her hoarse smoker's voice, she answered the question she knew I wanted to ask.

"That is your brother, Clark. He died."

I held my breath, trying to process what she was saying.

The pattern of her voice was off beat, like a video when the words didn't match the mouths. "We never talk about Clark in this house. Never. It was a very long time ago. He is gone."

She wasn't looking at me just staring out at the shadows on the porch. Her voice returned to her normal monotone. "Sunday, we will not discuss this again." She paused. "Never, ever mention it to your father. Do you hear me?"

Frozen in place, I went mute.

"Sunday, do you understand me?"

I nodded my little head, and as soon as I did, her eyes glazed over and she walked out of the room. I'm sure she put one of those little white pills in her mouth that turn her even more into a zoned-out zombie. I shivered.

The words "your brother" vibrated in my mind. Maybe there was someone else like me; maybe they'd killed him. My young mind created murderous scenarios.

The word *brother* penetrated my heart and has become a warm blanket I put on when I need companionship. In *THE DARK*, I pictured his smiling face and sea-green eyes and whisper to Clark, asking him questions he never answered. The mere idea that I wasn't alone in this world gave me courage.

I heeded the warning SHE uttered that day. I have never brought up Clark's name again. Never. But at no time do I stop thinking about my brother. My brother Clark.

I knew I would have to figure out exactly what had happened to Clark. It took me five years to find him.

The Sea Watch Library became my second home, a quiet place where I could investigate in the computer lab and discover the truth. And eventually, I did.

HE and SHE used to live in Fenwick Island, Delaware, where my father had a small law practice and my mother was his paralegal. SHE was an only child, twelve years younger than my father. From the marriage certificate, I learned that my mother was pregnant when they married, just like Marcia and Ed. Actually, nothing like Marcia and Ed. Later, when I heard HE yell, "I should have never married you, you scheming bitch!" I knew what he was referring to. It finally made sense—he never wanted any children.

I have no aunts or uncles, as HE and SHE were both from a one-child family. However, on ancestry websites, I tracked down what no one could tell me. All four of my grandparents passed before I was four years old. I have no memory of ever meeting them, if in fact I ever did. What I desired above all else was information about my brother.

I celebrated the day I found him.

His name was Clark Charles Foster, and he had died in a drowning accident near Ocean City, Maryland, at the age of five. Three months before I was born. It made some sense. Possibly, I was conceived when HE and SHE were a happy, smiling couple wearing khaki and white on the beach, with a son named Clark. Otherwise, they would not have another child; but I was already there, created before they'd stopped smiling and went to the dark side. I assumed the reason my name was Sunday was not just because I was born on a Sunday, but because HE and SHE couldn't think or care enough to give this new, unwanted baby a name. Who picks out a name for an unwanted child?

A child's giggle brings me back to the present. A mother and her children are playing on a blanket by the water's edge with their family dog. The boy is trying to build a sandcastle as the shaggy dog keeps running through it. The family's laughter is true and good.

Yes, I know losing a child must be heartbreaking—but I'll never forgive HE and SHE for never smiling with me. For never loving me.

Looking at the water makes me feel closer to Clark. I wish he was alive.

The last bus leaves in twenty minutes. I have to deal with what is happening right now. Even if that means more lies to Jack. The crowd below is picking up coolers, toys and blankets, and for a moment, I wonder what it must be like to have a family, a brother. I'm certainly not ready to have my own family.

Oh God, please don't let it be true. I can't be pregnant. I just can't. I need a brother to talk to. I wish I could talk to Jack but I don't know how.

I try to calm myself down. As the sun falls lower in the sky, the monstrous Bay Bridge is illuminated on the horizon, hundreds of cars are crossing the water.

Where are they all going? I'm transported to the summer I turned twelve, the last time I crossed the Bay Bridge.

Tara, Jack's sister, drove Jack and me to the offices of *The Dispatch* in Ocean City, Maryland.

I marched into the newspaper office, ponytail on top of my head, shoulders back clutching my research folder, determined to find the answers. "Do you keep copies of old newspapers?"

The woman at the desk rolled her eyes, her chewing gum smacking against her lips. She studied me, peering over her glasses. "We keep one issue of every paper since 1984, but we are a little busy today. Can you come back tomorrow?"

I hesitated, trying to determine my best course of action. Thoughts of Clark overwhelmed me. So, instead of pasting on my fake smile, I decided to be real. "Is there any way I could look through the old issues? I will be very careful." A lump formed in my throat. "We drove the whole way here from Owings Mills, just for this."

"Is this a school project?"

I locked eyes were her, no longer watching her chew her gum. "No, I'm looking for my brother's obituary."

The word "brother" engulfed my voice and took ownership of my eyes. I could barely see her as they became full. I didn't plan it for effect; it just happened. One large wet tear rolled down my cheek. I didn't wipe it away as it dripped off my chin.

Her tight expression softened. "What date are you looking

for?"

"November 2000."

She stood up and motioned for me to follow and took me to a back room, an overstuffed library of papers. "Here it is. You can look at it here." She gestured toward the table.

I wanted to walk, but my feet stopped. *Breathe.* I attempted to swallow this unfamiliar tightness overtaking my body. I blinked my eyes, as my hand wiped my face and my feet moved forward.

She stayed with me and helped me locate both an article and the obituary. "Honey, I can copy it for you."

Clark died November 8, 2000. The article was prominent on the fourth page of the paper, with two photographs. One picture was of HE and SHE. SHE had a crooked smile on her face, and HE was grinning like a puffed-up idiot with a head full of thick hair (crazy different than the spiky, thinning strands he sported now) in a form fitting suit, his arm tightly around SHE. A gesture of love I never witnessed. The other photo was a small picture of Clark, a smiling five-year-old, young, happy, and carefree. My heart stopped when I saw it. *My beautiful brother.*

Leaving the office, with the copied article, I stood tall as I walked over to Jack and Tara.

Jack grabbed my hand. "Are you okay, Sunday? Did you find it?"

"They were having a picnic on the beach in Fenwick Island."

"A picnic?" Jack asked.

"A picnic, and Clark went missing." The article shook in my hands. Jack gently took the paper, his eyes scanning the article.

Whispering, I barely got the words out. "He drowned. The paper stated they didn't call the police for five hours."

"Five hours? How do you lose a kid on the beach for five hours? What were they doing that they weren't watching a five-year-old as he goes into the ocean?" Jack tucked me into his arm, handing me back the article.

I shook my head back and forth, swallowing the anger inside me so I could find the words. "After an investigation, it was ruled an accidental drowning. They found him on the beach, dead." I clenched the article to my heart like a prized possession. "They let my brother drown."

My breath came out in quick bursts, intense pressure built as angry words fought to come out and I pushed them away. "I need to go to Fenwick Island Beach."

Tara, who had just received her permanent driver's license, hesitated.

"Please take me to where Clark drowned."

My eyes locked on hers, Tara relented.

The air in the car was thick with emotion, heavy with silence. Finally, Tara let out a sputtering of muttered swear words and hand motions aimed at the crawling beach traffic.

I'm not sure how you're supposed to feel when you lose a sibling you've never met, but nausea washed over me. Thinking about my older brother Clark and his fate caused a sharp pain in my stomach, as if the arteries of my heart were ripping open, inflicting a stabbing ache as I breathed. As a tear ran down my face, I wondered what would life be like if he'd lived. Would I have had a brother to shelter the disastrous storms of our parents?

Tara pulled in the empty parking lot, parking beside the weather-beaten wooden Fenwick Island sign.

When she shut the engine off, angry waves snarled as they hit the shore. I flung the car door open and ran towards the sea, alone. I fell to my knees on the warm sand, grabbing handfuls of grit and staring at the waves, it's roar muffling my cry. The bright fiery ball in the sky reflected off the charm bracelet Jack had given me like a signal, casting diamonds on the water. Did Clark even have a grave? A tombstone? My eyes fixated on the prisms in the ferocious waves. Flip-flops off, toes dug into the sand, I searched for closure in the enormous sea.

I wondered how he drowned, not wanting to picture that sweet face gasping for air, yelling out, but I couldn't erase the movie playing in my head. Did he know how to swim? How could this happen? Why did this happen?

I'm not sure how long I sat there, but the reflection of my bracelet no longer caught the sun. Jack and Tara stayed at the car, leaning up against the hood with the back door still flung open. In that moment, I knew I had the power to alter my life. THE PLAN was conceived, my escape route.

Chapter 6

Blue Sticks, Nicotine, and Cocaine

This is not my life. Not the life I belong in. My life is supposed to be better than this. Different. I don't know how I know this, but I've never possessed such instinctive knowledge that I'm right. Sitting on the edge of the tub, I jiggle the flusher on the toilet, the constant noise of the tank refilling is my music. A running toilet. I want to run.

I will change this life. Whatever it takes.

I close the page of my journal as the timer goes off on my phone.

Two lines show up on the stick. I gasp. Two lines. One is really strong. One is faint, but if I squint, two lines. Everything that's been pent up inside me comes out in a rush as I muffle my cries with a towel. Time passes. I have no idea how long I've been in the bathroom. I wash my face. I scream into the towel. Steady breaths to try and calm myself down.

I catch a reflection of my pink, wet, swollen face in the bathroom mirror as I head out into the living room. I'm still holding the blue plastic stick in my hand. SHE will never notice.

I stand there, my eyes focused on her, daring her to look up. *Look at me*, I scream silently. SHE is staring at some crazy reality show on the flat screen located on the wall above the gas fireplace—a fireplace we have never turned on; not even once to warm the house on the occasional snowy night in a Maryland winter. No cozy family gatherings happen here, sitting around the orange flames, drinking eggnog, singing carols at holidays.

I dare her. *LOOK AT ME!*

You can tell a lot about a person on whether or not they will look directly in your eyes. Not a millisecond glance, but making contact with your eyes and sharing that pupil-to-pupil interaction.

SHE is wearing her daily uniform: black leggings and a tight black shirt with the mask of no emotion hanging on her face. Her features are blank and expressionless like a department store mannequin with a bad bleached-blonde dye job. I bet if I touch her skin, it will feel plastic, hard and cold. But I have nothing to fear. SHE will never touch me.

Holidays are definitely worse than a typical day. And it's Easter weekend. HE's at home today, downstairs in the basement office, drunk or high on cocaine. It must be coke, because he is obviously snorting something up his nose. When he speaks— which is rarely—his glassy eyes do not quite connect to my eyes. The protruding artery in his neck slightly jumps and little specks of white residue stick to his nose hairs. Sniffling, always sniffling.

HE lives in an imaginary coked-up world. A world without a child, or a wife. HE tells no one of the deep hole of debt he has dug for himself and his family, and he keeps wearing these stupidly expensive tailored suits. I'm waiting for him to fall into the hole, his pit of despair and debt.

SHE knows. I'm certain. SHE has to. Deep down inside that hollow heart, that lost façade of a human, she knows our family is a sick disaster. But she blocks it out, just like she blocks out a daughter desperately searching for a normal or responsible mother or father. She barricades my presence with antidepressants, little white pills that paralyze any sense of rationality she might have lurking in her empty mind. She blocks it out with every puff of nicotine she inhales into her body out in the screened-in porch. I dump the overflowing ashtrays on a daily basis, so I know she's up to at least two packs now. Smoking her life away, and she doesn't even care. No time for her daughter, but time to smoke forty cigarettes a day.

SHE won't even glance in my direction. I'm screaming inside, *look at me. Ask me what is wrong. Ask me what I'm holding in my hand.* Nothing. NO response.

I'm only here surviving because I can succeed without them. I plunge forward and I live a life which looks somewhat normal on the outside. I wash my own clothes, I cook my own food—that is, if we have any food in the house. And if I do have food, it's because I went to the grocery store and bought it with the money I've earned from my job at the courthouse.

The courthouse. Tyler. Everything is ruined.

I've had it. It's not supposed to be like this. Parents are supposed to take care of children. Children. I can't believe after everything I've planned for, now this is happening.

I really believed with a little more time, a little more planning, I could make THE PLAN work. It's only my junior year. I just needed to survive for the last few weeks of this semester, work like crazy at the courthouse all summer, spend as much time as possible with Jack and his family, and push forward through senior year with the prize ahead.

My PLAN was almost here. it would've worked, and now I've blown it. My actions did this.

I'm gripping the blue stick, holding it up like a surrender flag. I wipe the tears falling off my face. It's not only about me anymore. In this moment, everything has changed. I would rather die than end up like SHE.

I would never want to trap Jack.

I say it to myself. Because for a second, I think maybe I should tell him I no longer care about saving my virginity until I graduate from high school. One night, maybe when Ed & Marcia are out, I would sleep with him. We could do that. It's not like he doesn't want to. It's because of me that we don't. Or at least the me before Tyler.

The me before Tyler is a me I can never get back. She's gone.

Could this new me tell him I was pregnant? It can accidentally happen even if you use a condom, it tears, we make a mistake. I could lie, the biggest lie of my life. Jack would believe me.

Marcia, his mother, would help us figure out what to do— maybe we could give the baby up for adoption to a good loving family. THE PLAN could still happen. She would help us. I know she would be disappointed but she would help. She would help me. It could work.

But I can't. I can't do that to sweet Jack. I won't. I am not my parents. I might lie about everything else in my life. I might be the best liar ever, but not this, not to Jack. He doesn't deserve a lying slut like me.

SHE walks right past me out to her smoking porch without any idea I'm in the room.

The trees on the edge of the yard are swaying. My bed pushed up against the window, allows me a glimpse of the outside. THE

PLAN doesn't matter. I know without a doubt, I am not going to end up like SHE. NEVER. I'll run away. I'm leaving. I'm smart. I can do this.

Thousands of pregnancy blogs exist on the web. I scroll, click and read until I can no longer see clearly.

Most women start showing in three to four months, I have at least 95 days before I will start showing.

Twisting my hair on top of my head, I wander down to the creek. I find myself biting my lower lip like Amir. When I bite hard enough, I can taste the metallic taste of my blood.

Make a list. Make a new plan. My pen is poised over my journal. There is another option, I know, but it's not really an option for me. I can't think about abortion. I understand it is an option for women, and I'm glad it exists, but I am an unwanted child. I don't have it in me to do it to another living soul. But, if I'm going to have a baby, I have to be a good mom. A word so foreign to me, it's hard to speak it, even in my head. I keep teetering on the right choice. I wish I could go back in time and never go to dinner with Tyler. Erase it all. But, I can't.

Pseudocide is my answer. I like how the word sounds. Crazy but clever. Nobody dies. No one gets hurt. I reinvent myself and get away from them. On Wikipedia, it states that the faking of one's death is not necessarily illegal, so I figure if I don't hurt anyone in the process, I should be okay. I don't want to start my life as a criminal. I still want to go to college. I want to graduate with a high school diploma. I want this baby to have a chance.

My number one obstacle: I need to find a way to fake my death without an actual body.

There are different ways to go about this. I'm going to find the right way to pull this off, disappear and never look back.

Chapter 7

New Plan, DNA, and Someone Else's Blood

If you want to do anything well in this world, you have to understand it, know it like a savant. Research. Good research is what will make this happen.

I study the girl at the front of the bus. Her boho hat covers the majority of her face, and with the oversized sunglasses, she could have any color hair under that hat. I make a note to buy a selection of large hats at Good Will. It hasn't been easy, but I've changed my looks on each bus ride to the various public libraries in Baltimore. They have fifteen different ones, and I've discovered several internet cafés in areas I didn't even know existed, where I can safely gather information to begin my future. I'm careful these last few weeks. I've erased my path.

Other pseudocide folks are not careful. Grown adults who have degrees and serious life experience do stupid things as they try to fake their deaths. I read an article about a man who was both a banker and a preacher. He faked his death by leaving rambling notes that he was going to jump off a ferryboat. His church, his family believed it to be true. He had pulled it off. He ended up in

Colombia, working at a cocaine factory before he finally came back to the United States and got pulled over by the police on the highway. The media speculated he wanted to be caught.

That is not going to be me.

I have a new plan, one that will watch my digital footprint. I now own two burner phones for any phone calls I need to make. They can't be traced to me. I've purchased chocolate brown hair color and ten samples of brown-tinted contact lenses. And, I now have seven prepaid credit cards. I've watched my digital footprint from day one.

The next step: find a storage locker to keep the suitcase full of the hair dye, contacts, identification, gift cards, gold jewelry, and clothing for my new life.

Outside the Greyhound terminal in downtown Baltimore, I wonder why bus stations are so dirty. They have lockers. Rentals are $150 a month, but I'm afraid to rent it myself; afraid someone will recognize me if I am presumed missing or dead. I leave without talking to anyone and start walking.

A truck stop not too far away from the bus terminal has a somewhat private bathroom. I could dye my hair and materialize into my new identity before hopping on the bus. It will work. I feel more confident every day that I can do this. WE can do this. It's not just about me anymore.

My first priority, and maybe the most important one is a new me; an identity I can use for the rest of my life. An identity so I can take and pass the GED, apply to college, and become a real person. I'll have a name to pass on to the baby.

The internet has answers and solutions to anything I can think of. I've been checking out a few darknet sites on how to buy a new social security card. I spend way too much time incognito, on a forum discussion, trying to find out how to buy new identification. My burner phone buzzes, someone named GoneBoy, who has been a wealth of information, can help me. He can get this done for me, if we meet tonight.

I text back, **somewhere public**.

He texts a location in Inner Harbor.

Done.

I need pictures of the new me. The one I'm going to create with brown eyes and brown hair. The itchy wig I'm wearing, since I can't dye my hair yet, is expensive. My new identity, is taking a huge chunk out of the last of my savings, and it's risky, but this will be my new life. Good fakes cost money.

As I walk into the CVS, the woman at the makeup counter looks at me. Does she know I am wearing a wig? I picked this particular photo center because of the old woman behind the photo counter. I'm in luck, she is working, and repeats the same motions as last time, head down, she shuffles back to the camera, barely looking at me as she captures the new me on digital. When she hands me the prints, I can't even recognize me.

Goodbye, Sunday Foster.

It's a long bus ride back to my old life, and it affords me time to make the final decision. So, how does one die without leaving a body. I mean a believable death, one where no one questions foul play.

Two scenarios circle around my mind. The first involves taking SHE's Audi, cutting my hand in the car, throwing my blood around like a struggle occurred, even strands of my hair and then leave my phone, ID, and credit cards, and just walk away. I've even read that if I could obtain another source of blood in the car, blood that is not mine, they would be searching for a DNA match. I thought about putting HE's DNA somewhere in the car, but then the police would just think that HE's DNA was in there because it was SHE's car. I could never falsely accuse anyone else. But, If I could get blood from someone who already died, it might just end up blowing up on the internet as an unsolved murder. Rabbit blood and even chimpanzee blood is the most similar to humans, but there is an easy test to confirm if it is human blood. How can I get someone else's blood to leave at the scene? Research tells me nurse's stations, blood banks, even blood drives.

The second scenario would really drive a stake through HE's and SHE's hearts—if they still have a beating heart. I imagine the suicide note I would write. An in-depth inside look of my sickening family would expose their lies, debt, and drugs. I could tell the world about my poor dead brother Clark, declaring they killed him. Then I would go to the bay, leave my clothes and my belongings on the shore, and hopefully they would think I drowned.

The drowning death seems more appropriate and effective. Bodies get lost at sea, water can carry bodies to many other places, and they might not turn up for years. Water, the sea, the bay can be a good cover. In the past, many older people tried to use this one, but because they had a reason to flee. I mean they were either running away from debt, a crime or running with stolen money, it seemed too convenient. I don't fit into any of the obvious categories. My age, minimal digital footprint and the fact everyone thinks I'm a normal high school student works in my favor.

Water. The bus crosses the bridge at Liberty Lake, and I think I might just go with the drowning death, in honor of Clark. But first, I need a new identity before I can fake my death. With good identification, I can set up an out-of-state bank account, buy a bus ticket, and start creating my backstory. My list seems impossible. I close my journal, careful not to miss the bus stop by the high school. I can do this.

Like the baby growing inside me, the NEW PLAN is born.

Chapter 8

Amir, Lucky Star, and Hard Liquor Boys

My NEW PLAN is falling apart. Shredding.

"Sunday, is everything going okay?" Mr. Cable asks as I zone out in class. He hands me a test with a big red circle on it. I scored a solid forty-two on my biology exam. I can't get the new movie of my life to stop playing in high speed in my head. I'm constantly trying to picture the alternative endings, depending on the choice I make.

"Yes, I'll do better next time." I smile, without meaning it. I'm obsessed about the NEW PLAN, and for the first time in forever, I couldn't care less about my grades. I can't take grades with me. I am certain this is really going to happen: Sunday Foster will no longer exist. It scares me to think that everything I've struggled and pushed for will be thrown away, but the alternative is incomprehensible. If I stay and end up like SHE, I will be facing a life sentence of darkness and despair.

In some respects, I want everything to appear as life as usual; however, failing grades might help paint a picture of depression for the suicide. It's hard to throw the car into reverse when it's been speeding down the good-grade-highway.

I'm definitely not worried about my grades for the first time in my life, but what I am worried about is the greasy-haired Italian guy, Tito, whom I met at Inner Harbor last week. I playback the meeting, wishing I would have trusted my instincts.

I waited on the bench in front of the street vendors for thirty minutes before he approached me.

"You Emily?" he said from the bench next to mine.

I nodded. Emily was my chosen name for my favorite author Emily Dickenson.

He slid a newspaper over. "You got the money?"

I slid my envelope in the paper.

Two seconds he had the paper. I gave him one thousand dollars for my new identity... one thousand dollars of my hard-earned cash, and five painstakingly difficult-to-produce photos of me wearing a brown wig and brown contact lenses.

He took the envelope, opened it up, and glanced inside. A magic trick completed in less than a minute. I had to give it to him he was quick. He mumbled, "It'll take two days. Meet me back here, same place, same time, two days from now."

He never showed up. I've sat on the bench, now for three nights in a row.

I've called his phone ten times and texted about 30 times. I'll try it again after class, hoping I'm mistaken; that this time it will work. But, yeah, I'm screwed. I just don't know how to deal with it.

After class, I try it again. His phone number no longer works.

My stomach hurts and I'm queasy. I'm not sure if it is because of my pregnancy or because I have $1000 less in my quickly-depleting fund.

I need help, but I don't know where to get it.

I've tried to chat with Goneboy, but he doesn't respond, either. It was probably all a set-up and I was stupid enough to fall for it. I'm sick with fear and I'm so angry at my stupidity. But how can you ask for a money-back guarantee on purchasing a fake identity? I went with my gut, even though it didn't feel right. I need to toughen up and realize no one can be trusted. I'm determined not to give up, for me and the baby.

"Hey, there's my girl." Jack offers me a bright smile as he walks up to my locker, and then it diminishes. He rubs my collarbone, bringing me back to reality.

"What's wrong?" he asks.

I see his worry in the drooping corner of his mouth and as he runs his hand through the top of his hair. I see it in his eyes, which lately I find myself avoiding. His kind brown eyes. I wish I could tell him about my NEW PLAN. I wish he could be my Cinderella story, my happily ever after. The fairytale version of my life plays through my head in which I tell him everything about Tyler and the baby, and he grabs me tight and says, "I love you so much, we can do this together and be happy." He isn't disgusted or disappointed. "We can rent a little cottage near the beaches of California and make a life for all three of us. I love you, Sunday. We can do this."

My dream scenario vanishes. Where's my fitted glass slipper? I gave up fairytales a long time ago, but it doesn't stop my innocent inner child from wishing.

"Sunday?" Jack is staring at me as I shut my locker. I realize he is waiting for an answer. What was the question? His beautiful mouth is slanted in sadness and confusion. I'm the only one in control of my future. It's up to me. Fairytales are not real.

"I beat my dad in poker. I finally got it. I know what my tell is and I definitely know his." Jack is rubbing his hands together. "I'm going to wipe him out."

I hear him, but I can't focus.

"Everyone has some sort of tell. My dad pulls on his eyebrows. I think I move my thumb back and forth. I'm not going to let him know I figured it out and I'm going to use it against him."

"Use what against him?" I'm confused. Is he still talking about poker?

"What's up with you, Sunday?" He looks at me with questions in his eyes, demanding an answer. "I've been patient, waiting for you to tell me and I get nothing. Excuses, you're busy. What is it. What are you not telling me?" I am hurting him. I've been emotionally empty, and of course he notices. Suddenly, a glimmer of a bad idea forms. I should break up with him. That way, when I fake my death, he won't blame himself. That's what I should do. Make him mad enough to not care anymore.

The last thing in the world I want to do is cause Jack pain. His milk chocolate eyes make me lose self-control; I can't break up with him. I can't even get in a fight with him, at least not now. He's the one good thing in my life—he's always been the only good thing, and, selfishly, I need him a little bit longer.

"I'm sorry. It's not you. It's just my parents, nothing I can't handle." A lie. "If you're biologically related to someone does that mean you might turn out like them? "

"Sunday, is it him? Did he do something?"

"No, he's stressed at work and he's getting on me about everything." I put my hands on his shoulder, lean in, and kiss his scar on his cheek. My scar, the one from saving the dog Harvey on the ice. Another lie. Everything seems like lies. I trace his scar with my finger. My life is a lie. Lies. More lies are coming.

Jack grabs my finger and holds my hand. "Are you sure you're okay? He hasn't..." I know what Jack wants to ask. In seventh grade he had seen the bruises that I desperately tried to hide from the world.

"No, and he never will again. Don't worry, I have it under control. Honest." I perk up, paste my actress audition face over my confused emotions, and give him the award-winning smile I have perfected over the years. He buys it. It's probably my tell, but nobody knows I'm bluffing.

"So you'll go with me to Ohiopyle on the rafting trip?" He reaches out and grabs both my hands.

"Do you really want to go?"

"Yes, I really want to go, and I want to go with you, Sunday Foster. Remember how much fun we had with my family last year? Come on, you know you were a pro white-water rafter. I mean I was of course better than you, but you were pretty good."

I laugh. Jack is of course good at all things, but by the end of my first rafting trip, instead of hating it, I loved it. I loved the smell of the water and the earth that held the looming trees that lined the curving river, like spectators bending and cheering to the groups of rafts that dared to take the wild ride. Something about the roar of rushing water, that whispered in my ear as the whoosh of air swirled around my face, I wanted more of the unknown danger that greeted me at every turn, because I wasn't alone. This danger we battled it together as a family. The day was awesome. Simply perfection.

It is my favorite memory, and the closest thing to a family vacation I've ever experienced. Even the guide told Ed what a great family he had, and Ed said, "Thanks they learned it all from me." I was part of they.

We celebrated our triumph in a lively Mexican restaurant, with warm out of the oven homemade tortilla chips and salsa, and an overflowing platter of cheesy burritos, tacos and quesadillas. Jack tried to get everyone to taste a dark red chili pepper, finally convincing his mom it wasn't hot. I laughed so hard that I cried tears of joy as she hid her face in her hands and the waiter rushed over with milk for her to drink. The best was when we realized Marcia didn't really eat the chili, but snuck it into Jack's rice. Jack ended up standing, fanning his mouth and drinking the milk. The perfect day ended when Tara, Jack and I snuck out to the hotel pool, lying on our backs under an open canopy of a million stars. We talked for hours debating Tara's choice of college, and each one admitting our secret adventurous hopes and dreams of a future full of whatever you wanted.

I so wanted to be back there, and repeat that incredible day all over again.

"Where did you go?" Jack bends down, eye to eye.

I laugh. "I was thinking about the raft trip with your family. I did love it. I'm in. But, can I pay by credit card?" Every bit of cash I possessed had to be saved. Every dollar.

"Moneybags, are you worried about the cost?"

I don't answer. I know he's teasing me about my obsession with saving money. If he only knew why, it wouldn't be very funny.

I lean into my locker, trying to catch my breath, while I mask the lies from my face, stacking books at the bottom. A notebook full of papers becomes airborne.

As I bend down to pick the papers up, I know my fake suicide will break him. It'll torture him. He will wonder why he didn't see the signs. He'll stay up night after night, trying to put the pieces together, trying to find the ones he didn't have for the Sunday puzzle. It will drive him crazy wondering what he missed. I know this because it would destroy and devastate me if he was not the Jack that I thought he was. If he ever went off the deep end and tried to take his life, I would question everything.

Maybe someday in the future I could contact him, let him know I was still alive, apologize for what I put him through. As quickly as that precious dream enters my mind, I throw it over the cliff of Never Going to Happen. From everything I've researched, the number one reason people who fake their death get caught is because they try to keep in touch with *one person* from their previous life. Jack would be my one person. I can't. Sunday Foster must be dead, gone forever. Letting go of Jack and his incredible family is the ultimate price I have to pay. It's my punishment for what I let happen.

Jack hands me the last of the fallen papers. "Well, my mom and dad just gave me $300 for painting the shed, so I'm paying. Consider it a spring fling present. Now you can't say no. Sunday, are you listening? Are you in?" His eyes wide, he gave me that extra special cute puppy look. "I miss you already, and you're standing right here."

His eyes always get me. The eyes are the windows to our souls; and his overflowing with goodness, love, and happiness. Everything I always wanted. Calm Jack: never reactive, never in a hurry. Knowing we have little time left together—I decide my pseudocide will occur one week after the school trip. This will require every free minute I have. No shortcuts, no digital footprints, every last detail has to be in place for the plan to work. But we can have this one last memory. One last time together. One final goodbye.

I miss him already too. "Count me in. I can never say no to you."

"Oh, really? Hmm. That gives me ideas..." Jack's beautiful face beams as he whispers, "I love you, Sunday Foster."

Three words. Three words I so desperately want to hear, and at the same time I want to ignore. I want to say, *Take it back.*

Jack told me he loved me last year. I never said the three words back instead I started using three words: "miss you already." I can't say the words back. I just can't. When I was younger, I used to tell my mom I loved her and she would ignore me. One day I said it as nice as anyone could say those three words. She grabbed my arm, lifted me out of the kitchen chair and pushed me in *THE DARK.* When I asked, sobbing, "Why, Mommy? Why? What did I do?"

"Stop saying you love me; you don't even know what that word means," she screamed.

I never say it. Not to SHE, HE, Jack or anyone else in my life.

Everything is moving so fast. I need to find a solution to my identity issue. Yesterday.

I slam my locker, kiss Jack, avoid his eyes and turn. "I'll call you later. I need to run. Miss you already."

The Hard Liquor Boys are at it again. Amir and Eric stand in the middle of the pack at the back of the school parking lot. Bunnies being circled by coyotes. From a distance, it doesn't look threatening, but I can't hear what they are saying. Eric stares at the ground and Amir continues to push his glasses up his nose, slippery in oil and sweat. It can't be good.

Amir hands his iPhone to the biggest bully of them all, the leader of the Hard Liquor Boys, Cody. My fist clenches. During the day, in the hallways, girls swoon over Cody hoping for a second of direct eye contact as he swaggers down the hall. But the current cruelty on his face makes him appear monstrous. The low-toned laughter from the group sounds dangerous. Cody, now in mime persona, acts like he is going to drop the phone and then catches it, casually throwing it back and forth from one hand to another. Great, now he is taking photos of the two of them, their shoes, their crotch and then he puts the phone right up on Amir's face.

I can't watch this, but I can't walk away. As I get close, I hear the shouts.

"Pose for the picture, Towelhead. Terrorists!" one of the boys shouts.

"ISIS called, and they want you to go back to your own country. America doesn't want you," another voice yells.

My gut clenches, compassion lighting a match to my pity, mixed with a rising anger at the stupidity of the chosen words. *Amir was born in America, and his father was in the military, and fought for our country, assholes.*

They cower close together. Amir, in his pants that are way too short, towers over Eric. If he would only stand up tall, he would probably be taller than Cody.

Cody vehemently throws the phone on the ground. A sickening loud crack, is followed by flinty sounding laughter from the other boys. Amir bends down to pick up the phone and Cody plucks his glasses off his face. The glasses are now the new sports equipment to toss back and forth. Cody grabs Eric's glasses next, and I know what is coming. Both pair of glasses are going to be shattered just like the phone.

That cracking sound and the smell of sweat created by cruelty infuses me. Bullies, just like my father. *Where did this depraved sickness come from? Could you be born cruel?* I hope to God my child will not be like this.

I storm across the ground, my tangled long blonde hair picking that moment to fall loose from the top of my head. My hand doesn't even shake as I hold my phone up and started to record a video.

"Hey! Cody Maxwell! Want to say hi to the camera?"

He glances in my direction and back to Eric.

"Seriously, dude, what are you doing right now? I'm filming you. Do you want this video to be all over the entire internet?"

His face twists in a snarl, barely acknowledging me. For a millisecond, he resembles a rabid dog. But it's okay, I'm used to rabid dog faces. This one will show up great on video.

"All it takes is for me to push this little button right here, and believe me, it will go viral. In fact, it's already uploading to the Cloud. And you know what the best news is, Cody Maxwell, besides being famous for a second by breaking someone's iPhone and glasses? Perpetuity. Have you heard that word before? It means, the video will be there for the rest of your life. Cody Maxwell, the Bully. Good luck getting into college, a good job... I mean, every company wants to hire a bully, right?"

He sneers at me, and for a minute I think he is going to lunge at me, grab my phone, and smash it on the ground, but one of the smarter Hard Liquor Boys grabs him.

"Oh look, I sent it to my email, just in case you want to smash my phone." I hold it out.

Cody gives me the once-over, starting with my scuffed-up leather boots, to my fringed jean skirt, all the way up to my face. No direct eye contact, only mild curiosity, as if I were a wild animal at the zoo.

"Pay him a hundred dollars for the glass screen you just broke, and give their glasses back, and I will delete it." I try to make him meet my eyes, thinking that if I could make contact, I could reach him.

I hear a noise behind me. A small crowd is rushing over to check out the commotion. Spectators with phones in the air: a cavalry of hope.

His eyes flick over my shoulder. "I don't have a hundred bucks."

Cody needed a nudge to find a solution.

"Well, borrow it from your buddies, or I post it. Now."

I'm crying again. I'm blaming it on the pregnancy and hormones. What did I ever do to deserve this? My fingers are digging in the dirt of my special place, I'm transfixed watching the tiny little waterfall trickle, the water running away over the smooth round pebbles, to a new destination. Running water never stays in one place. I want to run somewhere new. My fingernails are full of brown dirt. I don't care.

The snap of a branch alerts me. Amir is behind me.

After the incident at school, I knew he would seek me out. But I'm not ready for company.

I'm blaming it on the changing hormones. My face is wet as I wipe my chin with the back of my dirty hand.

"Thanks, Sunday." He breaks his ten-foot personal space barrier and touches my shoulder and I jump. I didn't realize he was so close.

Maybe he's wants to talk about the incident at school, but as terrible as that was, it isn't my most pressing issue.

"I hate them." A stone hits the bank and plops into the running water.

I don't even have to ask who 'them" is.

"I would have lost it if I had to deal with one more inquisition from my father about why I need a new pair of glasses." He pauses. "Eric is thankful, too, even though he will never tell you. He hates them more than I do. Hates them." He picks up another larger rock and pitches it in the water. "This is not supposed to be happening in our senior year. This is not how it's supposed to be."

I don't turn around. I use the back of my hand to wipe my face one more time. I'm sure I have dirt streaks. Amir is definitely right. We sit in silence for about five minutes.

"Sunday, maybe I can help you." I hear him swallow. "I know something is wrong."

His words make the lump in my throat grow ten times bigger. Why is it when someone tries to be nice to me at my lowest point, it turns me into a basket case? I use every shred of control inside me to hold back more tears.

"Sunday, I owe you one. What can I do to help you?"

I swallow my sadness, sniffle, and breathe in. Just breathe. Facing the creek, I wonder if I could trust Amir. I mean really trust him. I vowed not to trust anyone again, but what other options do I really have? Help. I need help. Amir is a genius with technology. Brilliant at computers.

"Can you make a fake I.D.?"

"What, to use in a bar?"

"No, to use for the rest of my life. I want to change my identity and start all over fresh and new, but I need a real identity. Can you do it?" The words flew out without a struggle. This is a moment I will regret or rejoice over.

Chapter 9

Ghosting, Cemeteries, and West Virginia

Amir is a savior. A surprising rescuer.

Tapping his hand on the steering wheel, I notice how different he is.

I laugh. He stops tapping.

It's funny how much time we have spent together. I know I'm breaking one of the rules of faking your own death by confiding in someone, but I don't see another way out. Amir knows many things about HE and SHE, and in the last six years, he has never told anyone.

After I told him my whole plan on pseudocide, he promised, swearing on his life he would keep the secret. I need help, and Amir is here.

Jack thinks I'm working. Another lie. He has no idea, how much time I'm spending with Amir. The last few days, we have spent more time together in public in mere days than we have for six years.

I trust Amir, but I don't want to tell him about the pregnancy. I can't imagine even saying those words out loud. I love Jack, but I can't tell him either.

Now, here we are, on a road trip, to find a cemetery in West Virginia.

"It's called ghosting," Amir says, interrupting my thoughts. "You need to find a baby girl who died and assume her identity. Most states keep poor records of births and deaths, and definitely not in the same office. It has been an unorganized tracking system for a long time. It's the government. They are not quite up to speed on technology. West Virginia is the worst."

"That sounds awful, looking for a baby that died."

Amir rolls his eyes. I think about the baby inside me, now almost a month old. I let my focus go back to the country road.

"So, you're looking for a baby girl who died at least sixteen years ago. Sixteen years ago, maybe seventeen. Birth and death records are not all digital, even today only a few states have digital records in full automation. In the future, ghosting will become much more problematic. A couple of years from now it will be harder to do this, maybe even impossible. And, it's much more difficult for adults who have to explain wages and taxes, but most sixteen-year-olds most likely never had a job. And, technology can help us as well as we can create social media accounts to start a digital footprint for your new identity. You'll create more digital shadows than the real baby."

I like his quirky confidence and his new authoritative vocal inflection.

"Wow, Amir, thanks for all your research. I think West Virginia is a good choice, since it's slower to go digital." Someone discovering my fake identity would be like looking for a grain of rice in the sand: you might find it, but only if they knew there was a reason to look for it.

Purple and yellow flowers dot the empty two-lane road with

thick green leafy trees, as we circle the narrow curves that banish any chance of a cell signal.

A cemetery scavenger hunt.

Up ahead, we are rewarded with an old brick church, its sidewalks cracked and the welcome sign missing the letter W. Sprawling out behind the peeling wood building we find our prize: dozens and dozens of tombstones.

"Let's stop and check this one out." I have a feeling.

As we trample through another grass field with rows of graves, I am amazed at the number of little tombstones. Sad. Time and weather have not been kind to the slabs of marble. One large cluster of stones are turning brown, underneath the dirty, hard-to-read names the dates have one thing in common—the year of death, 1918.

"All these are from 1918, there must be a hundred of them." I am wiping off the year 1918.

"Spanish flu, also known as of 1918 Flu Pandemic. It was the world's most severe pandemic. Historians estimate about 500 million people or one third of the world became infected. Hundreds of thousands of people died in the United States."

"That's terrible. I never even heard about that. I hope it never happens again." I can't even imagine a pandemic. I guess things could be worse.

"Oh, don't get your hopes up, it probably will happen again, and be even worse this time around."

"Look at this one." I stop, Amir almost runs into my back.

"This is the right one." I kneel down beside a little slab of beautiful marble; a pretty angel is engraved on the front.

"You will always be with us, we love you, Angel. Mom and Dad." My new identity once had a loving family. I immediately like it. "Hannah Williams is the angel's name, and she would only be one year older than me, almost ready to turn eighteen."

"Yeah, that's good, eighteen is a good age to start your new life. Hannah is a common name and, Williams is a perfect common surname. She'll do."

Surname. I laugh.

But I'm no longer laughing at Amir. When we return, brilliant techie Amir creates a replica of a West Virginia driver's license so accurate a policeman would be hard pressed to identify it as a fake.

Now, one last step, one last lie to Jack about working on a special project at the courthouse. I called my boss and quit weeks ago which really sucks, since I needed the money, but I can't face Tyler, can't even bear to look at him, and work is a great cover as I finalize my new life.

One more road trip to the office of Vital Records in Charleston.

This time, Amir plays music in his father's car and sings the words.

"Pull over here," I say, as I point to the worn country gas station sign. GAS, BAIT, FIREWOOD in large black letters. Amir pulls in front of the gas tank, and I jump out to use the restroom.

The smell inside almost makes me gag. Afraid to sit on the dirty toilet, I begin my transformation after laying out a row of paper towels on the counter. When I'm done, my brown curly wig, and brown eyes almost dark chocolate color, greet me from the smudged bathroom mirror. When I put the final touches on the elaborate make-up, a stranger smiles back at me.

I walk into the convenience store, and stand behind Amir, picking up a bag of potato chips. In a southern twang, I ask in a slow voice, "Excuse me, do you know how far away I am from Charleston, West Virginia?"

Amir in a slow turn, gives me a once over. For a second, I see a strange look pass over his face, and then he gives me a simple nod. He doesn't play along or answer my question, just takes his soda to the counter and pays.

In less than five miles, Amir turns into the parking lot. I pull down a baseball hat, with the words, 'Slay it' embroidered on it. As I wait my turn and shuffle up to the counter, my hands shake. I clench them together, certain at any moment, I will be arrested. I slowly hand the large woman behind the counter my fake driver's license. Knowing I'm wearing my messy wig under a baseball hat and brown contacts in my eyes, I look guilty.

"Hi, I need a copy of my original birth certificate. We moved and my parents have no idea where it's at." This is a moment of truth. My voice sounds odd in my head, almost like an echo.

The woman glances at my driver's license for all of two seconds, and takes my completed form from my sweaty hands.

"Twelve dollars," she says, I flip through my wallet and I try to ignore the tremble in my hand, as I pass her a twenty.

Easy and uncomplicated.

Fifteen minutes.

In fifteen minutes, I am the recipient of an official stamped birth certificate. My new me.

Amir researched both of Hannah's parents' names from the maker of the tombstone. Tom and Jan Williams. Amir went online and applied for my Social Security card. We had it sent to a P.O. box we'd rented in Baltimore using the West Virginia license.

Simply amazing how easy it is to become someone else. I'm holding it in my hand: my new Social Security card for Hannah Williams.

Upon arrival in California—that's where I'm going—I'll establish an address, take Hannah's birth certificate and Social

Security card to the DMV, pass the driver's test as Hannah Williams, and boom—I'm legal in the system. Amir takes lots of pictures of me with my new brown wig and brown contact lenses. He creates Hannah Williams social media accounts, with a few random facts about Hannah, and arbitrary photos of friends he stole from some Orange County, California site. He even makes a timeline using some random photos of a younger fake Hannah and uses a cute photo of a puppy as my profile picture.

And there you have it, just like that: in a matter of days, Hannah Williams is alive and breathing, once again in the world. A pang of guilt makes me rest my head in the palm of my hand. She had good parents who called her an angel.

"Sunday, I've been thinking, why do you have to do it now? Why not wait until after the summer, and then maybe I can help you from college? Just stick with your parents a little bit longer?" Amir asks.

He doesn't understand why I have to go now. I can't bring myself to confide in him about everything. I can't even vocalize the words *I'm pregnant* aloud. Sitting by the creek, he flicks rocks into the water, agitated.

Silent, I grab his hand as he picks up another rock. We lock eyes. "If I have to tell you, then I don't want your help anymore. You promised I could trust you. You're the only one that knows what I'm going to do."

Amir studies me intently as if he could read my mind. His gaze rests on my hand on his. I'm thankful for Amir, he's been a loyal friend almost like a cousin, but I've told him enough.

When I finally let go, he says, "Okay."

After that, Amir seems to have become consumed with my covert mission—maybe a little too much. His excitement at my project electrifies him. The next day, I overhear him tell Eric outside school that he doesn't have time to play their zombie killing game.

Eric scowls. "When will you?"

Amir snaps back, "I don't know, Eric, maybe never. Leave me alone, coward."

Why would he call Eric a coward? It doesn't make sense.

I trust Amir. I think so. Why am I questioning it? I'm not sure.

I believe him when he said, "Sunday, I promise I'll never tell another living soul, no matter what happens."

The illusion is to assemble everything in place for the NEW PLAN and act normal. That's why I'm going on the school trip to Pennsylvania. That and the sad fact that this will be my last good memory with Jack before I proceed with the rest of the plan.

We made special memories in Ohiopyle white-water rafting with his family, and we would have one more happy time in a beautiful place. One last time. If I close my eyes, I can smell the wet leaves, hear the rush of the rapids and see Jack's great smile. Jack loves Pennsylvania woods, and at least he will have this fun trip to hold onto. Even though I loved the whitewater rafting part with his family, it's not so much about the thrill of the ride this time. I relish having one special day with Jack, when I'm gone. It sounds like a sad love song. I can picture the video of Jack and I walking through the woods, his hand holding mine.

One of my prized possessions is a photograph Marcia gave me from the trip. The five of us, Marcia, Ed, Tara, Jack and me, with our arms around each other, smiling. Love, warmth, and belonging consume me every time I study the photograph. At least I know I was once part of a bona fide family. I wish I could take the photo with me, in my new life, but I can't. It will stay imprinted on my heart forever.

What comes next, the part of the PLAN that freaks me out the most, makes me sick in my stomach, is when I have to stage the scene. I struggle with the where and when. To fake my death, I need to plan a disappearance at the water's edge that will resemble a suicide. Amir offers to drive me to the bus station after I stage it, but I'm not convinced I want him to know the when and where. Again, from everything I've read, I have to be cautious and meticulous. I'm still leery of anyone being part of the actual day I change into another person. When I shred my Sunday skin, I need to do it alone. My deadline is looming—I don't want to be close to showing my pregnancy—and I decide I will definitely fake my death before May 25.

I'm torn between two scenarios for my perfect pseudocide site—Sandy Point State Park, just an hour bus ride, or Fenwick Island beach where Clark drowned. I need to make a decision. A drowning disappearance at Fenwick Island would be the stake in the chest to HE and SHE, but I'm concerned about the three-hour drive time back to the Baltimore bus station.

A locker in Baltimore holds all my Go items. They are ready, safely stored inside. Amir rented the locker at the Greyhound bus station in case anyone might have remembered me. In it, I stuffed a suitcase I purchased at a thrift store, full of necessities for my new life. I'm prepared. When I handed it to Amir to take to the bus station locker, I almost didn't want to let it go. The next time I held that suitcase in my hand, I would no longer be Sunday Foster.

For the first time in my life, time is flying by.

Chapter 10

American Flag, Whitewater Rafting, and Carpe Diem

Deep aqua skies, a soft wind that pats my cheeks, and warm brightness all make it a perfect day to go rafting.

This moment is mine, at least for a half a day. I will get lost in the smell of fresh earth and let the roar of the rapids block out my inner voice fearing my future.

I rest my eyes on Jack's sweet face as the last of our group gets in the raft, and inhale the scent of fresh.

"Get ready, hold tight!" the guide yells.

I glance back once more to smile at Jack. I spot a figure perched on a large rock overlooking the twelve rafts. A bad feeling wipes away any bit of joy. Eric? What's he holding? More like cradling something wrapped in red, white, and blue.

"Let's go!" the guide yells and pushes the raft out of the eddy.

The words are stuck in the back of my throat, as panic swells up inside. I want to stand and scream.

BOOM.

A loud *bang, bang, bang.*

Movement, flashes, a piercing noise. A horrific scene unfolds in slow motion.

And then that sound again—what a horrible noise! A chilling evil boom of rapid gunshots echoes over the river. Incomprehensible. What is happening? It feels like a bad dream, a very bad living dream. I can't tear my eyes away as the gun dances in all directions. I try to stand and fall sideways against the gear.

"Sunday, Sunday What is..." Jack is trying to move towards me.

As he stands to offer me a hand, I accidently push him off the raft. "No!" I scream.

The rest of the group panics and jumps off into a deep pool. The rocky area up ahead is turning into rapids. Too late to jump. I cover my head, not sure what is coming next.

I fall to the bottom of the empty raft. Lying on my stomach, the raft slams against rocks as I bounce down the river. An ear-piercing sound blasts a ringing noise in my ears.

My eardrums pound.

The rush of water consumes me.

Something hit the raft, I'm almost certain the sound is a bullet, so close to my ear.

I'm shaking all over. God, it's cold.

The booming noise is still throbbing in my ears. A sickly, smoky mist surrounds me.

I'm trembling.

If I could only stop the shudder; clear my mind. It smells like something is burning. The frigid water is not the cause of my uncontrollable quivering, even the blood seeping out of my arm isn't alarming. Darkness colors the pool of water inside the raft. I watch it spread out, and circle around me. Nothing hurts.

A dark red color swirls.

How is this happening? Oh Jack. I pray he didn't get hit.

Focus. I know what I saw. I think I do. My mind connects the elusive dots of time of what just occurred.

Eric.

Eric Beck is the shooter. God, it happened so fast. Can that be possible? One minute, I see him perched on a rock overlooking the twelve rafts floating down the waterway, cradling something wrapped in an American flag pointing at the river—at me, at us, at my classmates. I wanted to scream at Jack to turn around. I froze instead.

Did it hit me? Muffled ringing is all I hear now. Images flash in my mind of members of the Dream Team and the Hard Liquor Boys falling into the rapid waters of the Youghiogheny River.

Cody. The horrific image etched in my mind. Cody and Jason Johnson, not jumping into the river but falling sideways, like tin duck targets at the State Fair shooting gallery. One hit and they go down, slanted, the water around them stirred up, churning, moving dark puddles of color.

The raft moves down the river at a fast pace, but I can't get up from lying on my stomach. Is Jack okay?

I'm going to die. The irony of it all.

I can't help it, in the middle of this horrific moment, I can't help but think of all the hard work I've done to set up my own fake death. Weeks of putting everything in place to eliminate Sunday Foster. It seems deliriously hysterical as I bounce along the raft, and I almost want to laugh or cry. I must be hallucinating. Suddenly, my mind controls itself. The baby. My mind flashes to the baby inside me. I am responsible for this child, no one else but me in charge of this life growing inside me.

Will I die?

Certain a bloody bullet hole is bleeding profusely in some part of my body, I move my hands over my stomach. No pain. As I pull myself up to the side of the raft, a thunderous roar, a fast-swirling rapid looms directly ahead of the raft. Trees and sticks float by in the water. This is it—I'm now going to flip over on an uncontrollable raft that's leaking air. No strong family unit to save me.

Jack. I see his face, at the same time, the raft plunges forward and straightens.

It straightens.

I'm okay.

I grab a section of my torn sweatshirt and try to rip it. My arm hurts, I mean throbs, but it's almost like it's asleep with pin pricks and I need to shake it back to life. It's bleeding. Sopping up the blood, I see the cut is not deep enough to hold a bullet. I don't think I was shot.

Thank God. Thank YOU, God, I pray. *Please let Jack be okay. He's one of the good ones, he's one of yours.*

Get out of the raft, my inner mind yells at me, unless it's God trying to help me. *Move.* I test and lift my right leg, and then my left. I seem to be okay. As I sit up, I vomit.

Jack. I'd pushed him out of the raft. I know I did. I'm certain.

Just breathe. I wipe my mouth and crawl along the bottom of the raft toward the edge, away from the vomit, remembering what the guide had said about not standing up in the river; you could die. Really? I bet he never envisioned a school shooting on the river. I've grown up with the aftermath of the historic Columbine, Sandy Hook, Parkland, and all the other hundreds of school shootings and terrorist attacks on the news, who can keep track anymore, but nothing had prepared me for this.

The blood from my arm is leaving a trail across the dry bags in the bottom of the raft. I lean back and for a second, my head yanks back. My hair gets caught in something as the raft hits a large rock. I now have to yank out a clump of my hair to get myself loose. The dry bags—I have a small pack in the yellow rubber dry bag. I press forward, sliding over to reach the waterproof bags. *Think, Sunday!* I hesitate for only a moment, open the dry bag, and grab the most valuable possession in my life: a little pack that holds my future. Inside, beside the tampon, lip balm, and hundred-dollar bill that I've carried everywhere for the last month, is my most valuable possession: my Greyhound locker key. I grab some guy's hat and a black jacket in the dry pack. My phone is also in the pack, I turn it on and there is no service. I stash it in the jacket pocket, and wonder if this is really a waterproof phone. I place the small pack in the winter ski hat (who brings a winter ski hat on white-water rafting trip). I'll have to thank him and yank it over my wet head. I'm shaking. I jam the balled up black jacket under my life vest, and pain shoots through my arm.

Shaking uncontrollably now, I struggle to the edge of the raft, watching the blood mix in with the water. I need to get to the bank. I can do this. I tumble into the water, and go under. The life vest bounces me back and I spit out the river water.

I try to keep my head above water and maneuver my body to the bank. I grab at several tree limbs, their jagged edges cutting my cold hand until finally, with everything I can muster, I hold onto a thick branch. My hat is still on. In either direction on the river, nothing moves except for the rapids and the shrinking raft that is floating down the river. *What am I doing?*

Adrenaline soars through me. I reposition myself, both hands atrophied from the cold water, but they lock on the branch with a death grip. Someone will rescue me. I'll stay here and wait for someone to find me. I repeat it, brainwashing myself with the idea. The other voice in my head reminds me of what is under my hat. That untethered voice inside me grows louder: *this is it.*

This is it: this is your shot a new life without any questions.

Do it, do it, do it now!

Is Jack okay? Is he alive? I need to know this one thing before I even think of trying to make my escape. I love him now more than ever. Can I leave him?

I play out every scenario in my mind as I hang onto the bent branch. If I go to the hospital—the baby. My pregnancy will no longer be a secret. My life will collapse. I'll destroy this baby's life with HE and SHE. The cycle will continue.

It's amazing what freezing cold water can awaken. My mind is programming, coding an outcome. I believe, no, I know, that if I can find my way back to the Baltimore Greyhound bus station, I can make it.

Everything I need—my I.D. and money—is padlocked in the Greyhound bus station. I have the key. I can feel the pack in my hat.

I push back all the horrific images that haunt me. Block out the sickening image of Eric holding the gun, and try not to think about Jack. Once again, I had a plan. I had a way out that would be best for everyone. I'm determined to figure a way out now.

Chapter 11

Angels, Deer, and Greyhounds

My hand quivers as I slide the key, my lifeline, into the locker. I hesitate, convincing myself it's not going to work, but it does. The vein in my forehead pulses so hard, everyone must be scrutinizing my every action. My hair is tucked up inside my ski cap. Sunglasses perch over the hat resting on my forehead, and I have earplugs in, wires hanging on my face.

No music plays. The headphones weave into my coat attached to nothing. I'm hoping for less interaction; my attempt at mimicking the kids at school who want to shut out the world. My attempt at depicting a normal teenager. *NORMAL.* Nothing is normal about this moment. Nothing is normal about my life, the shooting, or me. I pull the beat-up brown suitcase out of the locker, it's heavier than I remember. My fingers curl so tight around the handle, a pain shoots through my arm. A lifeline. It's the last thing I have left in my life. No. I correct myself. It's the first thing Hannah Williams has in her new life.

The hair dye, the colored lenses, and the clothes in my suitcase are the catalyst to become Hannah.

Am I really doing this?

Uncertainty washes over me. My head is pounding like a club beat. Everything changes now. I want to go forward, but I'm frozen in place. I'm filthy, exhausted, numb, and not thinking straight. I'm trying to let my gut dictate this moment.

Focus. Head on over to the truck stop's private bathroom and take care of it.

Make the transition. Do it, move. Right now. Move your legs. MOVE.

Eye contact. I can't make eye contact. I don't mean for it to happen, but I look up and this old man meets my dead stare, my eyes fill with water. He studies me as if he can see inside me. He smiles, revealing a broken tooth. I back up. Concern: it's there in his eyes. I have to get it together.

I squint my eyes to block out the gunshots, the students, the blood, Eric, Jack. Oh God. I'm praying for Jack. I don't know if God is listening to me, but I prayed for his safety on my long walk through the woods. I prayed for Jack's forgiveness, for God's forgiveness. My heart is cracked. Jack has to be alive, but I have no idea what happened after I pushed him out and floated down the river. I can't go back there; can't think about the shooting.

Focus. Focus on the PLAN at hand.

The old man is no longer staring at me. He's moved on to the next person of interest, I step forward.

I'm walking. Just trying to move forward and function.

I've been practicing my name and my story. As I trekked through the Pennsylvania woods, I talked out loud to the birds and the trees. Hannah Williams. Hannah Williams. Last night, when I could not take one step more, I dropped to the forest ground. Nightfall came fast and even though it was May, I shivered for hours, wondering if my clothes would ever dry.

A few spokes of light poked holes through the tree canopy. Alarmed, I hid at first, frozen behind a bush, terrified thinking spotlights were looking for me in the forest. It was only the moon.

Exhaustion finally took over as I collapsed against a tree, my body wet, my face glistening with tears. When I woke, clarity found me with a strong odor of wet wood and soil as the morning light discovered me. I dug a hole, buried the life jacket and gear from the whitewater rafting company, and forced myself to eat one of the three waterlogged protein bars I had rescued and started walking. I walked and walked—at least ten miles, maybe twenty. (Who knows? Time had no meaning anymore.) I no longer had my phone, if there was a way to track it, they would find it somewhere in the Youghiogheny River in Pennsylvania.

Like discovering an oasis in a desert, it must have been early morning when I heard the sounds of motors and the smell of exhaust. A truck stop! It could have been a pot of gold. I cleaned up myself and my bloody arm the best I could, bought a cheap jacket, t-shirt, and sunglasses, and approached a relic of a truck driver who was headed to his truck. Inhaling, shoulders back, I surged into my actress persona, something the years of hiding and abuse had taught me. I repeated my mantra: *I can do this.* In my mind I relive the scene, making sure I didn't miss anything.

"Excuse me, sir, would you give me a ride? My boyfriend and I got in a fight—he made me get out of the car. I've been walking and I just need a ride."

Six feet of wrinkled clothes froze in place. The trucker wore a grey flannel shirt, and worn faded blue jeans. His kind hazel eyes circled from my hat to my muddy shoes. He stared me down.

Did he know who I was? Was there some video on the internet already? Paranoia almost buckled my knees.

"Sir, I just need a ride. Are you headed anywhere near Baltimore?" I wasn't giving up.

He studied me for what seemed like an eternity. Nodding his head, he broke the frozen trance and motioned to his truck. He walked with a slight limp. I followed keeping three feet between us. I don't know if he could speak. He was silent during the drive. Not one word. Thankful for no questions, I watched the countryside fly by as I tried to block out the smell of mildew, tobacco, and sweat. I offered him a protein bar and he nodded and turned up the old-time country music on a dusty cassette player. I didn't even know they still made cassette tapes. The words of the sad ballads stung my heart, adding water to my eyes. Stories of a man losing his wife, his life, and his dog.

What was the media was saying about the shooting? I blocked it out of my mind to stop shaking. The innocent baby inside me, the child I needed to save, gave me strength. When we got close to the city, Thomas Powell (that was the name on the ID hanging on the dashboard) pulled over at a truck stop in Baltimore.

Miracles do happen. Maybe Thomas Powell was an angel. Lucky for me, he picked the truck stop closest to the bus station. My truck stop. My bus station. I took it as a sign.

The rain makes everything colorless, almost like it washes away the brightest hues from the sky, the flowers, even the trees. Leaning my cheek against the window, I watch the muddy countryside flash by. So here I am, the new me, Hannah Williams, sitting on a Greyhound bus en route to Los Angeles. I'm near the back of the bus, but not the very back, trying to blend in. My fervent wish is to be left alone. A used California tourist guidebook I picked up at a garage sale for a dollar a year ago, rests on my lap. I need to be a typical bus rider.

Be unnoticeable. I can't curl up in a ball and cry: that would definitely draw attention. As soon as they hit, I wipe the tear drops off the cover of the State of California, hoping no one notices.

The bus is filling up and an older Hispanic woman takes the seat next to me. She appears to want the same thing, privacy. She doesn't even say hello. As we pull out, a twisted elation fills my chest. I glance cautiously at the woman beside me. It's nighttime, her eyes are closed, she is trying to sleep, and a strong smell of garlic emits from her skin. No one is staring at me; no one looks at me.

I squeeze my eyes shut and my stomach muscles tighten as I try to block out the flashbacks of the river. I need to sleep. My body is exhausted, but my mind is terrified. In the woods, I slept for a little bit when I leaned up against a tree and passed out.

Glimpses of last night come back to me. I don't know how long I lay there crumpled, but I opened my eyes to the trees, crying out loud for Jack. Covered in a sticky sweat, my body ached as I gulped for air, unable to catch my breath. In my dream, Eric was standing in the trees. I could see him holding the gun wrapped in the tattered American flag, staring at me. I couldn't let him into my brain.

Get out.

Amir. How is Amir? The question has been circling my mind. The best thing is to let him think I died. I've convinced myself of this. Being Eric's only friend, he must be going through some terrible times. He doesn't need this. Amir was a true friend when I needed it. I'm genuinely sorry I can't be there for him, but he will bounce back and soon he'll be away from all of it and graduate. I'm glad he didn't go on the school trip. He'll be okay.

In two days, fourteen hours, and thirty minutes, I will arrive in Los Angeles, California. I picked the bus schedule with only one transfer: Pittsburgh, Pennsylvania. The bus, a moving bed of material seats, shuttled a load of strangers from city to city. After Maryland, the bus will travel to Pennsylvania, Ohio, Indianapolis, Illinois, Missouri, Kansas, Colorado, Utah, and Las Vegas, the last stop before California.

I don't care about seeing the country. I did, before. Maybe someday I will see the United States of America, but now all I want is to head west, far, far away from Maryland, Pennsylvania, and HE and SHE. I give them one minute of my thought and wonder about their response to the shooting. Would they play the role of mourning parents? Join the outraged mothers and fathers of the HLB and Dream Team? Hug the families of the students killed in the school shooting? They will probably try to sue the school because I signed the consent form.

I try to steer clear of even thinking about Jack, blocking his beautiful face from my mind, blocking his name, and trying to shut up that incessant voice that shouts his name in my head. As soon as it enters, I try to think of the mission at hand and my new plan. He has to be okay. I think I would know if he was gone.

Gone. I'm gone. Does he know?

If I think about it one more minute, I will fall to pieces.

My mind goes back to Amir, and I deliberate whether he really believes I'm dead. I hope so. I know he'll be sad—our weird friendship has grown strong—but with this new turn of events, he might honor my memory by never telling a soul of my original plan to fake my death. I pray he will keep my secret forever.

Just in case I'm wrong about Amir, I took no chances at the Baltimore Greyhound station. I knew if I left the key in the storage locker, he would figure out the truth. The key is now in the bottom of a toilet in the bathroom of the truck station, hopefully on its way down the sewer. It's better this way; cleaner. Amir has to believe the PLAN never happened.

Sunday Foster is dead.

Chapter 12

Smells, Saltines, and First Jobs

"If the smell doesn't kill us, the junk food will." He is smiling, this happy-go-lucky personality.

Please stop smiling at me.

He sits next to me on the hard-orange chairs at the transfer station in Pittsburgh. I can feel him watching me. I pretend to be engrossed in my California guidebook, the pages wrinkled by my tears. He appears to be about my age, maybe a little older, his brown, razor-cut hair dyed blonde at the tips. His UNLV t-shirt exposes tattoos on both arms, and his beat-up brown cowboy boots are actually somewhat cool.

I target an empty chair away from him, give him a sideways glance, inhale and exhale, and get up and move. He continues to glance my way—not that I'm watching, but I know he's studying me. Time drags on waiting for the bus to depart. Finally. As I get into line to board the bus, he walks right behind me. My super power nose can smell him. Not bad. Better than the man that sat beside me earlier, almost clean like dryer sheets.

"I'm sorry, but the guy on the last bus stinks. I mean, reeks:

a body odor that creeps in your nose, and it's hard to breathe. I can still smell it. I've been blessed with a good smeller, but sometimes it's not a good thing. You know what I mean?"

I refuse to answer him, or even acknowledge my super sensitive nose, or that I know exactly what he's talking about. I'm not answering, no eye contact, and I start to count to ten in my head, hoping by the time I reach ten, he will walk away.

Seven. Eight....

"Since we are transferring buses, maybe we could sit beside each other. This is the last transfer, and it looks like a crazy full load, so we could be safe from strange-smelling seatmates. I'm Hudson, and I showered." He sticks his hand out. I ignore his hand. He isn't giving up. "I'm going to Vegas, which is the next to last stop." A no response from me does not dent his confidence. "I'm going to start classes at UNLV this summer. This is just the beginning of everything. Everything great. The story of my life starts now."

I continue to ignore him and step in front of him, but he still stands there, moving forward in line with me. Now, he's slightly behind me but I know he's smiling like I'm interested. The woman in front of me carries several blankets, a jumbo pillow, and a bag full of crackling plastic-bagged junk food. The man to the left of her is quite large, wearing crumpled clothes and a dirty baseball cap. I imagine my superhero nose will be on high alert with the majority of the passengers.

Would it be less conspicuous if I sat beside someone my own age? There's a chance people will think we are traveling together. Again, I survey the variety of folks in line. Yes, a few are sketchy. Smelly, dirty, possibly even intoxicated people.

I can do worse.

Make a decision.

I turn around, forcing one of my fake half-smiles. A Hannah smile. She is now alive and making her mark on the world. I step off the ledge I've been teetering on, with my first word. "Okay."

That one word is all it takes to start hearing the life story of Hudson Wagner.

Hudson most recently lived in Ocean City, Maryland, and was raised by a single mother, whom he obviously adores. He never met his father, who split when he was three. "My mom and I didn't have much, but we had each other. Sometimes that's enough." Hudson went to eight different high schools all over the country, and because of the constant moving, had a hard time being, as he says, "college material." But UNLV accepted him for a summer session, and with success in those classes, he's confident he'll receive full admission in the fall.

"My mom's happy. It's all she ever wanted," he says, almost as if sunlight beams dance in his eyes. I try not to focus on them. If I'm silent, Hudson just keeps on speaking.

"She might not be too happy about UNLV—she hates Vegas, or Sin City as she calls it—but as long as I'm enrolled in college, she can handle it. It's her thing, you know. I've heard it a thousand times. She would tell me 'you can do anything, but first do this for me and you. College only takes four years and then you can figure out the rest of your life, but no one can ever take that college education away from you.'"

He waits for me to speak, like he'd asked me a question. My head is turned in his direction but I'm half listening, looking at a stain on my seat. It reminds me of blood. The stain. I rub it with my fingers like I can erase it. I grimace, I need to stop the scary thoughts from growing, stop the flashes of memory from surfacing.

"I'm doing it for both of us. I mean, my mom finally has a real job. After years of moving around from ski resorts to beach towns, waitressing, housekeeping, and doing front desk work, she is now Assistant Manager at Harrison Hall in Ocean City. I'm so proud of her, and now she can be proud of me. You know what I mean?"

I nod my head, then look back out the window.

"It doesn't matter what my first job is. Did you know that Brad Pitt used to dress up like a chicken in Hollywood? He handed out flyers on the street to El Pollo Loco. Sylvester Stallone used to clean lion cages at Central Park—he made $1.12 an hour. These are facts. Truth. So, it doesn't matter what you start out as; just what you become."

Hudson stops talking. The silence is a reprieve, but terrifying, as I know he expects me to contribute to the conversation.

"You're so quiet. I guess I'm boring you, and it's late, and you probably want to get some sleep." Hudson pauses as he holds up a bag of chips and a bag of pretzels. "Hey, I don't even know your name."

This is it. Who do I want to be? A rude, depressed introvert? I choose the cautious skeptic. Hannah is going to be careful, but she can be careful and personable. I need to lose myself tonight and find Hannah.

Hannah who wasn't part of a school massacre. Hannah who never met Tyler.

"My name is Hannah, and you're not boring me. This ride is boring me, and we have another fifty-four hours to go. I'll take the pretzels, thanks."

"Okay, Hannah, nice to meet you. So, what's your story—and you can give me the long version, 'cause we've got plenty of time." Hudson settles back in his seat, crosses his inked arms across his chest, opens the bag of chips, and smiles.

It could be worse.

My cheek is warm, and I squint in the sunshine, trying to open my tired eyes. I made it through the night. Hudson and I talked for a few hours last night and then I faked sleep. It's amazing how much you can learn about someone on a bus. Besides Jack, (a sharp pain radiates from my chest just thinking his name), I have never talked to a boy this much. Well, maybe Amir. I wonder how Amir is. I'm sure it is even more difficult for him, since Eric was his friend. I hope he's honoring his promise of keeping my secret.

Hudson is a factoid nerd. He knows every famous person's first job. I name a dozen celebrities, and he knows what they did before they made it big. Exhaustion must have crawled into my entire being, brain, and body somewhere in the early hours of the morning. I realize now, my fake sleeping turned into real sleep.

Thank God, I don't remember dreaming.

We are coming up to a one-hour lunch stop in Indianapolis.

Hudson eyes flutter open. He looks around like a lost deer, a kind lost deer, and his green eyes focus on my face as he runs his hand through his hair and his lips split open, revealing his straight white teeth and a smile. His inner joy makes him cute. He pulls out a stick of gum, unwraps it in a flash, and it disappears in his mouth. He offers me a piece. His mother taught him well.

"Good morning, Hannah." Even his eyes look happy. "We have an hour lunch stop coming up. I'm going to get something to eat, I'm starving. Wanna join me?"

I can do this. I force on my fake face. "Sounds great. I'm

hungry, too." And it is the truth.

This thing, the two of us being seatmates, walking into a truck stop together, might not be so bad. In some way, it is easier than traveling by myself. As we walk into the restaurant at the truck station, we talk like two friends traveling together. Hudson laughs at everything and his energy is contagious. Anyone glancing our way may have thought we were girlfriend and boyfriend, possibly college students. I'm explaining my California plan: get a job, establish a one-year residency, then go to college the next year.

"I hate California," he says before continuing, "well, I don't hate the whole state, really. Just southern California, except for the beautiful beaches and ocean. And, I don't hate it but it's just not one of my favorite places."

I can't imagine Hudson hating anything.

"There's too many rules. I mean, most beaches, you can't even take your dog to the beach, or collect seashells. It's very expensive and people are nosy and fake. Like South Beach in Florida, a lot of plastic people."

Hudson loves the Wild West: thus the cowboy boots and the glitter and dazzle of Las Vegas. I'm glad he's not into the plastic.

"When my mother and I lived in South Beach, I met this great guy, George, who left one of the big resorts in Florida to manage a casino and restaurant in Vegas." His warm voice is like a happy melody of excitement as he speaks. "A part-time job while I go to school would be perfect. Or maybe I could even swing full-time. But if not, I'm not worried. Jobs are plentiful in Vegas, and the cost of living is low." He leans close as if sharing a secret. "You can eat breakfast, lunch, and dinner for 99 cents, and I found a cheap, cool youth hostel for a week."

Hudson seems organized. He pulls up the hostel on his phone, showing me the pics and the rates.

"You should think about Las Vegas," he says like it is the greatest place on earth, and the greatest idea.

"I have my sights set on California. I'm ready for the beach, LA—you know— California Dreaming."

He opens the restaurant door for me. "Well, the thing about Vegas versus LA is that an 18-year-old girl like you could find a job that probably pays good money and you can live cheap without a car and save up your money for college." He cocks his head. "And you know, in Vegas you don't pay any state income taxes, so you make more money." Hudson pauses. "Madonna worked at Dunkin' Donuts although she didn't make it past the first day; she was fired for squirting jam into a customer's face." He smiles, checking to see if I was listening. "And the most important point to remember is that it's the capital of second chances."

Startled, I slowed down. "Why would you say that?"

"That's a nickname for Las Vegas. I like it better than Sin City, and I remind my mother constantly of that nickname instead of Sin City. Another favorite is: 'What happens in Vegas stays in Vegas.'"

My chest constricts. In the truck stop, I'm out in the open. I have a sudden flashback to the river. I've read that fight or flight feeling is innate. The smell of food is in my nose. I think I'm going to throw up. I stop walking and drop my backpack on the floor. I am going to throw up.

"Hannah, you okay?" Hudson stops, a strange look on his face.

"Must be something I ate. My stomach's upset. I need to go to the restroom."

"Are you sure you're okay?" He hesitates, picks up my

backpack and hands it to me, holding on to it, until I give him a look. I nod my head afraid to speak or I'll vomit.

"I'll get us a table." Hudson says as I dart back outside to the restroom.

I barely make it to the bathroom stall, and I throw up. I suppose this is morning sickness. Great. I clean up, brush my teeth, and try to pull myself together. My arm has stopped bleeding, I change the bandage. I've always seen in movies that Saltine crackers help when you're pregnant. I guess the little life inside of me is shouting at me to eat. I will order some soup and crackers, and maybe even some orange juice.

Hudson is at the counter, his eyes focused on the flat screen above the counter. I lower my body onto the stool beside him, my backpack between my legs.

"You know what really gets me is the news media. I don't know why they keep showing his photo." His speaks slower than usual, and anger edges his voice.

"I mean change the guns laws or something, but don't keep telling the story of the shooter. It's probably what all those sick psychos want—some kind of gruesome fame attached to their name. They shouldn't even put their pictures on television. Give them all a name like Loser #126, and cover up their face. I am sick of school shootings and no one doing anything about it."

I almost fall off my stool; my fingers grip the counter to steady myself. I was so into thinking about the baby and eating, I didn't even pay attention to the television mounted behind the counter. Filling the television screen, there is a photograph of Eric. In slow motion, the light in the restaurant dims, I hear the news anchors voice.

"A shooting rampage in this small Pennsylvania town left 29 people dead, 25 students and 4 adults. Two missing students are

believed to be dead. Friday's shooting became the second-deadliest school related shooting in U.S. history."

I have to get out of here. My legs are shaking. *Breathe. Focus.* As I exhale, a sheen of sweat emerges from my pores. Wetness pools under my shirt. I don't want to pass out. Hudson touches me and the darkness fades.

"Hannah?"

Yes, I'm Hannah, not Sunday.

"May I have a sip of your water?" I say, trying to control the tremor in my voice. Hudson has to hear it.

Hudson holds his glass in his hand, eyes still glued to the television. He passes it to me. "Sure, Hannah, are you okay?"

The glass shakes in my hand, the water inside the glass looks like a wave. I attempt to take a sip. "Yes, I think maybe too much junk food on the bus. I'm going to take a walk, I'm not really hungry right this minute." Afraid to stand up, I force myself to exhale the tight air in my chest. Using the little grit I possess, I dig in my backpack, grab a ten-dollar bill, and force my mouth up in a smile. "Would you mind ordering me a cup of soup to go with some Saltine crackers?"

Hudson takes the bill from my hand, studying my face. "Are you sure you're okay? You look white as a ghost."

"I'm fine." I am no longer an Oscar-worthy actress. "I just need to move, walk around, and get some air. I'll be back in thirty minutes."

Back on the bus, Hudson doesn't utter a word. When he's about to speak, he stops. He stares at me. I pretend not to notice. Does he recognize me from pictures blasting on the news?

The soup is still in its container, cold by now. I open the Saltines, and for the baby, I force a bite.

"Hannah, I think I figured it out," he says.

My heart accelerates. I suck in my breath, almost choking on the Saltines.

"I don't mean to get in your business, but did you know someone from that school?" he asks.

"What?" I answer quickly, the dry crumbs of the bland cracker stuck in my throat. I'm coughing Saltines everywhere. I take a sip of water, calming myself down. "No, did you?"

"No. I didn't know anyone. But when you saw the shooter, you started shaking and turned white as a sheet."

The shooting was real. I know it really happened, but seeing it on the news reinforced reality. Nothing about this minute, this hour, this day, makes sense. For a minute in time, I was trying to be someone else, somewhere else, a false existence. Sunday Foster is missing as the news anchor stated, but soon, if all goes to plan, I'll be declared one of the casualties.

Faking my death, was my PLAN. Yes, it's what I wanted, but not like this. It was just supposed to be MY tragedy down by the beach. This is a nightmare. Most of all, I need to know if Jack's alive or dead. My heart tells me he is alive, but I need to be certain.

I need to get online.

Hudson is patient, adding nothing else, waiting for my response.

"It does shake me up: some high school kid takes a gun to a school outing and shoots kids on a river. I mean, they need to do something. It happens too much. I mean, why? I can't believe no one noticed he was going to snap."

"Someone had to know he was sick or violent. They mentioned radical terrorism; maybe ISIS got to him. Usually, they will find some clue on his social media. Some manifesto." Hudson bends down and fiddles with his backpack, digging for something.

"ISIS, they mentioned ISIS? Why?" I can't imagine Eric writing a manifesto.

"Something about a magazine his parents turned over to the police."

I think about the zombie death game Eric played with Amir. Was that a sign? Radical terrorism? Should I have noticed something? Eric had an American flag. Why an American Flag? None of it makes sense.

Thinking about Eric makes me want to throw up again. I just thought he was a lost kid, a bullied nerd. Who was I to judge? I mean, what about his parents? No one knows what goes on behind closed doors: trust me. I think about Amir again, wondering how he is holding up. He plays the zombie killing game, as well. Did Amir ever suspect what Eric was up to? I can't imagine what Amir must be thinking and going through right now. It makes me cringe, imagining him being picked on. After all his help, I'm not there to help him. For a minute, I wish everything was like it was a month ago, me sitting by the creek, Amir throwing rocks and everyone alive at school.

I know the best thing is that Amir thinks I'm a casualty of the shooting. I know it will hurt him, but Amir can't know I'm alive. Amir is tougher than he looks. The Saltines are smashed in pieces all over the tray table. In pieces, that's me. I eat the ones I can and clean the rest up and throw them in the bag with the soup.

Hudson has an iPad mini and the bus has Wi-Fi. I can't take not knowing. I need to know about Jack. I need to see the names of the victims.

"Can we look up the story on your iPad?"

"My battery's dead, but I just checked the Wi-Fi on my phone.

It's not working."

"Okay. I don't really want to think about it anyway." I force my lips to smile, my stomach broadcasting nausea and a dull pain thumping in my head. "Tell me more about Vegas." I need to think about anything but the shooting. I need Hudson's soft low tone and cheerfulness to take me away from the horrific images circling in my mind.

We pass an old cemetery and it makes me think of Hannah's grave. The *real* Hannah Williams. Hudson notices my fixation on the roadside graveyard.

"Rod Stewart's first job as a teenager was a grave digger in Highgate Cemetery in London. Can you imagine doing that?" Hudson lines up little chocolate doughnuts on a napkin on his tray table.

"No, I can't imagine." I turn quiet, picturing the green grass and slanted hill of the West Virginia cemetery Amir and I had visited. Amir. At least I knew *he* was okay, since he didn't go on the school trip. I put on my headphones. Hudson offers me a doughnut and his phone playlist to listen to music.

Music has a smell. I'm listening to Sweet Home Alabama and I'm taken back to Jack's kitchen, Marcia baking homemade bread mixed in with the odor of dryer sheets from the laundry, the scent of the family I coveted.

As the bus pulls into St Louis, Missouri, an American flag billows in the wind. A flash of a flag wrapped around a gun, washes away the smell of my good memory, and ignites anxiety deep in my chest, tiny beads of sweat form under my hair. Eric had an American flag wrapped around his gun. How could he be an ISIS follower? It makes no sense. For a moment, I smell the smoke of the gunfire. I practice breathing slow small breaths as

I take the earbuds out and unplug them from Hudson's phone. Sweet Home Alabama will never smell the same again.

"Are you done listening to music?"

I nod.

"You're looking funny again," he says, "maybe you need some more food?" Hudson takes his phone and puts it away, and offers up a bag of mixed nuts.

"Sure."

"Another stop's coming up. Do you know why it's called the 'Gateway to the West'?"

"No, but I'm sure you're going to tell me."

Hudson laughs and chatters away as he proceeds to tell me a funny story about him and his mother touring the St. Louis Arch. His warm eyes glisten with sparkly happiness as he describes his mother. I can't relate, but maybe someday, with my child, I'll understand.

"The Gateway to the West" stop (Hudson's trivia fact of the day for St. Louis) allows the passengers two hours and ten minutes for dinner.

"Want to grab a real meal in the restaurant?" Hudson asks.

I hesitate because I want the company but there are things I need to do. Alone. "I'll catch you back on the bus. I need to make some calls."

Hudson shrugs, "Okay "

I am on a hunt to find a newspaper and locate a store where I can buy a tablet. I don't have any credit cards, which actually makes me laugh out loud, thinking about HE and SHE surviving without credit cards. However, I have three prepaid credit gift cards for emergency situations. My money is hidden in my shoes, and some in the backpack. I carry it with me on and off the bus.

A tablet isn't an emergency, but it seems like a good investment. I can follow the news, look for jobs, and create my fake resume. There will be no digital footprint on my tablet unless someone confiscates it, and it will be Hannah's tablet. I hate to admit it, but living for two days without any technology is strange. Wi-Fi spots are everywhere, so I don't need a service contract, and I have my relic burner phones in the back pack that I can activate if I need to make a call. But who would I call? I can't call Amir or Jack. Jack. Saying his name is like a knife in my gut. *Please be alive and okay.*

The area around the bus station does not look touristy. The air smells foul with trash strewn on the ground, graffiti on the walls, and boarded-up buildings down the street. I hug my backpack closer. I need to find a store where I can buy some type of tablet. The Greyhound bus worker told me there's an Office Depot less than three miles away, and a city bus is coming in ten minutes. Perfect.

"Can you hurry? I'm trying to catch the bus back to the station," I ask, sizing up the slowest clerk in the world, at Office Depot.

"Too late, it just pulled out," he says matter-of-factly in a monotone voice. He continues slowly taking the stickers and security band off my Kindle Fire and activates the code. I want to grab it from him and yell, *HURRY* but I can't. There is only one thing on my mind.

My heart races, I'm laser focused on the new tablet in my hand as I sit on the curb, outside the store. I need to know about Jack, now. Thank God, Office Depot has Wi-Fi.

I completely forget about the bus, transfixed by every news report I read.

Eric is dead.

He shot himself as the police tried to apprehend him.

Jack, my sweet and loving Jack, is not listed as injured, dead or missing. *Thank you, God,* I silently pray. I read the list of names five times, and tears of joy and relief roll down my face. I'm elated for a minute and then, with my head in my hands, I cry for the kids who are on the list: the Dream Team, the Hard Liquor Boys, our National Honor Society advisor and English teacher, Mr. Alexander, and two Ohiopyle whitewater instructors. My grief racks my shoulders, my face slick with tears. A keening sound startles me. I stop crying and realize it is me. I'm making that sound. I try to stop to avoid drawing more attention to myself as I gulp for air. Sunday always held it together, but Hannah: she's a basket case.

I need to stop. Now.

My head between my knees I'm trying to catch my breath. I smell something sweet and can feel someone is there.

An older, pretty blonde woman bends down beside me, gently touching my hunched-over shoulder.

"Honey, are you okay? Do you need help?" She inches forward. There is true kindness in her eyes. Even through my swollen eyes, I can see something resembling compassion. For a split second, I think: yes. What if I spit out the whole story? Tell her everything, and go back to Jack. Can I go to Ed and Marcia's house? Would they help me?

No, HE would never allow the pregnancy. I can't imagine the explosion that would erupt or how I would be able to get away from them and raise the baby. I've gone too far. I wouldn't know how to explain any of this. What if they think I had something to do with the shooting?

Hannah and Sunday fight with each other in my head.

Call Jack.

Jack is Sunday's, not Hannah's. I want Jack's arm around me.

I am Sunday. No one but Hudson knows Hannah.

I must be losing my mind, but who can blame me. I can't explain any of this. The brown hair, the escape to the greyhound bus, leaving the scene of a school shooting. They'll think I had something to do with it. I can't go back because of the baby. The life inside me deserves an environment of love.

I bring out the actress, wipe the tears off my face and attempt a smile. "I'm fine. I just need a cab to get back to the bus station. I missed my bus."

The kind woman cocks her head and looks me in my brown contact eyes, "The bus station? Like the Greyhound station down the road?"

"Yes, my bus leaves in ten minutes."

She pulls a tissue out of her purse, passes it to me, and offers me her hand. "I'll give you a ride." She steers me to her car, not taking no for an answer. A gold cross twirls from her rearview mirror. She seems genuinely concerned.

Wiping my face with the tiny pack of pink baby powder scented tissues, I clean myself up in her front seat and in minutes she pulls up in front of the bus station.

The woman meets my eyes once again. "Can I help?"

I study this compassionate stranger with small wrinkles around her lavender–blue eyes, sitting in her red Prius with a stack of grocery coupons in the cup holder.

For some reason, I want to assure her I'm okay.

"No, I'm just missing my boyfriend. He broke up with me. I'm going back home to California because he doesn't love me. He wouldn't even take me to the bus station. I thought he was the one."

She seems satisfied with my reply, then puts her hand on my arm, the one that is cut. I hold back my yelp. "Just remember this. If you love something, set it free; if it comes back to you, it's yours. If it doesn't, it was never meant to be."

"Thank you." I open the car door wanting to believe every magical word she says.

The bus is starting to smell like rotten eggs and gasoline, plus the toilets are gross. I don't feel like talking right now, and Hudson somehow gets this and has EarPods in. Out of the corner of my eye, I can see his chin drop. For the next ten hours, I try to sleep. When exhaustion takes over, nausea wakes me up. We don't have another long break until morning, when we arrive in Denver, Colorado.

The sun wakes me, and my contacts feel stuck to my eyeballs. It's a clear day with turquoise-blue skies and I can see the stunning Rocky Mountains out the dirty bus window. The enormous jagged rocks jutting up to the sky are beautiful and massive. I realize that what I'd always hoped for, actually existed. Big skies and beautiful mountains. This was a far cry from the green hills and city streets of Baltimore with space to roam. It feels like the further West we travel, the bigger the sky gets. More space to breathe.

"So, this is Denver? It's so beautiful," I say.

"It's a great city, but you should see the mountain towns. Madeline Albright's first job was a bra clerk at a Denver department store." Hudson lifts his eyebrows with a cocky grin.

I can't help but laugh. "Who knows this stuff? And who is Madeline Albright?

"Who is Madeline Albright? She was Secretary of State from 1997-2001." Hudson pops a mint into his mouth and offers me one.

"Of course you would know that." I say, as I plop the mint in my smiling mouth.

The battery is dead in my Kindle Fire. I'm hoping to find a place to charge it in the bus station and clean up in the bathroom. My colored contacts are killing my already red, bloodshot eyes, but of course I can't take them out. I put my sunglasses on.

Every seat in sight has a half-asleep traveler. Tablet charged, I sit in a corner on the floor. I have some time to myself. Hudson proclaimed he is tired of sitting, and left to go walk outside. News reports, there's dozens of them. Sunday Foster is presumed dead, lost in the river. Everyone else has now been accounted for. I hate that I secretly wish someone else would be missing, so it wouldn't just be me, but I'm sure their families have comfort in knowing the truth. If I had parents who cared, the pain of not knowing if your child was alive or dead would be awful. Jack, Ed and Marcia. Maybe someday they will forget all about me. I feel terrible I caused them a shred of pain.

My junior year school picture, which I hate, is on every news site. The only positive thing about the picture is, my hair appears long, straight and very blonde, and my eyes are vibrant blue, even though they look far too big for my face. I'm sort of smiling, and I look happy. Real happy, not fake happy.

Jack had stood behind the photographer, making faces. I worry about people recognizing me, but when I look in the bathroom mirror, I barely know myself, and I'm certainly not smiling.

Cutting my hair brought out curls and thickness, I never realized existed. My short, dark hair has a certain messiness, my face is thinner, and the dark circles under my eyes look even darker reflecting off my dark brown eyes. The girl splashed across the internet, has morphed into another person entirely, she no longer exists.

Hannah Williams, a sad, curly-haired brunette liar, is eighteen, pregnant, and free.

Chapter 13

Blood, Truth, and Facebook

The cramping starts around 8:30 p.m.: a sharp pain in my stomach and my pelvic area. I try to ignore it, pushing the discomfort out of my mind. At around 11:00 p.m., I'm in severe agony. I nudge Hudson, sleeping in the aisle seat, to let me out to go to the bathroom.

I'm bleeding. Bright red. We don't have another stop longer than five minutes until we reach Las Vegas. Exhausted, in pain, and dirty like a little kid playing in the woods, I fight like a soldier to stop the tears from coming. *Suck it up, Sunday.* I make pads out of rough toilet paper folded five times. *No, suck it up, Hannah.* What should I do? I want to give up. I want to talk to Jack. For once in my life, I just want things to go my way, and again, it isn't happening. The bus pulls into Las Vegas at 2:45 a.m.

Hudson bounces awake, his mouth spreading to a wide grin, excited about arriving in his new home. In goes the gum, and the offer to me. He barely notices my struggle, his positive energy bouncing off the windows. I force a smile, take the gum, and tie my hoodie around my waist. I'm a pro now at masking reality.

Hudson's bursting excitement is on the exact opposite scale of my exploding pain and discomfort. He leans closer and studies my face, searching for something, I know he'll never find. "Hannah, can I get your info? I mean, who knows, maybe you will want to visit Vegas sometime, or maybe I will find myself in sunny LA." He takes out his iPad.

"I don't have a phone number right now, but I'm on Instagram. You can check out all my stories, and all the new ones to come."

He tilts his head, his smile growing small. "What's wrong?"

Wrong. Where do I start? Hannah's first and only friend is getting off the bus. I'm bleeding and I don't know what that means. Am I losing my baby? I need help. Suck it up. Say something; act normal.

"I'll friend you." I wonder how many Hannah Williamses there are on Facebook. Amir had helped me set up a page at the library with very little info and a few pics and I haven't even thought to check the account.

I open up my tablet and log on, trying anything to create a distraction from the pain. I gasp as I open the account Amir created for me.

"What?" Hudson asks.

Amir had messaged me three simple words: *Are you alive?*

I panic, and slam the case, certain Hudson read the three words. "Nothing, just that an old boyfriend messaged me." Amir knew my password.

Of course, he set it up. If I change it, he will know I'm alive.

"My battery is dead again. I'll send you a friend request when we get to Vegas. But Facebook's so old school, I barely check it so give me your cell when you get one."

He buys another lie. Probably because his laser focus is on his big moment, the one he has been waiting for is here, and his excitement is propelling him to the city of second chances.

Hudson gets up to use the bathroom. Closing my eyes, I lean over, my head touching my knees, I try to talk myself through the cramps and the bleeding. *Is the baby okay?*

I need to get my suitcase and get off this smelly old bus now.

As I wipe away a tear, Hudson's face is inches from mine. I didn't even realize he was back in his seat.

"Hannah, are you sick?"

I run my hand across my wet forehead. "I'm not feeling so good. I need to get off with you. Will you help me get my suitcase?"

Hudson doesn't hesitate. "What's your suitcase look like? I'll take care of it."

As we get up to leave the bus, I see Hudson looking at the dark wet spot on my seat. He helps me out of the bus, grabs my backpack, and sits me down on the nearest bench. He leaves to get the suitcases.

I don't know what to do next. I'm bleeding and cramping like a bad period. Does that mean I lost the baby? *Lost the baby, just like Clark.*

"Hannah, do you need to go to the hospital? You don't look so good."

"I don't know. I just need to lie down. I don't have any insurance. I don't want to go to a hospital."

"Okay, but I think you need help. Can you tell me what is wrong?"

What do I do?

I try to breathe slowly, but I am in pain with every breathe. I squint my eyes and try to hold back the wave of emotion, about to explode. Everything is a mess. A mess.

"Please, please, do not take me to a hospital. Please, Hudson.

I'll be all right just as long as you don't take me to the hospital."

I think that's the right decision. If I go to the hospital, what if they find out who I really am? Did I do all this to save the baby and now...

I can't think straight.

Hudson sits down beside me and grabs my hand. He is now taking deep breathes trying to calm me down or calm himself down. A pain shoots through me and I squeeze his hand hard.

"You're coming with me. I already have a room booked for tonight. First night splurge at an old casino downtown, the El Cortez."

Chapter 14

It Happens, El Cortez, and Fear the Buttons

"I'm not pregnant. *I'm not pregnant?*"

"You're not pregnant now, nor have you ever been."

A nurse with no eyelashes and dark circles under her eyes flips through papers in a folder. The white concrete walls seem to be coming closer, the faster she flips the pages, the smaller the room gets.

I don't even know how to respond. The smell of disinfectant is strong in my nose and mouth.

"But the pregnancy test was positive. I never got my period."

"It happens. You should have gone to the doctors."

It happens? My entire existence changed because *it happens.* I'm hollow inside, like an Easter chocolate bunny you break open and there's nothing inside, just dead air.

In Nevada, they have a free medical clinic. Hudson brought me here after I crumpled on a bed in the hotel he booked. He saw the bloody sheets. I was certain I had lost the baby. It never even crossed my mind that it was my period, because I was convinced I was pregnant. The second line showed on the dollar store test, faint but I didn't imagine it.

As I walk out to the clinic waiting room, Hudson is sitting in an ugly plastic chair. The waiting room smells like body odor. I'm exhausted, my mind must be playing tricks on me. I was certain this was all some nightmare. Any minute, I would wake up and everything would be back to the way it was. Yes, certainly my life before wasn't great, but at least I had Jack, a job, and a plan. But, seeing Hudson made it real. I can't believe he stayed. Stunned, I can't wrap my head around the news that everything I thought was my reality was no longer true.

I don't remember anything after that, except Hudson took me back to the El Cortez Hotel.

Exhausted, lost, and empty, I sit on the bed in a trance.

"Are you going to be okay?" Hudson asks in a soft voice. "Do you need me to get you anything?"

I barely remember the nurse telling me I might have the beginning stages of endometriosis, a condition where tissue grows outside the uterus. The tissue can cause severe pain and heavy bleeding. Even as I try to replay the conversation it doesn't seem real. Her matter-of-fact gruff voice relaying the results of the ultrasound—no pregnancy, but two small fibroids. She states the combination of the two and stress might cause a skipped period, but there could be other factors. She tells me to make an appointment with a doctor to discuss treatments.

Stress.

A sad laugh bubbles up inside me. I can't contain it. I'm laughing at the sheer impossibility of my situation. The laughter turns to tears, then to sobbing, and here I am, with a guy I'd just met on a Greyhound Bus, sitting in a hotel room in Las Vegas, hiccupping and crying on the bed.

Hudson, in a white t-shirt, his tattoos exposed, paces the room trying to avoid direct eye-contact. Hudson tries to mimic a tough boy persona. At first glance, his clothing, ink, and cowboy boots paint a snapshot of a street-smart guy. The resilient outside appearances mask his kind interior, which always comes out when he speaks of his mother. She must be a saint, teaching him all her life lessons about right and wrong. I am grateful for this tough, kind boy, who just three days ago was a complete stranger. Now his kindness is a part of my journey into my new life. He deserves the truth, or at least a part I can confess.

"I thought I was pregnant and lost the baby."

"I'm sorry." He shifts forward awkwardly, as if to hug me. We don't touch.

"Don't be. I'm sorry for all the trouble." I stand up, more like a crouch. "I'll go now. I'll figure out when the next bus leaves for LA." My voice trembles. I want to curl up and cry. "Can I give you some money for the room?"

Hudson walks over, put his fingers on my shoulder, and gently eases me back onto the bed.

"You need to rest. You need to eat. At least stay here tonight. I paid for one more night. It was only $39 to book online. I'll leave you alone and give you some time to yourself. I'm going to meet the guy from South Beach to find out about a job."

I turn my face away. I can feel the tears building. In one minute, everything has changed; nothing makes sense.

"There's a ham and cheese sandwich and a granola bar on the dresser. You really should eat something. Oh, and I bought you some orange juice." He hands me a bottle of water and a bottle of juice. "Unless you want me to stay?" He massages the back of his neck, confusion and concern written all over his sweet features.

"The nurses gave me a bag of some things you might need. You know: feminine items. They are in the bathroom." His face flushes pink. "I can stay with you, Hannah."

Afraid to speak, I shake my head from left to right, terrified that his kindness will open the floodgates of my sorrow.

"Okay, then, you sleep. I'll be back."

For the first time in the last few days, I'm not on a bus schedule. As the world stops moving, the stillness and my aloneness engulfs me. It's just me now, whoever I am, sitting in a tacky Vegas hotel room that smells like SHE. The life I tried so desperately to save had never existed. I scrub my skin red in the shower with a bar of Dial soap. The letters DIAL stands out on the bar and as each letter vanishes, I wash away my old life. I wash away the baby that never existed.

I scour my skin, desperate to get rid of the past, the shame, the cruelty, the lies. Cigarette smoke wafts in from the hallway, reminding me of SHE. I scrub harder. The soul I tried to save had NEVER EXISTED. The pregnancy is why my plan changed. The pregnancy is why I left Jack. The Pregnancy never existed.

Hudson is off on an all-day job search. I'm finally alone. An emptiness swells in my body. Hannah Williams, a mother of no one. Is it too late to go back? I hate to think what a stupid idiot I am.

"You're a stupid, stupid, stupid girl!" I can hear HE shouting. For the first time, I agree.

I can't even verbalize it in my brain, but the thought creeps around the corners of my mind like a stealthy pickpocket. What would happen to me if I just miraculously appeared back home; maybe I can make up some crazy story about how I couldn't remember who I was. A headline flashes in my mind: "Student from shooting lost in the woods with amnesia." What would Amir think? Based on his messages, he already thinks I'm still alive. I would think he would help me. Why wouldn't he? Pragmatically, how could I explain any of this? My hair was now cut short and dyed dark brown. It's been days since the shooting.

I can't. I don't know how to make any of this right.

I also can't conceive what HE would do to me. With all the media attention, HE is probably a rupturing volcano ready to explode chunks of hot fiery magma. I don't want to be caught in the burning lava. Not ever again. Instinctively, my hand goes to the three scars above my elbow. I've always said they were from a rare spider bite. It's hard to make up stories about cigarette burns. Things have changed. I am different.

Everything happens for a reason, right? There must be a reason. I know my early existence in the menacing house with HE and SHE was not my life; it's not who I am or will ever become. That house, HE and SHE, and THE DARK are not my destiny.

I study the vintage hotel room. A cheery, cheap rendition of a time gone by brings strange comfort to me. I am without them. They no longer have control. The past is no longer my truth. I want Sunday back, but I don't want the surroundings that made up the world of HE and SHE or the memory of Tyler. I want Jack, the one human on this earth who loved me and believed in me... but I can't have one without the other.

If you love something, set it free.

I am setting Jack free. I don't want to, but I am. I still wish I could talk to him, hear his voice, tell him everything. Maybe he would forgive me. But this is stupid thinking. He can never know where I am, and therefore he can never forgive me. I can't imagine his grief. I can't hurt him anymore.

Tomorrow, I will catch the next Greyhound bus to California and block Jack from my mind. I owe him that. He needs to get over me and move on. Tomorrow, I will stop torturing myself wondering if he would ever forgive me for Tyler, and for not letting him know I'm alive, and for leaving him.

I'm alive.

While people are searching for my lifeless body back home, I'm resting in a Vegas hotel room, living and breathing, exhausted, the grit of everything lying on top of me. I'm afraid to close my eyes for the nightmare of the shooting to replay. The smell, the sound of the gun fire and the screams. Lately, I hear the screaming.

I need to see Jack's face. His kind, cheerful and loving face.

Tomorrow I'll stop looking, but today I need to see his handsome face and remember my every day Jack, not the Jack falling into the rapids, confused, and concerned. I flip open my tablet and head to his Instagram. There he is, crooked smile, pink scar on his cheek, and hair that looks like he just ripped off a ski hat. God, I love his hair, his smile, his face.

Then my eyes go down the page and get stuck on a photo of me—well, the old me. My hand goes to my short brown hair and tugs. I wrap my arms around myself as I stare at the picture: long blonde hair, a real smile, and Jack's head next to mine. Jack had created a video, "Looking for Sunday."

Oh my God. *Oh Jack.*

I hit play on the video and Jason Mraz's "I Won't Give Up" starts playing. I'm a mess. I can't control my sobs as they escalate. I grab the pillow and try to muffle my cries. It seems like an eternity before I catch my breath.

Oh Jack, I'm so sorry. I miss you so much. I trace his handsome features on the screen.

He can't forgive me and he never will, for I am gone. I keep my face covered with the pillow.

Where am I?

I wake up and for a minute, just one minute, I forget who Hannah is. I smell smoke and think SHE must be near me. I flinch and then the room comes into focus, like adjusting a lens on a camera. Hudson is staring out the window, deep into the early morning dawn of Vegas, shirtless. I study his naked, lean, muscular back, a tattoo on his left shoulder. He's wearing Levi's. His hair is wet from the shower; it's not all spiked up, and I notice it curls at the end by his ears. From behind, he looks different. He turns around and glances over at me as he goes to put his t-shirt on.

"How are you feeling?" he asks.

"I'm better." I sit up, picturing how I must look with my red, puffy eyes and swollen face. "Any luck with the job?"

"I got it." His white teeth gleam. "It's not quite what I imagined, but it's a job. I start tomorrow."

"That's great, Hudson, really wonderful. What type of job is it?"

"It's a little bar and casino, east of the strip. Nothing fancy, but not horrible. Meet the dishwasher, cleaner, and errand boy." Hudson smirks and takes a little bow. "Michael Dell, founder and CEO of Dell Computers, was a dishwasher at a Chinese restaurant, making $2.30 an hour, so it could be worse."

"Well, congrats, you never know what it will turn into. That's really good." I mean it, I am happy for him. He is a good person. He deserves all his plans to work out.

"They're hiring cocktail servers," Hudson states. "Jennifer Aniston worked as a waitress while she was starting out."

"You interested in serving drinks?" I ask.

"No, they only hire females: young women like you. Hannah, if you are interested in sticking around Vegas, I could introduce you to this guy, George. He's all right, a little more slippery than I remember as a kid, but I'm sure he'd hire you." Hudson moves his suitcase and backpack on the bed and keeps talking as he packs up.

"We have to be out of the room by 11:00 a.m. I'm moving to Hostel Cat. It's a shared dorm room but they have free Wi-Fi, breakfast, and a laundry room. I just paid $100 for a week and I'm going to try that for a while until I find a roommate or an apartment." Hudson walks into the bathroom, collecting the miniature soap and shampoo bottles from the hotel. "Why don't you come with me? Check it out for a night. It's safe, clean, and cheap."

I stand up and close my eyes steadying myself. "Thanks, Hudson, but I'm headed to California. I really want to thank you for helping me. I don't know what I would have done without you." I'm awkward, trying to say the right thing, as I lean against the bed. I can see the pink-tinted sheets from when I'd tried to soak in cold water to get the blood out, hanging over the shower curtain rod.

"Really, thank you, Hudson." I am having difficulty finding the right words. "Your mom would be proud of you for the man you are." I want to hug him, but I don't know how. Hugging is foreign to me. Jack is the only guy I ever felt comfortable hugging.

Hudson stares at me for a second, his mouth opens, but no words come out. He tilts his head and bites his lower lip as if fighting an internal struggle with an imaginary wall blocking the words from coming out of his mouth. This full-time chattering optimist is for once solemn.

"I'm just glad you are okay." He reaches into his pocket and throws a bent business card on the other bed. "Here's George's number in case you change your mind." He pauses. "Hannah, you sure you're going to be all right?"

I nod. Hudson picks up his things; and with his hands full, he stands right in front of me. We are inches apart. I smell his distinct clean scent. I like it.

Again, awkward silence. It's as if he is daring himself to do something, but he can't pull it off.

"Hannah, it's going to get better. My mom always told me you have to fight through some bad days to earn the best days of your life."

Tears fill my eyes. This boy, this sweet boy, who was just a stranger three days ago cares about me—or at least about Hannah. He has no idea of who I am or who I was. He doesn't care. I move closer to him and clumsily hug him and his belongings. It feels good. I will never forget him. I hold on a little too long. I have no fear, because he is nothing like Tyler. He drops his bags, leans into me, and lets me hug him, and he hugs back.

I'm showered, packed and ready to get back on the bus to California. I need to look at Jack's Instagram one more time. I convince myself that seeing his face will give me strength.

Sixteen messages pop up on my Hannah social media. One is from Hudson, a short note but it makes me happy: "Hope we stay in touch. I'm here if u ever come back to Vegas. Good luck in LA."

The other 15 messages make me sick to my stomach. All fifteen are from Amir. They start out calmly:

"Sunday, are you alive?"

"Sunday, are u okay?"

"Answer me, Sunday."

"I see someone messaged you. Sunday, where are u?"

"Sunday, please answer me; I need to know u are OK."

"Sunday are you in Las Vegas or LA.?"

Each message seemed angrier. The very last one took my breath away.

"Sunday, if you don't fuckin answer me, I'm going to tell your parents. I'll tell them everything about Hannah Williams. They will know you are in California. Just answer me."

Stupid, Stupid, Stupid me. Amir created the Hannah Williams accounts; he knew my password and had friended himself. I click out of Facebook and Instagram as if it burns me. He can see if I'm online right now. I am so stupid.

Oh shit, I have compromised my new identity. Connections: I had been so careful about my digital footprint and now my internet connection was my accomplice. The world was intimately connected by our digital trail. I remember reading in 'my how to fake your death' books to fear the buttons. We press buttons every day on our phones, our laptops, our tablets, and it all leaves a trace of when we get on and where. Amir was so convincing when he created my social media accounts, asserting I had to have an existence online to be real. Back then, I was concerned about the phone number/email you had to enter to register, and you had to have a phone line so they could send you a text. Amir used my prepaid cell phone and then called to delete my number. A record still existed. I hunched my shoulders, rocking back and forth.

If I close the account, he will know; if I change the password, he will know. Amir will know I am alive, and my gut tells me this is the wrong thing. If Hudson messages me again, Amir will know I am in Vegas. If I don't do anything, he might think it was random or a wrong message.

Amir knows too much. Will he guard the secret he vowed to keep?

Now doubt, anxiety and Amir are making me question my California plan. Should I stay or should I go?

Chapter 15

Everything stays in Vegas, Sleeping in Closets, and Stalkers

The stench of cigarettes and alcohol fill my nostrils as my eyes adjust to the dim light. The smell is overwhelming, almost suffocating. The dinging of slot machines drowns out the piped-in music, the temperature about forty degrees colder than the hot Las Vegas sun. Inside the casino feels like a meat locker. Goosebumps instantly appear on my skin. Outside, Las Vegas breaks temperature records and the high today is close to 107 degrees. Dry heat, not humid like the Baltimore summers, but burning hot in my tight black uniform as I walk to work, careful my feet do not slip out of my sweaty flip-flops and touch the scorching concrete. Slow roast, Hudson jokes.

Hudson was right about the job. George hired me and now I have survived my first week as a cocktail waitress at the Magic Hat Casino. The best thing about this dark den of drunks is the fact that George, my new boss, pays me under the table for my trial period. The worst thing is the tight, revealing leotard uniform and the black top hat that I had to buy for $50.

I think back to the interview. Before he would hire me, George, with his sweaty olive skin and greasy long black hair, asked me to change into a two-sizes-too-small uniform behind a thin wooden room divider. I wanted to leave, but I also know I need some fast cash, and I walked out with the mantra that this is just a means to an end. All this as I tried to pull the shiny tight black fabric over my underwear and bra. My skin crawled, just thinking about him watching.

But I sucked it up. I've had worse things happen. I'm no longer that naive girl, they won't happen again. Forcing my expert fake smile, I walked out to show him.

"You need to wear more makeup," he barked as his eyes zeroed in on my chest. "Slather it on, Hannah, and keep your shirt low. I'm giving you a break because of Hudson. He's a hard worker."

It's a job. I'm thankful to have one. I already am way down on cash, after I made myself pay the medical bill from the clinic. I don't want any debts in Hannah's name. Money goes by so fast when I have to pay for everything. Rental prices in California stresses me out. It's five times higher than Vegas. The anxiety of living on the streets in California gives me anxiety. Hudson thinks I can make fast money here and be better prepared for my new life in California. I'm going to stay for a little while. I know Amir knows exactly where I want to go in California, so I have to readjust and take some time to find a new place with enough money saved for a few months of rent.

I'm determined to make some money and think this through. Something about this glitzy façade of a city makes me think it might be easier to hide here. After all, they created a city in the middle of a nowhere, and it is a thriving. If they can dress up and hide a desert with lights and fake attractions, I know I can create a new identity in a never-ending stream of tourists.

Since this decision, Hudson, my one and only friend, hovers over me like a mother bear watching her cub. He's found me a room for rent with two other girls he met at the UNLV summer school. Jamie and Adriana. It's actually more like a walk-in closet than an actual room (there are no windows). I have a twin mattress on the floor with a door I can now (thanks to Hudson), close and lock, a small cardboard dresser, and a long rod to hang my clothes over my mattress. But, it's my space, and the rent's cheap and the bathroom and kitchen are fairly clean.

I hide everything—money, prepaid credit cards and gold jewelry—in a tampon box in the cardboard dresser, praying it will stay safe as I lock my door each day.

When I first met my new roommates, Adriana and Jamie, they were somewhat friendly, basically just happy to have a little more cash towards the rent. I can tell they are curious who I am and my relationship with Hudson. I'm almost certain Adriana has a crush on Hudson. I don't care.

Today, despite our opposite schedules we meet in the kitchen. I'm throwing the last of my groceries in a lunch bag for work.

"Hudson said you have a job?" Jamie asks. She sports a huge mane of hair that is always on the top of her head with the ponytail swinging. Adriana, the younger and always half-dressed of the two, gets up from the futon looking couch to listen.

"Yes, Hudson helped me get an interview. I'm working at the Magic Hat."

They toss a cynical look back and forth to each other, their eyebrows raise, and their eyes meet as if they speak a secret language.

"You're only eighteen, right?" Jamie asks.

"Yes, I'm eighteen," I say because Hannah is eighteen, even

though Sunday is not quite seventeen.

"Can you dance?" Adriana moves her bare shoulders in a graceful move, her Hispanic accent exaggerated, laughing and looking at Jamie.

"I guess so," I answer with a half shrug.

"Great," Adriana smirks, swaying her hips low to the ground. "If you lose your job, you can always dance for the rent." I don't get the joke. I would never strip.

Jamie, the motherly figure of the two, and very matter of fact, takes in a sharp breath. "You can dance naked at eighteen, but you can't serve alcohol until you're twenty-one. If someone asks you how old you are, you're twenty-one. You better be careful, because you can get in a lot of trouble waitressing underage." Jamie is twenty-one has a huge crush on Adriana, and seems to be a proud cocktail waitress at Bally's. Hudson told me she'd worked hard to get the coveted spot.

Adriana, nineteen, is a hostess at Hooters. No surprise there. The first time we met, it seemed obvious she liked Hudson and obvious to everyone but Adriana, Jamie's in love with her. She flashes a fake smile and says, "Just pay the rent on time and we will all get along fine." She dances around and wraps her arm around Jaime and dips.

Just then, there is a knock on the door. It's Hudson. We are on the same shift today and are going to walk in together. Adriana answers the door and she flirts shamelessly while Jamie watches her. Her low-cut uniform makes it impossible not to notice her chest.

Adriana has it bad for Hudson; probably the only reason they rented me the small bedroom (aka the closet). I can see the desire in her eyes when he talks to her. It reminds me of how I'd once looked at Tyler, but Hudson is no Tyler: he has a heart. I don't care why they rented the closet to me. I have an address without any credit check, rent that covers all the utilities, a bed, a job, and I am starting my new life, even if this is now Plan C.

Go for it, Adriana.

My new life consists of long hours of waitressing in the meat locker, sleeping during the day, and creating digital dirt on my social media.

I need a plan, although I know where plans get me, but I have to do something. Amir is going crazy with the messaging:

"Sunday do not ghost me."

"Sunday call me. Call me."

"I need to talk to you."

"Sunday please do not ignore me. Contact me NOW."

"YOU BETTER RESPOND TO ME."

I'm sure the shooting and Eric hasn't made his life easy. With Eric dead, I must be his only friend. He must be lonely and stressed. But he has to let me go.

I can't help but wonder what it is like at school with local families. I can't let myself imagine or I'll think of Jack. I have to block it from my conscious voice when a memory pops up. I can't go there in my heart or in my thoughts. If I did, I will break, I won't survive.

I confided in Hudson last week and told him I didn't want my old boyfriend to find me, so I was going to act like I was in LA on social media. I know he thinks I'm talking about the boy who I thought got me pregnant, but regardless, he was eager to help. He posted a few comments about visiting me in LA next month and we even copied some photos off other people's social media in L.A. to complete the charade. I friended a few guys in

Los Angeles and told them I just moved there and asked some questions about the area. I kept it up, posting a few times a week.

Yesterday, after not sleeping because of Amir's messages, I decide the best thing to do is write Amir a personal message from Hannah Williams. He was on my side before, and I'm sure he is going through so much with the shooting, though I need him to forget about me and be my old friend once more.

Amir,

I thought it would be easier for you if you didn't know anything. I'm okay and I sincerely apologize for not responding after every- thing you did to help me. I can't imagine what you have been going through. I'm so sorry I can't be a friend to you when you need me. I appreciate everything you helped me with in the past, but please let me go. It's the only way. Remember what you taught me: no connections, no footprints. Do this for me. Please.

And then I block him as a friend and change my password again. This will surely make him angry, but I hope my old childhood friend will be relieved I'm alive, and let me peacefully go.

I was wrong. So wrong.

He doesn't let me go. He friended Hudson. Then Hudson blocked him on my request, after I created another lie about Amir being some weird friend of my ex-boyfriend.

I check social media. He isn't stopping. He isn't moving on with his life. I can now see he created other social media accounts and is trying to friend anyone I friend and follow anyone I follow. Amir is stalking me.

My gut tells my brain that this is not normal behavior. I make up excuses about Amir just being concerned and try to push it away. I need to close all social media. My addiction is looking at

Jack, and I need to stop.

From everything I learned about facing a threat when faking your death, you have two choices: stay and hope for the best or get the hell out of town.

Amir knew I was in Vegas at one time, but does he know I stayed, or did he believe I was in California? If I start all over again, I will have to lose my Hannah identity. It seems unfathomable to begin again.

One week later, I log in to close down all my social media when a new private message and friend request comes in from an unknown Facebook account—the message stops my heart.

"Sunday, I'm coming to Las Vegas with my father on his business convention next month. I know where you are living. Meet me or I will go to the police and your parents. There are things you need to know."

Chapter 16

Trapped by Computers, Footprints, and Digital
Shadows

The envelope trembled in my hands, its crisp edges taunting me with possibilities. Five days. Five days since I'd walked into the fluorescent hell of the Motor Vehicle Department, clutching my identity in a manila folder—Social Security card, birth certificate, employee ID with freshly inked address.

The memory of Jamie's decrepit Toyota Corolla made my nose wrinkle. That day, waves of heat had shimmered off its black paint, promising an inferno within. As I'd slid into the driver's seat, the scent hit me—a pungent cocktail of rotting fast food and stale cigarettes. My eyes had darted to the floor mats, daring not to imagine what horrors lurked beneath.

The steering wheel had been slick under my palms, a combination of cheap vinyl and my own terror-induced sweat. Each turn of the test course felt like a tightrope walk, the examiner's piercing gaze burning holes in the back of my neck.

But I'd done it. Aced the vision test with a confidence I didn't feel. Breezed through the computer exam, my finger hovering over each answer like it knew a secret. And now, this envelope. This innocuous paper sleeve holding the key to my freedom—or my downfall.

With a deep breath, I slid my finger under the flap. The plastic card inside felt cool against my skin, my own face staring back at me. Official. Legal. Mine.

A driver's license. My ticket to anywhere but here.

Or is it? Can Amir hack into the Motor Vehicle Department? I know he's brilliant, but the MVD?

I'll keep this identity and figure out how to deal with Amir. I want this to be a happy day for me. Hannah Williams is a real live person with a genuine driver's license. Now, I can do anything. I can't bear the prospect of running again.

Hudson, Adriana and I are going down to Fremont Street to celebrate my new Nevada residency. They think I'm just getting a Nevada license to replace my West Virginia license, but I laugh, smile and dance over the fact I now legally exist. My next step is taking the GED. After cocktailing for two weeks in a dim, smoky casino and being gawked at and touched by old men, I have to get back to the origins of THE PLAN. My sights are set on college.

So, Amir had to have found me in the system.

Amir. Why is he doing this? What is he hoping to achieve? If he continues, he will ruin everything. My stupid mistakes are going to cost me everything. Amir is a computer genius. My new address is on the license. Amir knew THE PLAN. We had spent hours together down by the creek, figuring out how I could make Hannah Williams legal in the system. My new identity is the singular component that will allow me to start my new life. Why would he jeopardize this?

"Connections," Amir had said. "You will never ever be able to speak to Jack again. You will never be able to speak to anyone you have ever met, or at least not as Sunday, and you better hope you never remind them of Sunday. Connections, Sunday. It's all about losing all connections forever."

Is he in trouble? What in the world are the things he needs me to know? I have to meet him. And, he probably knows that I don't have it in me to flee again.

In less than three weeks, Amir will be in Las Vegas.

While counting my money and stashing it in the tampon box, Amir continues to fill my thoughts. Was Amir trying to tell me something to do with my escape from the shooting? My presumed missing body? I long for him to be the boy next door, the nerdy computer geek who remembers my birthday every year.

What happened to my Amir since I've been gone—the one who'd kept his distance at the creek? Who is this new Amir, who threatens my existence? It just proves what I always knew:

Trust NO ONE.

Chapter 17

Terrorists, Birthday Candles, and Bunnies in a Cage

It's a good thing the internet doesn't have a way to track those who have been looking at your profile. I've studied Jack's Facebook and Instagram page like an obsessed follower. I can't help myself. It's the best part of my day. I love reading about how he is doing. Seeing his smile makes me happy.

Last week he wrote:

Sunday is my hero. She pushed me off the raft just as my life jacket was hit. The police suspect the bullet that grazed my life jacket hit Sunday. She saved me. I wish I could've saved her. Sunday, I miss you.

Jack downloaded a video filmed by a bystander on the banks of the river.

I hit play. The video is taken several hundred feet away from our rafts, after the shooting, and whoever's recording tries to zoom in closer, so the video is grainy and blurry. It's difficult to discern who or what is in the video.

Jack writes below the video: It's Sunday lying face down in the raft, lifeless, floating down the river. I know it. Sunday, I'm sorry. If you hadn't pushed me off, I'd be right there beside you.

If you asked me how I'm doing, I would say I'm doing just FINE. Sunday used to say she was FINE—Fucked up, Insecure, Neurotic, and Emotional. She had read that definition in some recovery book or heard it from some kids in rehab for addiction. She loved to use it when someone asked her how she was doing.

Yes, FINE is what I am. I still believe she is out there. I won't give up until there is a body.

Show me she is dead, show me she is no longer here, and then I'll give up, but I'll never forget.

Yesterday he wrote another post.

Sunday was it for me. She used to tell me I was born under a lucky star. She's right, because I was lucky to love her. She also told me I was her sunshine. She was wrong, because it's pretty dark without her. I miss you, Sunday. Did you know I would travel the world to be with you? I hope so.

I can hear our familiar banter.

"You're my sunshine," I would say, and start singing, "You are the sunshine of my life."

"You're my moonlight," he would answer. "My bewitching moonlight."

"Perfect," I'd reply. "Sunshine and moonlight make the day complete."

Today he wrote:

Sunday is alive. I know it. They have never found her beautiful body. Why is that? It has been two months! Where's her damn body? She saved me. I just want to save her.

Sunday, I'm sorry for pushing you to go on the school trip. If we didn't go you would still be here.

His posts break my heart. I stare at his handsome face and his kind puppy dog eyes. *I'm so sorry, Jack. I wish I could really talk to you.*

My stomach aches.

It's possible the police and rescuers have given up the search for my body. I'm presumed dead, and now I am included in the total number of victims in the shooting. I don't want to think about Tyler, but I wonder what they are saying at the courthouse. I wonder if Tyler feels bad for what he did to a dead girl.

I'm not sure what the proper procedure is for investigating a missing student in a shooting spree, but the search for my body is no longer front-page news. The focus now is on terrorism. A commercial airplane that has been missing for over a year was discovered in the middle of a poor African country, the surviving passengers now hostages of a terror group. The media focuses on this new trauma.

Eric, the shooter, is still plastered in the headlines on the internet. Anytime there is another school shooting, which unfortunately seems to happen, Eric is mentioned. Apparently, recently they discovered information in Eric's computer: he might have been supporting ISIS or some other extreme Islamic group. They uncovered al-Qaeda videos on his laptop and an internet magazine in English, "Inspire," reportedly published by al-Qaeda. If Eric was involved in radical terrorism, could Amir be part of some radical group? Could he have known what Eric was up to?

It doesn't seem possible. I hate that my mind even goes there. Yes, Amir's mother is from Kuwait and a Muslim, which, from everything I have seen and witnessed, is a loving and peaceful religion. She is definitely not a terrorist or some extremist, and his father served our country in Desert Storm. I rack my brain to remember. Was Amir a Muslim or a Christian? He celebrated Christmas. His father is Christian. I guess it never mattered to me. I have no idea if the Beck family is religious.

Eric. I don't want to, but I can picture him perched on the rock above the river with the gun wrapped in the American flag. My head hurts, pounding like a hammer, trying to solve a physics theory or equation problem I can't wrap my mind around. Why would you use an American flag if you were an extremist? It will never make sense to me. Never.

My new life is a revolving routine of time blocks. I work the late shift at Magic Hat and by the time I arrive home to my hot closet, I'm exhausted. The days and nights are both hot in Las Vegas, and when I get up in the morning, I only have a few hours to work on devising how to move forward from here. It's moving along at a snail's pace. Everything costs money, and money goes quick.

I'm scheduled to take the GED test at The College of Southern Nevada. It will cost me $95 to receive the diploma—that is, if I pass. Budgeting money is nothing new to me. I've been doing it for the last several years, but funds seem to deplete at a quicker speed than back in Baltimore. At least HE and SHE were responsible for the mortgage and the utilities and, even though they were maxed out, the use of a credit card was a luxury once tasted, never forgotten.

Amir will be here in less than two weeks; I pray I won't have to reinvent myself. As much as I ache for the death of Sunday Foster because of Jack, I want to be Hannah Williams and move on with my life. Getting the GED will be my first step to fulfilling my dream of going to college.

The bus ride to work is crowded today. Men and women dressed in their Vegas work attire, leopard leotards, three-piece bright blue suits and even a ballerina, anywhere else this group would be going to a Halloween party. Completing the GED and going to college is such the right path. Hudson is doing both school and work, which keeps him extremely busy. I'm looking forward to today when we will cross paths at work.

The Magic Hat Casino is a bargain-basement version of a drunk's vision of fun. The darkness and smoke mask the cheap decorating and cheesy theme. The bells and beeps of slot machines add to the old rock music piped in the background. I detest the tight uniform I have to pull on and force over my body and my daily ritual: coating my face with a thick layer of makeup, shadowy black eyeliner, false eyelashes, and dark brick-red lipstick. As I apply the paint, I pretend to be an actress going on stage. The set, a cheap bad movie.

As I slather on the thick foundation and powder, my mind centers on a fact from the past. Today is my real birthday—or, at least, Sunday Foster's birthday. Sometimes, I think I have a split personality. Although the driver's license in my purse states I am eighteen, my deep dark secret of the day—because I have so many—is that I'm actually seventeen, no longer sweet sixteen, which I laugh on the 'sweet' part. Happy birthday to me!

'Homesick' would not be the appropriate word, but something about my birthday makes me think of back home.

Of course, HE and SHE would not have even whispered the two words to their only daughter, but Amir would have shyly presented his annual present. This year, Ed and Marcia would probably have cooked me a birthday dinner. I remember last year when Jack realized I'd turned sixteen as I proudly flashed him my driver's license. He had been so excited to celebrate my birthday. Again, for the hundredth time, I let myself dwell on a memory with Jack. I could hear his voice:

"How long have you had your permit?"

"Four months."

"When do you turn sixteen?"

"I already did. I took the test last weekend."

"Well, when was your birthday?"

He grabbed me and jumped on top of me on his parents' couch and pulled the driver's license out of my hand, tickling me to let it go.

Reading my driver's license, he gasped. "Sunday, I missed your sixteenth birthday! Why didn't you say anything?"

"It doesn't matter, I'm not really into celebrating birthdays."

"Well, I am. Sunday, we will celebrate! You're only sweet sixteen once! Say it: every birthday is a gift."

He tickled me again, repeating those words over and over again until I couldn't breathe from laughing and I gave in. "Okay, every birthday is a gift!" We collapsed twisted together and, even now, I can even remember his cinnamon breath from his gum, the fresh smell of soap mixed with his deodorant, and the secureness of his strong arms hugging me. For a brief moment in the universe, I belonged.

Marcia baked a delicious cake, loaded with frosting and a little raspberry jam in the white cake. She stuck a hot pink waxy number sixteen candle in the center. As I blew the candle out, I made a wish. I held the tears back, as they all sang 'Happy Birthday' off key. My first cake with a candle. I felt deliriously happy, hoping my wish would come true.

It never did.

I shake that memory from my mind. That was then, this is

now.

I remember a quote I read: "If wishes were horses then beggars would ride." I never really understood what that meant until now.

The smell and lights of the casino bring me back. Walking through the slot machines, I watch the manic collection of women and men inserting their hard-earned cash into a machine, wishing they would win. It fills me with sadness and pity: the most destitute of people scrounging around in their purse or pocket for another dollar to slide into a colorful, musical machine. Wishes do not come true.

"Good evening, Miss Bridget," says Ward, a regular, looking up from his slot machine with a kind smile.

My name at Magic Hat is Bridget. I like having a casino name. Since everything I do at work is acting, it makes it seem just part of the play. George just happened to have a name tag with Bridget on it.

I put on my best fake smile, mix in a little genuine grin. "Good evening, Ward, can I get you something to drink?"

"Yes, my dear, the usual would be terrific." He stops playing to make eye contact with me.

Without fail, Ward sits in the swivel chair in front of his favorite slot machine, "Stinkin' Rich," at least four nights a week. Some nights he orders four or five beers and some nights he drinks the free ginger ale. Regardless, he always is kind, and tips me the same amount—a crisp twenty-dollar bill—at the end of every night.

Ward is soft-spoken, but boy, is he a talker. He shares with me that his wife died ten years ago, and he never found another to steal his heart. Emma was the heart stealer, and he mentioned she didn't like gambling or drinking very much; or as Ward says, only once in a blue moon. His eyes smile when he talks about her, and he looks off in the distance, remembering her, or possibly seeing her for a moment. I understand that vacant look, how memories can come alive in your mind, and take you away.

Ward tells me he recently retired from Waste Management for the city of Las Vegas after forty-five years.

"It's a dirty job, but somebody has to do it," he says more than once. "Although now I guess that makes me a dirty old man." He laughs at his own joke. I've heard it many times.

He tells me about his son. The pride in his voice lights up his face. "My boy tried to be a race car driver, and he was pretty darn good, but it's expensive, so he gave it up and went to law school, and now he's an attorney here in town. He's one of the good ones," Ward adds.

Ward is harmless and kind, a rare bird in the nest of vultures that perch around the casino. Even though his son is a lawyer, I sure hope his son is nothing like Tyler, who some at the courthouse called a good one. I like Ward, and when he hands me the twenty before he leaves for the night, he winks at me and always says, "Go have some fun, Bridget. Life's too short."

Fun. How do you define fun? I haven't had fun since Jack. Jack demands joy. He is the one soul on this planet who can make me laugh. Sure, I'm an expert at pasting on the fake smile at a moment's notice, but a real smile, my real laugh, hasn't emerged since the last time I saw his handsome face before the shooting began, before I was Hannah.

Jack always knew how to bring the best out of me. He teased me about how I would laugh, throwing back my mane, as he called my once-long blonde hair.

It seems like forever since that happened, and I can't imagine when real laughter will happen again.

In the break room, I visit Jack's page.

"George wants you in the back office before your break," Carla says, a blonde, blue-eyed cocktail waitress as she struts by. She has a pretty face and a great body, but she looks hard as nails. I haven't made friends with the other girls who work at the Magic Hat. They are all very territorial and push me to my one little section each night. I think they know I'm not twenty-one. They make plans to go out to clubs on their days off and they joke with each other with private innuendos. Hudson told me it was because they were jealous by my fresh young face. Whatever. It doesn't make sense, but I'm content to keep to myself, just as I always do. The thick walls I carry protect me from anyone getting close. It's all I've ever known, except for Jack. As I walk back to the office, I can't help but wonder if Jack is celebrating my birthday.

The door is half open, I knock.

"Come in." George leans back in his chair, his feet up on the desk. He carries around an unlit cigar, chewing on the end in an annoying fashion while he spits out his words and pieces of the cigar. His overpowering cologne irritates my nostrils, strong and vinegary. Hard to breathe.

"Sit down, Bridget." He sucks the end of the tattered cigar.

I sit on the small chair centered directly in front of his monstrous desk. The cheap plastic chair is shorter, a purposeful act so others look up at him while he looms over his employees. HE did the same thing in his office. Where do men learn these traits, some insecure man handbook?

"Your trial period is almost up, and I've been thinking about doing you a favor." He gnaws on the end of his mushy cigar, like a rabbit fixated on a carrot, staring at my chest.

I want to stand up so he can't see down my low-cut outfit.

"In the next couple of weeks, I'm planning on adding a little pizazz to the Magic Hat. I want you to be a part of it," he says, and smiles like he is offering me a present.

Silent, I dread what he has to say next. It can't be good.

"Can you dance?"

My gut constricts, thinking about what Jamie and Adriana had teased me about before: dancing in Vegas (aka stripping, of some sort).

"Dance? Not really. I don't have much rhythm."

The scowl on his face tells me he is not happy with my answer.

"Well, if you want to stick around the Magic Hat, start practicing your dance moves. I need waitresses to put in at least four to six hours of dancing a week. I'm thinking black hats, fishnet stockings, maybe a rabbit in the corner of the cage. Figure it out." He glares at me and snorts. "That is, if you like working here."

I examine the dark circles under his eyes and his cheesy shiny fabric outfit, his cheap silky shirt is unbuttoned too far down. His gross curly thick chest hair is exposed. He waits for me to reply. I don't understand why Hudson likes him. I need this job and even though I don't enjoy working here, I can't afford not to. I have to figure something out.

"Okay, George, I'll work on it. Thanks for the opportunity." Pushing my mouth up in a brilliant fake smile, I walk out.

Determined my life will not be another *Lifetime* movie of a runaway teenager turned dancer or stripper, I have to focus on the next phase. NO, I'm not dancing. I'm going to college. I need to take the GED and get going on my PLAN.

Chapter 18

Blindfolds, Cages, and Tests

Did I remember to put deodorant on? Beads of sweat form under my arms and my stomach aches. I want to run into the bathroom and vomit. Anxiety. I need to focus on this test and remind myself that I was once an outstanding high school student with honor classes and straight A's.

But that's a lie. Hannah Williams is nothing but a high school dropout, working illegally as a cocktail waitress in an off-the-Strip casino.

Like a thief, I've been secretly studying my exam prep workbook, hiding out in the Clark County Library, and keeping it inside a notebook so my nosy roommates don't see the cover. Taking the GED is more challenging than I thought: all the years of learning rolled into one computerized examination. No one around me suspects I didn't graduate from high school—hell, no one suspects I am only seventeen—but in order to move forward, I have to pass this test.

Hudson, playing the big brother role, is always checking my pulse. Not literally, but the scary thing is I could picture him putting two fingers on the side of my neck. He makes me paranoid about my brown contact lenses. I'm obsessed with the idea that he's trying to peek under my façade.

The proctor walks in, and the room is tense with nerves as he explains the rules. The janitor must have just sterilized this room: the cleaner flares up my nostrils, almost burning. It's not helping my nausea. Sitting next to me in this disinfected room in Las Vegas is a diverse smorgasbord of humans, a variety of ages and races, equal parts male and female. The older Hispanic man to my left catches my roving eye.

"Don't be nervous, we got this, right?" He leans towards me and smiles.

"Right." I paste on the fake smile.

His forehead glistens with sweat and the back of his shirt is damp with sweat. Wow. He may be more nervous than me, and I didn't think that was possible.

What happened to this random group of adults that they were unable to finish high school? How many of them were like me? Well, I can answer that: *Zero. I'm sure no one faked their death during a school shooting.*

Just then, the young beautiful Asian girl in front of me turns around and looks at me. She seems to be high school age, like me, and I wonder what her story is. She doesn't smile; just studies me and then the clock on the back wall. What interfered with her childhood to stop her from achieving one of the most basic rites on the way to adulthood? She showed up here, and I'm proud of her for that. For everyone here, no matter their ages or sex or past or whatever.

I have seven hours to take the test. I need to focus and stay on track.

This is a walk down the road to my new life, and if I pass, a new door opens.

Bleary-eyed, I walk out of the testing center to the bus stop. Unofficially, I passed the GED test. I want to celebrate. I want to shout it to the world. It is one of my rare days off, and I want to be a senior commemorating my graduation and throwing my hat in the air. Every day, I am lonely. I do not want to be alone on today.

I text Hudson, **R u free?**

From the posted schedule on the Magic Hat break room wall, he knew I had requested the day off and he asked me why. I snapped an answer, telling him it was personal; something I had to take care of. He left it at that, but I knew he wanted to ask if everything was okay. He'd just smiled and walked away.

He texted back in seconds. **Just chillin, why?**

I reply, **I need to have some FUN. Desperate for fun.**

His text, **Do you trust me?**

I trust no one, I want to text. Only Jack. However, Hudson knows one of my darkest secrets and has never breathed a word.

I trust him a little bit.

Maybe... I text.

I'll take that as a yes. Meet me at MGM bus stop in 1 hour.

The amazing thing about Las Vegas is—it doesn't matter how hot the temperature; there are still hordes of people trampling down the sidewalks. Crowds taking pictures, texting, talking, and staggering drunk. I am bubbling from the excitement of passing the GED test. The future seems brighter. I ignore the over-one-hundred-degree dry heat pressing down on me, making me feel like an oiled turkey walking around the inside of an oven. Although my plan has changed countless times, the future is going to be better. Today is going to be a good day; the first one in a long time. Since the shooting, Tyler, and the false pregnancy, I didn't think I could ever have a good day again, but I need to at least try.

I still have two weeks until the two things that gave me insomnia transpire: Amir's visit and dancing at the Magic Hat. Thinking of Jack always makes my stomach and heart ache and keeps me up most nights. I can't let my mind wander.

I just spent seven long studious hours taking a test—successfully, I might add—and my brain needs a break. Tired of scheming, planning, and answering questions, I need to be mindless. I need one day to be a normal teenager.

At least one goal is completed: a high school diploma. I form an image of a graduation ceremony, me walking down the aisle in my gown, throwing my cap in the air, Jack's dreamy smile as he catches his own cap.

It is a milestone in real life that I will never experience. My mind travels to images of the Dream Team and the Hard Liquor Boys, the majority of whom will also never walk down the aisle.

At least I am alive.

Hudson is the most comfortable company I can think of to spend a day within Sin City, and I'm actually excited about what he has in store as I step off the bus in front of the MGM Casino.

"So, you do trust me," Hudson whispers behind me.

His breath tickles my ear, making me jump at the invasion of my personal space. I am a split second away from taking my backpack and slugging him. I can still feel the remnants of his hot breath on my ear, and the smell of fabric sheets.

His face is consumed by a huge mouth of white teeth, and joy. Hudson is a happy-go-lucky kind of guy. Even when slimy George barks at him in the kitchen area, he nods, whistles and keeps stacking glasses.

"Maybe," I say. "Maybe I trust you." I smile, a genuine emotion that Hudson naturally brings out.

"Well, do you have ten bucks?"

"Ten bucks? Yes, I have ten dollars. What are we doing?" Money is tight. I am saving every dollar in case Amir destroys my world and I am forced to start over again. Unlike my old life, spending an unbudgeted $10 is a careful decision, but a girl must celebrate her high school graduation.

"Lions, volcanos, and gods." Hudson spread his hands, then held his fingers to his lips. "Let me show you the secrets of Las Vegas or, as I like to call it, 'Hudson's ten buck tour.'"

Hudson's excitement is contagious, a man on a mission, preparing to give the tour of the year. As we walk toward the entrance of MGM, Hudson takes out a blindfold.

"Trust me?"

I hesitate, and remind myself Hudson is nothing like Tyler, then give him the thumbs up, unsure. "Seriously? Do I have to?"

"Only if you want to." His happiness is hard to resist. I nod.

"Try it. If you don't like it, then no blindfold." He slants his head, studying me. "Hannah, escape from your daily existence, for a minute; let me show you fun."

In this moment, I do trust him. I am only seventeen, and this is what young people are supposed to do: be in the moment. I want to escape my burdens and be here now.

"Okay."

The silky blindfold covers my eyes and with gentle hands, Hudson ties it in the back.

"Can you see anything?" he asks.

"No." I giggle as Hudson grabs my hand. His hand is warm

and a little sweaty, but firm and strong as he maneuvers me through the crowds.

I sniff. What is that smell? Not necessarily bad, but different.

"Where are we?" I ask.

He unties my blindfold and pulls the silky black scarf off with a flourish. Golden hair, glassy eyes, and big yellow teeth. We are standing directly in front of two magnificent lions pacing back and forth. I step back from the sheer size of cat power. Their dominant attitude fills the air as they strut in front of me. Beautiful, fierce mammals, they are kings of the jungle in their world. The larger of the two cats, tilts his head to the sky, opens his exceptionally large mouth of teeth, and roars. I jump. These two magnificent beasts know how to tame all the animals of the jungle with one sound, and yet here they are, stuck in the middle of the Las Vegas strip, caged. Power behind bars.

The smaller lion moves closer to me. As I gaze into his unflinching eyes, I know we share the same pain: we both want to be free and in our own home.

"They're amazing," I say, and mean it.

From here, it's off to a shuttle. The blindfold goes back on. "Do you think they're happy?"

"The lions? Well, it's a good question. They probably are sad they are caged up and not able to roam free. You know to just be lions, free and in control."

I understand.

It's a strange sensation, to lose your sight in a bustling crowd. My chest rises and falls with rapid breaths as I try to enjoy the moment. Walking around with the blindfold is a bit awkward. I have no control and I hate the dark, but the light penetrates the blindfold, unlike THE DARK. Hudson tightens his grip on my hand, and I hold his arm as we walk together. A new lesson in trust. I'm trying it.

The next time the blindfold comes off, I am standing face to face with a mermaid. I always liked mermaids as a little girl and wished I could change my feet to a tail and swim away. I wore out the DVD of *The Little Mermaid*. This mermaid is wearing a bright orange bikini top with matching colorful fins, she twirls and dances around the fish and coral, her long blonde hair swirls around her face, and it reminds me of my once long blonde hair. Is everyone caged in their own little world? Two other mermaids join her in a spectacular dance, with spotted leopard sharks lying on the floor next to stingrays and bright, vibrant yellow and blue fish swimming back and forth. We are at the Silverton Aquarium.

The fish stick together in schools, each like-kind of fish banded together in a formation.

"It reminds me of high school, little cliques joining together," Hudson says. We watch the different pods swim away from each other and then back together.

"What clique were you in?" Hudson asks.

"I wasn't." I quickly change the subject, trying to steer my memory away from school, the Hard Liquor Boys, the Dream Team, and the bloody shooting. I wonder where Hudson fit in his school, and I can't picture Hudson in any group, just his own coolness. But I want to stop the conversation of high school. "Lions and mermaids are pretty hard to beat. What's next, my tour guide? This is fantastic."

"Just wait, the tour has only just begun."

Hudson, true to his word, is just getting warmed up.

Next time, I open my eyes to laser lights and moving statues. An amazing showcase of the Fall of Atlantis. For fifteen minutes, the gods shout and the sky rumbles. A moving play, with statutes that speak and move. Inside the Forum shops in Caesar's Palace, on the hour, statues magically come alive. It's an incredible light show, creating the illusion of stone moving and talking. When the lights and the music stop, I walk over to the statues to investigate. Enormous stone and concrete sculptures...if someone can make them come alive, anything is possible.

As the night continues, I witness a molten lava volcano erupt at the Mirage and a wildlife habitat with some of the world's most beautiful winged creatures fly and walk around a room outside slot machines at The Flamingo.

Hudson saves the best for last. Momentarily without sight, my ears try to pinpoint the sounds I'm hearing.

Outside, I'm definitely outside.

The scents are overwhelming—fried foods, booze, and perspiration of Las Vegas all mixed together, and then I hear the traffic and pedestrians, like a background musical of sound effects. My blindfold draws attention from the tourists. "What are they doing?" someone in a hushed tone.

Hudson laughs, and the unique melody of his happiness adds to the soundtrack. I smile. "It's my friend's birthday and I'm surprising her, showing her Las Vegas for the first time."

"Well, she can't see it very well." I hear a flirty girl's voice and sweet laugh. Yes, something about Hudson makes everyone happy.

"She will, it's the element of suspense that's exciting."

I stand there blindfolded and smile. It is fun not knowing where you are and trusting someone almost like I trusted Jack.

Before Hudson removes my blindfold for the last time, water thunders. The air changes and humidity blankets the dry desert air. There is a new fresh smell, almost like the air surrounding my special place at the creek. Water.

A few sharp booms make me jump out of my skin. Gunshots?

I claw at the blindfold, breathing hard. I want to run.

"It's okay, Hannah," Hudson says, wrapping an arm around me. Hudson's face is next to mine as he unties the silk scarf. His warm breath on my cheek. His forehead creases, concern written on his face. "I'm sorry that scared you."

The rafts. The river. The blood.

Soft flute music starts playing as fountains shoot up in the air from a huge body of water in front of me. I steady my breath. *"Near, far, wherever you are, I believe that the heart does go on."* Haunting music plays, with an entire lake of fountains shooting high to the sky and then falling back into the lake in rhythm. The water roars to life right in front of me, with a song that rips at my heart.

I am alive. So many are not. Hudson's arm rests against mine.

I bury my head in his chest and hug him. He envelopes me, wrapping his arms around my entire upper half. We stay entwined long after the song ends, the water recedes back into the lake, and the crowds scurry away to the next attraction.

"Are you okay, Hannah?" He wipes the tears from my face as they drip off my chin.

I turn my face to his. "No not really," I pause, "but hopefully someday I will be." I raise my chin.

Hudson goes past my brown-contact eyes, searching deep inside me. I can feel his breath and smell a soft musky scent; I back away.

"I have no doubt at all, Ms. Hannah Williams, that you will be more than okay."

"Thank you, Hudson. Thanks for being my friend and thanks for the tour."

He lifts his shoulder in a half shrug. "You're welcome, Hannah. I'm glad you liked it."

He holds my gaze, studying my face.

After a few seconds, I look away and change the subject. "So, what's the ten dollars for?"

"It's for the last bit of the tour, The Grand Finale. Are you hungry?"

"I am. Starving."

We end up at Mr. Lucky's Café at the Hard Rock Hotel. The menu looks pretty expensive amidst all the museum pieces of musical history and the old rock and roll legend's clothing. Hudson said ten dollars, but very few entrées are under twenty.

"Do you mind if I order for you, Hannah?"

I shake my head, worried about sitting here, in a place I can't afford. I can't spend twenty or thirty bucks on one meal.

As the waitress comes up to the table, Hudson puffs out his chest with an enormous smile on his face.

"We will take two 'Gambler Specials', please." Hudson put his hand on my arm. "We are celebrating this one's birthday."

The waitress smiles and collects our menus. "Happy birthday, honey."

My mind flashes back to the last time I went out to dinner to celebrate a birthday. I swallow the anxiety building inside and study Hudson, who I know is nothing like Tyler. Absolutely no similarities.

"Really, my birthday?"

"Yes, I'm celebrating your birthday—when is it?" Hudson asks.

He is asking about Hannah's birthday; I have to remind myself. "November 8. I have a long time until I turn nineteen," I say, which is true, since I really just turned seventeen. "What's a 'Gambler Special'?"

"You'll see. It's not on the menu, but if you know about it, you can ask for it anytime, and they will serve it to you. It's a precious secret only the locals know."

Hudson was spot on: for $7.77 we had a delicious three-course meal complete with a juicy flatiron steak, three jumbo shrimp, a beautiful salad, and buttery garlic mashed potatoes. The waitress even threw in dessert, a triple layered chocolate cake, which we shared. I ask her to please not sing Happy Birthday, as she brings the cake over with a candle, and her mouth forms into a chord, she obliges. I wish I could tell Hudson about my GED, but even without sharing my accomplishment, it is a perfect celebration for my secret graduation.

Stomachs full, we walk back to my apartment; the lateness of the hour doesn't faze us. Silence fills the air as the electric lights and constant hum of Vegas engulfs us. What has changed since dinner? I can sense something different.

"Thank you again, Hudson. It was an epic tour." I mean it.

"I was thinking about making some cash and doing a walking tour for first-time visitors. What do you think?"

"I think you can't blindfold them."

"No, it might get a little hairy crossing the street," he says, and chuckles. "I used to do this in every town we moved to. My mom would be working two or three jobs and when she finally had one day off, which generally took forever. I would have the house cleaned, the laundry done, and surprise her with a tour of all the best free things our new city had to offer. They were interesting tours, some hidden things you would be amazed at, but Vegas takes the cake. I could show you hours more of wonderful things. You just received the highlight tour."

"I bet your mom would love this."

"Yes, she would. Where else within a three-mile stretch can visitors gaze upon the Eiffel Tower, an Egyptian pyramid,

Imperial Rome, the New York City skyline, a dancing fountain, and," he pauses for emphasis, "an exploding volcano? When she visits, I'll have the perfect tour all mapped out." He rubs his hands together. "I would love for you to meet her. She'd like you."

Love and kindness surround Hudson's demeanor when he speaks of his mother. He reminds me of Jack. Do all good boys love their moms?

Hudson walks over to a bench in the park. This park, not too far from UNLV, has a nice playground area. Hudson and I have met here a few times and then walk to get the bus. I come here sometimes after work to think. It is the closest thing I can find to my spot back home by the creek.

Hudson is watching me. I can see his head is turned sideways. "I know the Magic Hat isn't your dream job, and is definitely not one of the spectacular Strip casinos, but are you sorry you didn't move to Cali?"

I inhale and let it out. "I don't know. I always dreamed of California: soft beaches, surf, sun. I'm sure what I have pictured is not even reality." I lean back on the bench. "But it's all right. I have a job and a place to stay, although now George wants me to dance at the Magic Hat. Not sure what to do about that. Me dancing..." I make a face. "I guess I have a couple weeks to figure it out."

"Yeah, I heard about that. I'm not sure he's really going to go through with putting cages by the Houdini Bar. He wants them high above the bar. I think it will cost him too much money, and insurance. George is cheap. I'm sorry, Hannah. I wish I could help you find something else. Help you..."

I put my hand on his arm. It's my turn to study his face, as the metal on the bench behind him picks up a glint of light from the dented moon hovering in the sky. I move closer and pull on his arm so he will look at me.

"You *have* helped me, Hudson. The apartment, the job...do you know how much you have helped me?" The truth of it fills my eyes, and my heart is full of gratitude. I close my eyes. I remember his concern and caring heart, openly displayed and written all over his face at the El Cortez.

Hudson moves close, stopping two inches from my face, so close the smell of spearmint gum tickles my nose. My eyes open. He kisses me gently, like a soft breeze, then straightens up with his back against the bench, looking out at the distant lights of the Strip. Just one soft kiss, nothing more. He's not Jack and he's definitely not Tyler.

We sit there in a comfortable silence, our arms touching the tiniest bit, taking in the magic of the moment with the twinkling lights of the Strip on display.

It was just like a movie.

Chapter 19

Stinkin' Rich, Butterflies, and Fried Eggs

I wake up dreaming of Jack.

Jack and Sunday.

In my closet bedroom, the night light casts an orange glow on my hanging clothes, reminding me without a doubt where I am at. It's a funny thing about dreams: for a minute, there's a crack in the universe, and the subconscious world exists. When I dream, I'm Sunday. Long blonde hair, blue eyes and the underlying terror of HE and SHE. It's always Sunday, never Hannah. My hand snakes up to the back of my head: yes, it is still short and curly Hannah hair. I wonder when I will start dreaming of being Hannah.

Last night was a lesson in acceptance. Admission of my new existence. This life I'm living is growing tangible. I actually had fun yesterday, a first for Hannah.

My mind wanders to the soft kiss. It was very innocent, but romantic without being overbearing. I am unsure of what category to put Hudson in. It bewilders my common sense, my intuition, and my desire. Do I like Hudson? I mean, *like* him, like him? In my logical mind, Hudson is like a big brother, what I imagine Clark to be: kind, accepting without being judgmental, and always on my side. Yet, thinking about the few seconds his lips touched mine creates butterflies in my chest. Happy butterflies. I intermittently go back to conjuring that moment in my mind until I sense the fluttering of little wings, relishing this new feeling.

I love Jack, but I have to let him go. Maybe Hudson is a way to help me get over Jack.

Groaning, I realize I need to work a double today at the Magic Hat. A cocktail waitress named Nell needs a day off for her daughter, Molly, and no one would trade with her. She seemed desperate. I agreed to work her shift and mine. It will make for a long day, but I'm hoping the tips will be better in Nell's section. And Nell seems to be somewhat like me, like she's a little lost and needs help.

The Magic Hat Casino, like all casinos, has no window to reality. The music and the pulsing sounds of the slot machine bang and ding all night long. The crowds change slightly, but only an experienced cocktail waitress or bartender can win the time game. If there were no clocks in the casino, no watch on anyone's wrist, and no cell phones, would any customer be able to tell *WHAT TIME OF DAY IT IS?*

I doubt it.

Vegas never sleeps: no siestas, no naps. It's an ongoing movie without an end. It is completely normal to leave my shift at five in the morning, walk down the street next to a drunk man and a woman, sweaty from dancing and gambling, their voices at high octaves, and then see next to them a jogger keeping his stride, sprinting down the sidewalk getting in his morning run before he starts his day. Completely different versions of a Vegas movie all playing at the same time. The difficulty is that sometimes it is hard to sort out what movie is playing when.

The taste of grit and the smell of smoke consumes my senses. Taking a break in the dry desert heat is not much better. Walking outside is like sticking my head in an oven. Opposite of the thick humid air of Baltimore summers, this fire heat is intense. Even this early in the summer, Las Vegas continues to break heat records.

Hudson texts me to come outside. I put my hand on my beating heart as I read the text. I've reconsidered the butterfly effect and I've concluded that it's the newness. The art of kissing someone new is exciting: it's curiosity and it's daring. I care about Hudson, but I love Jack. And even though I can't ever see him, I can't ever touch him again, I will always love him. I know that now.

I walk outside overwhelmed by the bright sun. It takes me a minute to adjust, and then I see him. Hudson is holding an egg in his hand, a mischievous smirk across his face.

"Hudson, it's blazing hot out here, what are you doing?"

"An experiment for your viewing pleasure..."

Hudson holds the egg by two fingers, as if it were a card deck in a magic show.

"It's an egg. I see it," I say. "What are you going to do? Make it disappear?"

"No. Welcome to Las Vegas, Hannah. I'm initiating you into the sweltering furnace. The summer is yet to come, it only gets hotter from here. Just watch and pay attention. Are you hungry?"

I shrug my shoulders. "I'm flipping hot."

"I'm going to fry you an egg, Vegas style."

Hudson hands me his phone and pulls out a spatula from his

back pocket. "Your job is to keep the video on the egg."

Hudson clears his throat and points his finger as if he is the director of a film, and I hit Record. "I'm Hudson Wagner and I'm standing on the sidewalk in sunny Las Vegas, Nevada. For your viewing pleasure, we are going to see if it is indeed hot enough to fry an egg on the sidewalk. Sin City is breaking records today, hitting 112 degrees. So, the question becomes, is it hot enough to fry an egg?" Hudson cracks the egg with one hand and we both watch the gooey liquid hit the concrete sidewalk. "Yes, folks, the concrete is probably registering hotter than 112; more like 117. The concrete absorbs the heat from all these monstrous steel buildings you see all around us. But, as you can see, the egg white is cooking instantly, with the yolk running a distant second."

Sizzling, the egg is frying on the sidewalk.

"Next, I'm going to flip the egg with a cooking spatula, because Hannah here wants her eggs over easy." I laugh and the phone shakes. Hudson places the shiny spatula on the concrete and gets under the egg and flips it. It is cooked, almost burnt at the edges.

"There you have it, folks: that's how hot it is here in sunny Las Vegas. You can fry an egg in under ninety seconds."

I turn the video off and a strange sound comes out. One of Sunday's laughs, my head goes back, and the laugh builds deep inside my chest bubbling out. An old friend reminding me of the old me with Jack.

"Hudson, you crack me up."

We both double over.

Hudson has a way about him.

It is more than his trivial knowledge of famous people's first jobs. His glass is always half full, and if he senses you are down and weary, with solid determination it is his mission to make you smile. He is one of a kind.

My second shift starts and I'm actually joyful on the inside, genuinely smiling because of Hudson. I am no longer pitying myself for not being a typical teenager in the summer before my senior year. It is enough, for this moment.

The double shift night drags on until my favorite customer comes in.

"Hi, Ward, the usual?"

"Good evening, dear Bridget. Tonight, I am going to have a drink for my friend, Bud."

"Oh, that's nice. Is Bud here?"

"I'm sure he is, but not that you and I can see him. I feel him, though. I think he is watching over us. Bud died last week." Ward pauses and swallows, and his voice becomes softer. "He drank Dewar's and water, so give me one of those."

"Coors and a water?" I ask.

Ward chuckles. "No. Dewar's is a Scotch whiskey. Bud's favorite beverage. That feisty Irishman."

His white hair and cornflower-blue eyes are a compliment to his sweet demeanor. Ward said he was originally from the cornfields of Iowa. I imagine he once had blonde locks with his eyes the color of the Iowa sky.

"I'm sorry, Ward. Was he sick?"

"Nope, a car accident on the 95. They think he might have had a stroke. My son is handling his affairs."

"I'm so sorry, Ward." His friend had obviously meant a great deal to him.

"Thank you, my dear. So, tonight I'm going to celebrate Bud."

"I'm sure he would like that. Let me know when you need another."

"Will do. I'm playing his favorite machine, 'Stinkin' Rich.' He used to always tell me when we were garbage men together: 'Don't worry, brother, things are going to change, and I will be stinkin' rich. That's why I always play it.'"

"Well, good luck for Bud." I smile and mean it.

Ward sits in front of the machine called "Stinkin' Rich" for hours. I bring him another Scotch as soon as his glass is empty.

I know loss. The shooting comes back in a flashback. It happens like that; one thing triggers a flash of terror. I envision the Hard Liquor Boys and the Dream Team floating in the bloody river in Pennsylvania. The vicious, violent images always lurk in the back of my mind, just waiting for a trigger to show up. I grind my teeth together and work my section harder, repeatedly yelling, "Cocktails, soda, drinks!"

About an hour later, I walk over to Ward to bring him one more Dewar's, I hear the cheering and whistles and see several people holding up their phones. "What happened?" I ask the man in the back of the crowd of patrons blocking my path to deliver my drink.

"Some guy just hit the jackpot! A big one."

I make my way through the crowd. There's Ward sitting at the "Stinkin' Rich" machine as it flashes revolving red and green lights, the loud music repeating its happy obnoxious tune, the melody of a winner.

"Ward, what did you hit?" I ask.

"I hit it all, Bridget! I'm stinkin' rich!" His blue eyes shine with moisture, his mouth turned up in a huge smile of disbelief. I walk over to pat him on the arm. He holds my arm for a second to stay and pulls out his wallet and counts out ten hundred-dollar bills and hands them to me. Future gold. "This one's from me and Bud."

I can feel a hundred eyes on me and see people with their phones out. Casino security is shutting them down, yelling, "No photographs please, cameras are not allowed on the casino floor."

Ward did it! He did it in the biggest way, a casino fairytale that patrons pass around faster than a fire. Ward hit the jackpot, the biggest progressive jackpot the Magic Hat (or even MGM, whom George bought the machine from) had ever seen. It's the Mother Lode: 1.575 million dollars all with a push of a button on a video screen. The flashes and music keep playing as I throw my head back, laughing, and hugging Ward. Another Sunday laugh bubbles out. Finally someone won other than the house.

Yelling and banging came from Slimy George's office.

The casino hums in chatter and hyped-up energy. All night, there's chatter that the progressive jackpot was only meant to draw the slot machine players in, like a fake bone for a dog, something to chew on, but not to ever pay off.

"Apparently, George flipped his desk and threw the chair into the wall. He might lose his position of general manager over such a big payoff. Who knows, it could possibly bankrupt the Magic Hat," Nell says to me as we pass by each other. Patrons keep feeding their dollars in the machines, spurred on by Ward's magic luck.

My mind is cheering for Ward and doing back flips. Maybe now Magic Hat will not have the money for the dancing cages. Oh, what a night!

Hudson joins the crowd for a quick moment, catching my eye. I still clutch the ten hundred-dollar bills tight in my hand.

"1.5 million, that's cray cray!" Hudson is electrified. "Your garbage man wins! Did he give you that?"

I nod, still speechless.

"What an awesome tip he gave you. That will help your shoebox money. Are you sure your friend isn't a Tommy Glenn Carmichael?"

"Who is Tommy Glenn Carmichael?"

"He invented the light wand, which was a way to blind a sensor inside the slots, causing it to pay out. His first job was as a garbage man."

"Seriously, how do you know all this?"

"It's all part of my education into the rich and famous," he says, and laughs. "So, where are we celebrating?" Hudson believes in the Las Vegas destiny. The city of second chances. He also believes good luck strikes three times in a row.

Chapter 20

Old School Minute, Vegas Wildlife, and Flip-Flop Flasks

Hudson, playing tour guide again, leans against the wall as I end my shift. He sports a beat-up black UNLV baseball hat and holey black t-shirt and a black backpack he bought at a thrift store. With little money, he is still cool. As we leave the casino together, I wonder what adventure he's conjured up. He pulls me on a bus, dumps the money in the fare slot and doesn't speak as we ride along the busy streets of Vegas. As the bus comes to a halt, and other folks board, he grabs my hand and we exit at the Sunset Park bus stop. Sunset Park, one of the largest parks in Las Vegas, according to Hudson, showcases a lake in the middle of the desert.

"It's closed," I say.

The hours are clearly posted at the entrance to the park: 6 a.m. – 11 p.m. The very last thing I need is to get arrested for breaking and entering.

"Not really, not technically closed. Follow me."

I hesitate, my feet stuck in place.

"Trust me, it will be okay," he says.

No way. Breaking the law is the last thing I need.

Hudson walks toward the tree line of the park. This is my should-I-stay-or-should-I-go moment. Sunday is always cautious and calculated every step, every day, but perhaps Hannah can be a little more daring.

Trees and darkness ignite my memories. My mind flashes back to the awful night I slept in the woods in Pennsylvania. That night of no return. My special place comes into focus in my mind. Maryland, my daily ritual of walking down to my tree lined creek and sitting on the bank. My safe spot.

Perhaps I need to take a step out of the hot concrete jungle of Vegas. Inhale the masculine scent of the woods. Lost in my memories, before I notice, Hudson has contorted his lean muscles through a hole in the enclosure. He is inside in less than a minute, motioning me to slide in between the fence line and a large pine tree.

The earthy smell beckons me. An enormous towering tree makes up part of the perimeter fence. Not one of the massive hardwoods like back East, but a tree, nonetheless. Nature. I trust my gut and squeeze into the opening. Hudson grabs my hand and pulls me through. In a matter of seconds, the tree coverage voids the light pollution of the city. My eyes begin to adjust to a night not illuminated by the neon of Vegas. Hudson, warm and sweaty, wraps his fingers around mine, and continues to pull me along until we come up to an opening in the dense thicket. He points and puts his finger to his lips. Movement, water, a small lake or a pond is in front of us. Hudson plops down on the ground at the edge of the tree line, the shadows still cover our silhouettes.

"No one will bother us here and we won't disturb anyone."

Hudson's white teeth glow in the light of the moon. He extracts two small shot glasses and sets them on the ground. He then proceeds to pull off one flip-flop with his right hand and with his left he reaches into his pocket and removes a tiny funnel.

"What are you doing?" I ask.

"Just watch."

He inserts the funnel into the heel of the flip-flop and pours liquid from a hidden flask in the heel, filling each shot glass to the top. "Let's have a toast." Hudson grins as though he had just performed magic.

"What is it?" I do not pick up the glass.

"Captain Morgan Spiced Rum. Have you had it before?"

His sandals have a flask in the heel and now he wants me to drink it? I lift it up to my nose and automatically grimace. The biting scent climbs inside my nostrils.

I'm not sure why people drink alcohol. It can't be the taste, or at least what I've tasted as I remember the bitter olives from Tyler's martini. I shake it out of my head. I don't want to go there.

Do they really want to turn mean and ugly? I'm sure somebody gets cute and happy, but not me. It has never been my thing. Marcia and Ed allowed Jack and Tara to try alcohol as long as they did so at home, but I never liked the flavor of it. One whiff— I gag. My nose smells HE, and the memory of his sour breath hot on my face makes me queasy. The red smoldering tip of a cigarette an inch from my face.

I've tried it. Jack and I snuck four wine coolers out to the creek one night, and they made me sleepy. I know I'll probably get around to liking it at some point in my life, but right now, I don't need drinking. I'm wrapped up in enough illegal deeds for the moment.

"You haven't even sipped it yet," he says.

I laugh, unsure what to do. "I guess I'm not much of a drinker."

Hudson pulls a Coke out of his backpack. "It's a little warm but try taking a swig of this after you down the shot." Hudson picks up both shot glasses and hands one to me. "To the luckiest cocktail waitress in the Magic Hat Casino." Hudson looks me straight in the eye and says, "Shoot it down fast."

He swallows the brown liquid in one gulp, and for whatever reason, I copy his motions. I almost gag immediately as the sweet bitter flavor warms my throat and trickles the whole way down my esophagus. Hudson hands me the Coke.

The park is intimately quiet, the buzzing of the Strip faintly plays in the background. The twilight cast shadows on the desert and branches of the trees, a radiance of light ripples on the lake. Through the darkness, the illusion of the holes of light poke through the trees, spotlighting sections of nature. It makes me think of the Pennsylvania woods the night of the shooting.

Ding. My phone flashes light and dings. I have a message. I don't want to think about Amir. I want to grab my phone and hide it.

"Turn it off."

"Why?"

"As my mom always said, 'Look up and around.' She's a big fan of the no phone zone."

I reach inside to silence my phone.

"Turn the power off. Be without technology for an hour. Free yourself." Hudson tilts his head to the sky. "My mother always talked about the days when people had to use payphones. I can't imagine, but it sounds sort of freeing."

"You're so old school, Hudson. I never see you on your phone.

I like that."

Hudson has a stick and digs in the dirt. "Yeah? I think I was born too late. I should have been born 30 years ago."

"Well, then, I would have never met you."

"That's true. You think you're going to hang around for a while?" He scrapes the dirt to draw the letter "H."

It's a good question. One I don't really know how to answer. With Amir coming to Vegas, my future is unclear. I lift my shoulders and sigh. "I'm thinking maybe for a little while longer, unless I have to dance at the Magic Hat. I'm not dancing. I mean, I'm definitely not dancing in a cage."

Hudson smirks. "George is a wacko. Who needs dancing girls in cages?" Hudson continues, "Although, you would draw quite a crowd."

I hit him on the arm, ignoring his laughter. The current from his arm to my hand silences me. I cross my arms. "How's the summer session going at UNLV?"

"Not bad. The most decent thing about it is my psychology class. The teacher is pretty cool; makes it interesting."

"I can't wait to start school. I just need to save up some more cash and who knows, maybe I can take a few classes in the fall. Psychology sounds interesting," I say, thinking about all the people from my past I could psychoanalyze.

"Well Miss Big Time Winner, you got a $1,000 scholarship tonight, which is worth toasting." Hudson is back to pouring the brown liquid into two more shots from his flip-flop. "Yeah, now you just need a few more." Hudson hands me the shot glass and hold his glass up in a toast.

"The scholarship or the shot?" I ask amazed at how much liquor the flip-flop flask holds.

"Yes." Hudson smirks. "Here's to the Hannah Williams

Scholarship Fund."

Why not? The second shot slides down a little bit smoother, still fiery in my chest. I gulp the sweet sugar of the Coke, trying to wash out the fuzziness of my mind.

I hear the rustle of branches behind me, my head turns, and for a moment I am transported back to my special place near the creek. Back home, it would be Amir sitting in the tree line watching me. I was never alarmed. But this can't be Amir. He wasn't due to show up for a week.

Hudson places his hand on my arm, and, with his eyes, he silences me and I freeze in place, my heartbeat getting louder.

He mouths, "Don't move."

My eyes widen in question. I can't imagine what will happen if we get arrested for trespassing. IS trespassing a misdemeanor? I certainly don't want to spend my newly acquired fortune on a fine or, worse yet, bail money. *Why did I drink? Nothing good ever happens when you drink.* I don't want to look around me and see the bad that is coming.

Hudson squeezes my arm hard forcing me to look up, and unexpected happiness lights up his face. Motioning with his head, he mouths, "Turn around."

He nods yes at my surprised reaction. I don't want to move, but I do. With little motion I shuffle sideways and turn to the woods behind me. Standing in the glimmer of the soft light, like a newly erected statue, a small skinny deer is also frozen in place, its head cocked, staring at the moon.

We are in its sanctuary, and if it could speak, I picture it yelling in a Vegas gangster voice, "What the hell are you kids doing in my territory? Get out, now. Beat it."

But it stands as if posing for a glorious painting. This beautiful deer isn't scared, angry or rabid; but calm like a golden retriever, someone's dog, sitting in the woods.

A wonderful moment until the ever-present nightmare flashes in my mind. In the woods after the shooting, I woke up to a pungent smell of wildness. On the ground beside me, an animal had marked the dirt with its footprints inches from where I was sleeping, as if it stood in front of my face sniffing me, trying to determine if I was alive. It might have been deer tracks or some other hoofed animal that lived in the woods. I'll never know what animal watched over me that night, but I'd like to imagine that a beautiful deer like this one stood beside me.

The deer lowers itself to the ground a few feet away, staring at us, calm and content. Large, dark eyes.

Transfixed, I return the gaze. Where was his mate or family? Sadness rips open my heart and the tears roll out without asking me. Hudson is silent and then in a sweet, gentle motion wipes the wet drops sliding down my cheeks with his hand, the deer sprints back into the thicket. I turn to Hudson, his mouth follows his hand, and he kisses me, a gentle kiss, first on my cheek, wet with tears, and next on my lips. I pull back, my heart thumping in my chest at a running speed. Warmness spreads through my body. I move away, studying the ground, my legs crisscrossed in front of me. *Sunday can't have Jack, but Hannah could have Hudson.*

Hudson leans his head sideways, trying to look at my turned down face. His rare serious expression erases his normal happy expression. Placing my hand on his cheek, I lean in and kiss him, trying to get lost in this intimate contact between two human beings. I've never been good at human contact, except with Jack, whose boyish, handsome face suddenly comes into focus. The kiss is long and intense, but Jack's face is permeating the images in my mind when suddenly Tyler's sick, sly smirk invades my brain.

"No!" I jerk back. Both of us are breathing hard. Hudson reels back.

Wow, is this what liquor does to your senses? Uncomfortable silence thickens the space around us. Hudson brings reality into the forefront, as he jumps up, concentrating on stashing the shot glasses in his backpack, and sliding on his flip-flops.

His voice is scratchy as he says, "We should be headed back. I'm not sure how early the park ranger gets here."

I force myself to stand, wobbly from the rum and exhausted from my two back-to-back shifts. The excitement of Ward's jackpot fades. I want to hold Hudson, but it is clear, his mood has changed, his insight into reading others' emotions evident. I did this. My actions confuse him. Hell, they confuse me.

"Hannah, I'm sorry if I make you uncomfortable. I know something is not right, and I never want to kiss anyone who doesn't want to kiss me. I'm not sure what happened or who you're thinking of or who or why," he stumbles with his words, "but that's not me."

Two shots of liquor and everything pent up in my crazy mind irrupts. I am a blubbering idiot. My shoulders shake as I drop to the ground. The dam bursts and the heavily armored walls I built up crack. Actually, they explode.

Hudson kneels beside me, his hands precariously on my shoulders. He wraps his arms around me, holding the sadness with me, whispering, "I'm here, let me help." He cradles me as I cry. It seems like we kneel in that spot forever. And then, the smell of him, the dryer sheets, reminding me of Jack's house, made me catch my breath. Inhaling deep breaths, I try to control my sobs.

I tell him about Tyler. I try to explain how I couldn't tell my boyfriend, Jack. I describe my shame, and that leaving was the only way to protect myself and the child I thought I was carrying from ending up like my rotten parents. I ramble. He listens, never really talking, just a few "Oh's" and "I'm sorry."

I cry. I'm exhausted. I release the entire dam, well, not everything but all of the Tyler stuff, and when all the tears run out, a rare peace settles in my heart.

Hudson stares at the sky, his hands behind his head, knees pointing to the moon. I follow his movements and rest against him, the side of my arm touching his, my eyes open.

"You could go back to your boyfriend, and tell him the truth of why you left."

"It's more complicated than you could imagine" Hudson has no idea about the shooting and faking my death, and there's no way I want to tell him that portion of my crazy screwed up life.

"The jerk forced himself on you. You are the victim; there's nothing to be ashamed of. Hannah, it's not your fault. You did nothing wrong."

At least in my moment of weakness, even in my liquor haze, I do not spill ALL the beans. Thank God, I didn't take another shot. I can't tell him my name is really Sunday. I can't verbalize the school shooting. I'd have to tell him about my fake ID, and my real age. I am seventeen, Hudson is nineteen, and I wonder what he would think about the real truth. Would he feel deceived? Lied to? Telling Hudson about Tyler, verbalizing the terrifying events of the night, helps weaken the sick feeling that twists my stomach.

"You could have gone to the police. No one deserves that. He forced himself on you. Date rape. Hannah, he raped you." Hudson throws the stick into the clearing.

I consider his words. Maybe it wasn't my fault.

Chapter 21

Amir, Blackmail, and Ugly Duckling Makeovers

I check the phone to see what I missed. Amir is coming to Vegas tomorrow.

Sunday, meet me at the lion at MGM at 10 am Wednesday.

I work the late shift, so I would be ready to meet him in the morning. What is he thinking? Is he going to jeopardize everything? Together, we had schemed and analyzed all the risk factors of the new identity. Why did he help me then, if he was just going to turn me in now?

Something must have happened. Crazy thoughts cloud my brain, and my anxiety increases by the hour. What if the police show up at the MGM while I'm waiting for Amir? What if this is a set-up?

My gut tells me something isn't right.

I can't take the chance. I pay Nell, one of the cocktail waitresses at the Magic Hat, twenty bucks and a night of babysitting her nine-year old daughter, Molly, to hand-deliver my note to Amir at 10 a.m. Nell has a mane of long blonde hair similar to my old hair. If someone was actually there to find me, they might approach Nell. I will be hiding in the crowds from afar and watching.

The note is simple:

Amir, walk outside the casino, get on the CAT 27 bus and get off at the first stop, turn right, and walk to the park. Don't use your phone, don't even look at your phone, and don't speak to anyone. Put this note in your pocket right now and start walking. Sit on the bench by the art sculpture and wait.

I know it sounds all James Bond and spy-like, but I want to be sure. I need to verify that the police are not involved.

The first problem in my elaborate plan is Nell. I watch her as she searches the crowd, she picks up her phone.

Mine rings a moment later.

"I can't find the dark-haired chunky techie dude with braces and glasses," she says.

I've been searching the crowd. "Neither can I."

Is it a set-up? Is Amir even here? Why would Amir make up the entire ruse to have me appear and not show up? Maybe the messages are not even from Amir.

My heart thumps so loud I can hear it. My chest is tight and my stomach aches.

Terrified.

What do you want me to do? Nell texts. She walks around the lion area, studying the single guys in front of the lion. She stops and speaks to a dark-haired slender guy with longer hair, tight jeans, expensive shoes, and a button-up long-white shirt. She smiles and even giggles as she hands him the note. WHAT IS SHE DOING? That's not Amir.

Oh my god, she is handing the note to the wrong guy.

He takes the note reads it and puts it in his pocket. Then his head pivots in each direction, I squint, examining the side of his face. Could that possibly be Amir? If it is Amir, it is a shocking transformation; as if he'd emerged from a booth on a home makeover edition, the dumpy outdated house, now house beautiful. NO way.

He takes off his sunglasses, and there is the give-away, he bites his lower lip and I swear he looks right at me. What an amazing shift in appearances. Braces off, cool jeans, and longer hair—way longer, almost wavy. He could have been in a skin commercial with his new, clear skin; and an "after" model on an infomercial for weight loss.

It hasn't even been two months since the shooting. What happened? I watch this fake Amir read the note. He stands still, searching the crowd, then jams his left hand into his front pocket, his head toward the ground. The mannerism is familiar to me. I've witnessed it a hundred times. He hesitates a bit longer, then picks up a backpack sitting on the bench and a bouquet of flowers.

Flowers. It hits me like someone threw a bucket of water on my face. Amir came here for me?

He heads out without giving any signal or picking up his phone. I keep my distance and follow him onto the bus. Like him, I am hard to recognize, wearing my Vegas fedora hat, a black skirt, black blouse tied at my stomach, giant sunglasses, and a massive fake tattoo on my leg. Amir doesn't look around. He gives the right change to the bus driver, steps on to the crowded bus, and looks straight ahead.

What happened to Amir? The ugly duckling turned into a swan. Apparently, the shooting changed all of our lives.

I follow Amir off the bus, careful not to be noticed. I stand next to a large woman as if we were together. He strolls right by me, focused on the first bench after the art sculpture. No one is following him, and with Amir's new makeover, well... I might just have it all wrong. Very wrong.

Did Amir come for me?

I don't know how I didn't see it before, but now his past actions make more sense.

I wait a full ten minutes, and he never takes his phone out of his pocket, just the note, which he rereads several times.

Nervous, I draw in a long breath and start walking in his direction. As I approach him, he casts a glance at me as I come closer. His face is amazingly clear of acne, still oily in the heat, but his longer hair gives him a certain sense of coolness. Amir, cool on the outside? It doesn't seem possible, but the clothes, the hair, and no braces transforms this boy who always wore nerdy dress pants and fashion-less shoes. This boy, who had no friends at school except for a dead killer and a girl who'd faked her death. He doesn't even resemble my old friend who quietly snuck up on me in the woods.

I sit down beside him, not saying a word, studying him behind my sunglasses. I search the perimeter just in case I'm wrong and the police are waiting for me to approach him. Nothing happens.

I take a deep breath. "You look different. You're wearing jeans."

He gives me a slow hesitant smile and I can see his white teeth straight and braces-free. Wow.

"That's what you noticed? I'm wearing jeans?" He turns an eye on the tattoo on my leg. "You look different, too."

"I'm supposed to," I say.

"Well, you do look different; very different. Is that real?" He points to my tattoo.

"No, it's not real." I tense my shoulders.

He picks up the flowers on the bench and says, "It's all Kaitlyn.

She helped me go shopping. She helped me with a lot of things." He holds out the flowers. "For you."

Kaitlyn? Kaitlyn Barbour? She was a member of the Dream Team who had survived the shooting. One of the first girls to laugh when the HLB boys picked on Amir and Eric. She'd dated Cody, who hated Amir. It's impossible for me to picture the two of them shopping. I take the flowers and lay them on the bench.

"Thanks." What is happening here? I lift both my eyebrows in question. "Kaitlyn?"

Amir shrugs. "A lot of things happened since you left. Things have changed. Everyone's become closer, friendlier... everything is different now."

I cock my head, transfixed by his words and the flowers on the bench. A sudden rush of emotion comes over me. I have to know. "How's Jack?"

Amir's face moves into the sulking face I recognize from before. It's a quick flash to the same face he made when he was displeased with his father's orders. His lips look stretched out, too big for teeth now free of braces. The sulking flash disappears as he smiles.

"He's fine. He's hanging out with Ashley Lindley."

My stomach constricts. I do not like Ashley Lindley; never have. She always flirted with Jack. She oozes with sweetness in front of Jack and every adult. When he isn't around, her words to me are as sharp and cold as a pointy icicle ready to fall from the roof line and stab your back.

"Why are you here, Amir? Why are you threatening me?"

Amir seems puzzled at my question. Shaking his head, he picks up the flowers and thrust them at me. "I'm not threatening you. I just had to see you. I'm here for you, Sunday." He slides closer to me on the bench, placing his hand on my arm. "Sunday,

I've always been here for you, always, and I want to help you."

Amir's fist clenched the stems of the flowers, his other hand on my arm. Something isn't right. Instinctively, I shift away from him on the bench.

"It's Hannah, now." The words shoot from my mouth. I press a hand to my throat, my pulse pounding.

I need to calm down. Think before I speak. "You were the only one I could trust, Amir, and I'm so thankful for all you did. But this meeting, here now, me and you, making me meet you, it's wrong. I'm possibly blowing everything I've worked for sitting here talking to you. This doesn't help me."

Amir's breath quickens and in a flash his hand plucks the oversized sunglasses off my face. His other hand on my arm adds pressure. "You don't understand, *Hannah*." He pronounces it odd, accenting the last syllable. "I can make things so much better for you. I got into MIT. I got offered a work-study job, a full scholarship, and I have an apartment. You can live with me in Massachusetts. You can go to college, start over, and I will help. It's everything you ever wanted. Ever since you..." He struggles with his choice of words "...umm, disappeared. I knew I was supposed to help you. It's my destiny. Just like you always had a plan, I have one now. I have it all figured out. This time, this plan will work. I'll get you the life you always wanted. The one we always talked about."

His eyes seem sincere, as his face flushes, he gushes the words without taking a breath. And for a brief moment my old friend with silver braces and spiky short hair who'd thrust a wrapped birthday gift in my hand every year since I was ten, is sitting beside me. He always did want to make things better for me. Suddenly, it becomes clear. I missed the fact that Amir crushed on me. Being with Jack, it never crossed my mind. I was too caught up in my own world—the world circling around Sunday syndrome—to even notice. His hand tightens on my arm. I believe he thinks he can save me, but his fierceness makes me nervous.

"Amir." I gaze into his black brown eyes, but his intensity or something else I can't describe, make me look away. "I'm going to be okay by myself. This plan I have is *my plan* and even though it's not as easy as I thought, I need to see it through. How could I go to MIT with you? Your parents would recognize me, or someone else would, and then I would be in so much trouble, and you would be in a mess for helping me. No, I've made this choice and I have to live with the consequences. Alone."

Amir's fingers dig into my skin as he grabs my shoulders and forces his lips on mine. His tongue darts on my lips, trying to break through into my mouth. His hand circles my shoulder in a vise-like grip, and it triggers a flashback of Tyler. I shove him back hard, as hard as I can, and he slides off the bench, his white shirt picking up the Las Vegas dirt.

"Amir, what are you doing?" I want to spit the taste of him out of my mouth. A sour and sad taste. My heart sprints in my chest. I want to run.

He looks away, bites his lip, and stands in slow motion. A tear rolls off his chin. His face is red. He slowly brushes the dirt off his shirt and jeans. Wipes his face with the back of his shaking hand. A ripple of defying reactions controls his facial expressions—almost as if he's fighting with his emotions to stay calm.

"Sunday, we are meant to be together. I know this with certainty. You're all I can think of, and if you're worried about MIT, who cares? I won't go there; we can go anywhere you choose. I will change my identity, even fake my death, and we can start fresh. THIS can work. No one needs to know. Ever. It's MY plan. We can do anything however you want. I need to do this for you." He sits back on the bench, more in control, nodding his head up and down as if he didn't hear a word I said.

I stare at him. Who is this aggressive Amir? In the past, he would never have kept pushing his ideas. He would never even have these ideas. I have to be straight with him. I don't want him to think for another moment that this is a plan that will ever materialize. Eric being the shooter must have really affected him, even more than changing his looks. Pity mixes in with my anger.

I'm not sure how to get out of this.

"Amir, look, I'm sorry. It's not going to happen. This lie, this life I created, is something I have to live with. It's my burden, not yours. You have to walk away and believe that I died that day, along with everyone else." Bent over, looking down at the ground, his hands tighten into fists. "Just believe that Eric shot me on the river. Like everyone else, you have to let me go."

He unclenches his fists but does not look up.

I touch his shoulder. "I'm dead, just like everyone else Eric shot."

Silence. Time ticks by. I don't know how to end this, but I know I have to get away from Amir. I want to comfort my old friend, but this is not my old friend. Maybe I will have to move. I hope not. I don't want to change my identity all over again. Something is different, and not just his clothes, contacts, weight-loss, hair, and white teeth—something inside, he isn't reacting normal.

"Sunday, you're not dead like everyone else, and I don't want to have to call the police and tell them you are alive and hiding. Can you imagine what they would think of you running, hiding, and changing your identity? I can fix this. Come live with me and no one will ever know."

A loud roar is in my ears, I can't move. Amir mumbles something else I can't understand, his head hangs down, and his right hand is still crunching the stems of the flowers. He sounds like he is repeating a phrase, but it's incomprehensible. Five minutes that seem like thirty passes as I sit there not knowing how to respond to his threats. "Amir? What? What are you saying?"

Amir stops the mantra and looks up, his face changes into some weird expression. My breath quickens. What is wrong with him?

"Eric would never have killed you because he knew how much I liked you. I told him definitely not to kill you, so it's impossible to imagine you're dead like everyone else."

His words chill me to the bone and the air around me seems to swirl. Did he know? Did he know Eric was going to go on a shooting spree?

I'm going to be sick.

Chapter 22

Thieves, Illusions, and Black Clouds

Impossible. The torn corner of my cardboard box of a dresser is all I can stare at as I sit on the floor like a broken doll. My dry throat makes it difficult for me to swallow. I make no attempt to stop my tears from dripping on the floor. It's gone, all of it. *EVERYTHING.* The gold jewelry I had purchased at the pawn shop, the cash in the tampon box, my Kindle tablet.

Gone.

"Someone broke in," Jamie says between hiccups. She's hammered. So is Adriana. In between their slurring words and weaving, I conclude that they had come home from a party and the door was wide open.

"My laptop is gone," Jamie slurs.

Adriana's backpack is also missing.

The old school television with the ancient over-sized DVD player, bought at the Goodwill, still sits on the box against the wall. Too heavy to carry out or just too old to want? My paper-thin closet bedroom door was broken, and my meager, valueless possessions were thrown around, but the stuff that mattered—

my whole life, all my savings, including the money from Ward—are gone.

Terror fills my chest cavity. It's hard to breathe in a normal rhythm. There is nothing left. I have no place to run to. I try to breathe; try to collect my thoughts. The gravity of losing it all is sickening. Everything. Gone.

My life is over. Now this after Amir's threats to make me come live with him.

Yesterday, after I stopped myself from throwing up, frozen in place in shock, he spoke quietly in a demented voice that frightened me into silence.

"I'm doing this for you. You'll thank me some day," were the last words he said. He acted like he was the logical one, doing me a favor.

Fear and disbelief held my tongue. I wanted to scream at him, walk away, tell him he was out of his mind. *Who do you think you are?* But I hesitated. I had to be smart, not reactive. Clearly, there is something wrong with Amir. Did Amir know Eric was going to go on a shooting spree that day, or did the horrific event make him delusional?

I wanted to run to the police. Why would he say that he *told* Eric not to kill me?

I can't go to the police.

I didn't know how to react or what to say. "You might be right," I said. "I need to think your plan through. Can we meet tomorrow to discuss our plans?"

I grimace thinking back how he petted my arm like a cute puppy he had just rescued. Amir was not right in the head. It took all my acting ability to remain calm, when what I really wanted to do was scream and run.

After the meeting, I went to work and had a terrible day with only a few tips which is all I have after getting robbed.

A black cloud. Somehow, I am caught in a twisting tornado which is collecting the worst possible things on the planet, swirling and circling me. I'm dodging the obstacles, trying to not get knocked down, but it's impossible. For a brief interlude, the clouds part and Jack pops into my mind. Oh, how I miss Jack, and wish for some magical scenario where he and I could end up together. He is my light in the dark. But Jack can't help me.

Wake up, Sunday, I yell as I look at the cheap Walgreens mirror attached to the back of the door of my closet. I'm amazed it didn't fall on the floor during the break-in. My reflection astounds me. How did I get here? My mascara paints black streaks on my cheeks, and my blonde roots are slightly visible. The whites of my eyes are bloodshot, and my nostrils and tip of my nose are red. Who am I? Sunday or Hannah? This illusion is not working for any name.

My whole PLAN is now destroyed. Not only did I lose Sunday and Jack and the imaginary baby that made me commit the whole pseudocide to begin with, but I lost every cent I saved. Maybe I should have been one of the casualties of the shooting.

I know my life with HE and SHE was not living, but I've spent my whole life working for something better, some grand plan that won't ever happen. Jack was born under a lucky star, and somehow when he was in my life, I thought maybe my luck would change. There's no reason things are the way they are, but maybe it's me, my fate. That is the heart of the matter. Things don't happen, they are this way because they are supposed to be. If chaos and commotion are part of my life, then who am I to fight it, to try to change it?

Amir's threat of turning me into the police is the worst

possible scenario I can imagine; it would ruin whatever life I try to create. HE might beat me to an inch of my life if I return home. I can't imagine how I could explain any of this to anyone.

Life taught me to pick myself off the floor; to lie through my teeth and not expect miracles.

I tried.

If Amir turns me in, I'm not sure I can get back up this time. But if Amir's responsible for the shooting, I don't know how to go on and keep this dark secret.

Chapter 23

Back to Vegas, Towel Throwing, and Sickness

My hard-earned money is now nesting in some thief's pockets. Everything I've worked so hard for is—Poof! —gone. Oh, I've learned that lesson before—one day you're on a school field trip, whitewater rafting down a beautiful river in the woods, and then suddenly, well, there's a crazy kid with a gun and an American flag and that's it; you're gone along with twenty-seven of your classmates.

Every brick I laid to build my road to the future led me straight back to where I started. I must truly be the unluckiest person God put on this earth. I've never had a mother's love, never had a family, and never had control of my own future. Now, the world I tried to create is a fiasco.

I'm flat broke, and what does it matter? I'm certain that if I save up money again, the pendulum will swing, and I will be back to where I started from. Who cares where I live, what I do, or even if I survive? The world thinks I'm dead, anyway. Ironic, 'cause I feel dead. In a moment, I might be homeless. My rent was in the tampon box safe in my dresser.

Last night, after my shift and before the break-in, I ran into Hudson waiting for the bus outside the casino. I think back to the conversation from last night, picturing kind Hudson, wishing I would have said something or did something different.

"Up for a walk in the park?" he asked. His glass-half-full of positive energy dialed on high increases is such a huge part of his attractiveness. I can see why my soon-to-be-ex-roommate Jamie thinks he's hot and talks about him constantly.

"I need to go home, I'm beat," I said, wanting to scream, instead: I'm being blackmailed about my fake identity and I need your help.

"Okay, get some rest, Hannah." And with that, he squeezed my shoulder and the conversation ended.

I let him walk away when I was exploding to talk to someone.

Then I arrived home to the break-in. Seriously, what else could go wrong?

I believed I could survive on my own, without anyone's help. I'm so wrong. I have $43.25 from tips to my name. I owe four hundred dollars in rent and one hundred dollars for my broken closet bedroom door.

My two choices: accept Amir's offer, or flee and say goodbye to Hannah Williams. This time, if I start all over again, I will have no money and no help. A true unidentified soul, a homeless runaway without an identity or an address. Who cares, right? No one does. That's the point. So, what does it matter?

I watch him light the cigarette and blow it up toward the neon lights of the Casino beside us, the smoke creating a hazy picture of the new Amir. I picked a well-lit busy courtyard. "When did you start smoking?" I ask.

His eyes half closed, Amir faces me, holding the cigarette in his hand as if he had practiced the pose to look cool.

"It helped me lose weight. I never wanted to smoke around you because of your mother." He takes another drag. "I knew you hated it. But everyone smokes in Las Vegas.... you must be used to it."

"I'll never get used to it," I say.

Amir moves closer to me, openly scrutinizing me, his eyes going from the top of my head to my shoes. "Well, in Cambridge, I will smoke outside. Or, if it's too cold, I'll open the windows. I can do that for you." He gives me a creepy smile.

"Someone broke into my apartment last night. They took all my money." I watch Amir's body language. He has no reaction. He blows out smoke and studies the cigarette, moving it to his other hand. With his other hand, he covers my hand with his.

I try not to flinch.

"Well, that's terrible." He flicks the cigarette ash on the ground, and then squeezes my hand. "But it will be okay. Lucky I'm here, we can ride the Greyhound together and head straight to Cambridge. My father will pay for the apartment a few weeks early and you won't have to worry about a thing. I'll cover you, Sunday. We will get an alarm. It pays to have one, that way, if someone breaks in, the alarm alerts the neighbors and scares the robbers away. You should have had an alarm. But, don't worry, you won't get robbed again. Not with me."

"Hannah," I correct him. How does he know I didn't have an alarm?

"Of course, sorry, I meant Hannah." He lets go of my one hand and shows me what he has beside him. It's a brown paper bag over a bottle. He holds it up. "Want some?"

I focus on my breathing, trying to control my emotions. My pulse has been in my throat ever since I sat down beside him. I have never seen Amir drink.

He takes another swallow and continues. "Things have changed. Since the shooting, my father basically does anything I ask. Are you ready for this? I'm not going to medical school; I'm enrolled in the Brain and Cognitive Science Department at MIT."

"Sunday, are you listening?" He slides his leg against my leg.

"Yes, I heard you, I thought your dream was computer science?" I need to find a non-obvious way to ask my burning question.

"It was, and is, but basically everything is computerized, and it's science. MIT has the latest technology. Just wait until you see the school. You're going to love it."

He pats my hand again. I swallow back the rising vomit.

"Studying the human mind is an extraordinary opportunity, an irresistible chance to unravel persistent puzzles of the brain and mind. Neuroscience."

He speaks as if he is reciting a college brochure. What happened to Amir? Everyone from our high school must be affected by the shooting. Amir, being such close friends with Eric, must have had an extremely difficult time. I must have misunderstood him last night. He couldn't have possibly known what Eric was going to do.

I take in a deep breath and swallow. "Maybe studying the human brain will give you some insight into Eric."

Amir, squishes the cigarette out on the ground with his new cool shoes, jerks his head in my direction. His face twists with anger.

"Why would I want to do that?" He balls his fists.

I touched a nerve. For a split second I empathize, but then I remember he's blackmailing me. "To try and understand what would make someone snap like that! Why someone would shoot a group of innocent students?"

"Innocent? Do you think the Hard Liquor Boys and the Dream Team were innocent students?" Amir's words are sharp; he spits them out one word at a time, as if they cut his mouth.

"Maybe innocent is the wrong word, but innocent enough not to be shot for their bullying." I can hear my voice going up an octave.

Amir stiffens and chuckles, a cold ominous low sound. "Eric couldn't be stopped—he wanted to be justified; that's the word he used. He liked that word, *justified*. He just wanted to belong to something, anything, and he was so easily addicted. I showed him ISIS and other radical group videos on his computer just to piss off my father, the Gulf War hero. Everyone always called me a terrorist at school, a towelhead, a Muslim lover, so I looked it up and I showed it to Eric, and he became obsessed with all the information that exists out there. He wanted to go out with a bang." Amir laughs a bitter laugh. "I guess he got his wish."

The bitter acid taste in my mouth almost makes me heave on Amir. I swallow, unsure of what to say next, and I stand up. Could Amir possibly have prevented the murder of twenty-eight people? I sit down on the bench as far away from Amir as I can without falling off the bench.

I want to run, scream, slap his face, and punch him.

I have to know. I have to know.

I swallow and focus on the tone of my voice, struggling to keep it level and as normal as possible. "Do you think he had it planned out ahead of time? I mean, what made him pick the school field trip?"

Amir takes a long deep swallow of whatever liquor is hidden inside the crinkled brown paper bag. I try not to stare. Every time I look at him, I can't fathom how he transformed, into this....

He motions for me to come closer, patting the seat beside him once more. "Everyone asks me questions about Eric, as if I'm the Eric expert. The press, the media. The fact is: no one ever cared or even took the time to get to know Eric before BOBB. And now, everyone wants to know everything. Always questions about Eric. It's a little too late to care, don't you think?"

"BOBB?"

Amir laughs and says, "That's what the students call it, BOBB, B-O-B-B—Before Ohiopyle Blood Bath."

"That's terrible."

"Well, for such a terrible thing, the school and the students have never been closer. Students are nice to each other. They've even befriended me. Eric would be mad. He wouldn't be happy." Amir finishes off the bottle, tilting it straight up.

"What do you mean, Eric would be mad?"

Amir moves closer to me, since I won't slide over, and I can smell the liquor and cigarettes on his breath just like HE. I start sweating. I don't know if I can sit here for another minute.

"Are you going with me, Sunday? Will you let me take care of you?" He is once again, touching my leg with his, this time with full pressure. "It will be easy to blend in, it's a town full of college students, and don't worry about my mother and father. They will stay away. I frighten them. They will do anything I want." A creepy laugh bubbles out of his mouth, as he smiles.

I want to run, hoping he can't see the perspiration on my forehead, but I have to know the truth. "Scared of you?"

Amir put his hands on my shoulder and pulls my chin to look at him. His eyes bloodshot and wild. "Sunday, I know you can figure it out. Eric was smart, but not as smart as me."

And with that, he lights another cigarette, takes a big drag, and blows the smoke out with a smile on his lips. The conversation is over.

Chapter 24

Wide Awake, Walk Away and Viral Videos

After the meeting with Amir, I walk like a zombie through my first half of my shift at the Magic Hat. A variety of scenarios flash in my mind as I try to figure out what to do. I'm not giving up or giving in, not this time. *You only fail if you give up.*

I'm wide awake.

I can see clearly now. I AM smart enough to figure this out.

I realize what I need to do. I cannot, will not, go to Massachusetts with Amir.

Let him turn me in to the police.

I'm done being a victim. I am getting my control back.

Ward, back in the Magic Hat for the first time after winning his millionaire jackpot, sits at the progressive "Stinkin' Rich" machine. The progressive jackpot is now only worth three hundred and twelve dollars. I don't notice him until he touches my arm. "Bridget, are you all right, darling?"

Why is it when someone asks me tenderly how I am doing, the kindness gets underneath my skin and overtakes me to the point of crying on their shoulders and telling them everything.

I turn my fake smile on high and say, in a forced happy voice, "Of course I am, Mr. Stinkin' Rich. What can I get you?"

"I'll take a ginger ale tonight." Ward lowers his voice. "Lately, I've had a little too much celebrating, if you know what I mean." He chuckles. "Did you see that crazy music video they made of my interview and you and me, when I won? I guess it was a virus or something like that."

"What video?" Ward has my attention.

"Oh, you didn't see it, did you?" Ward lifts his chin as he digs into his pocket. "Well, you are probably going to like this." He pulls out the latest iPhone. "I got me one of these fancy phones and I know I have it on here if I can figure out how to use it."

It takes Ward two long minutes to find the video, but when he hits play, I watch an auto-tune video of Ward's interview with clips of video footage from someone's cell phone in the casino. "It has over two million hits or something like that. A virus, is that what it's called? Now isn't that just plum crazy? Two million people know I won all that money."

There I am, plain as day, laughing in the video while Ward counts out the hundred-dollar bills to me. Yes, I have dark short hair, but still...Oh My GOD...my heart is thumping on the highest setting, making it difficult to breathe. What else could possibly go wrong today?

I sit down. "Can I see it again?" The clip of me was less than four seconds. My hand shakes as I hold Ward's new phone.

"Are you sure you're feeling all right, Ms. Bridget? You look a little peaked to me."

"No, Ward, I'm fine, only tired. Two million hits, that's a lot. That means the video went viral, not virus, meaning it just kept getting forwarded and viewed." I stand up. "I'll be right back with your drink."

When I come back, Ward is sitting with another gentleman quite a bit younger than him, with blonde messy hair and in a suit. He hands Ward a pen to sign something. Ward introduces him as his favorite son and lawyer, Devon, and introduces me as Bridget, his lucky charm.

"Yes, now I need an attorney and an accountant. Imagine that." Ward laughs.

"I'm his only son and he's always needed me." Devon extends his hand; I can see the resemblance in both the eyes and smile.

And as I shake his hand, which is warm and firm, a light bulb turns on in my head.

"Devon, do you have a card? I have a friend who might be looking for a lawyer."

Hudson is leaning against the outside wall after my shift. I'm terrified Amir will be standing outside the casino when I walk out the door. I am ecstatic to see Hudson's handsome, caring face instead.

"That sucks that you guys got robbed. Jamie said you guys didn't even call the police." He pauses. "What did they take of yours?"

Hudson's concern fills his green eyes, and for a moment I see Clark, an older version I've conjured up in my mind, of my brother fifteen years down the road. I imagine he would have been a happy optimist like Hudson. "They took everything."

And then it hits me. I can't help but smile. Even though my world sucks big time, I am wondering why I never realized the similarity between Hudson and what I imagine my brother Clark would look like. It's hard to explain, but a secure feeling washes over me, as I study him. "Did you have blonde hair as a baby?" I ask.

"What? They took everything?" Hudson cocks his head to the side. "And yes, I was a towhead, but what does that have to do with the robbery? And what are you smiling about? That rare Hannah smile... and after you just got robbed."

I knew it. "Nothing. I just wondered what you looked like as a baby. I bet you were cute."

"What is up with you tonight, Hannah? Did they take your brain?"

"They might as well have...I'm going to be homeless. The crooks took all my money, every last cent, except my tip money from the last two shifts. I'm finished."

Hudson stops and shakes his head. "Hold on. I'm sure Adriana and Jamie will give you some time, given the circumstances."

"No, they don't have the money to cover me since they got robbed too. So yes, I'm going to be homeless. I'm out tomorrow unless I come up with $400 in cash tonight. I think they have already found someone from school to move in. And Adriana will be happy to get rid of me"

Hudson shifts his weight from one foot to the other, unsure of what to say. "Well, you're in good company. Lots of famous people started out homeless before they became rich and famous. Charlie Chaplin lived on the streets of London and Halle Berry lived in a homeless shelter. Houdini, Cary Grant, and the millionaire New York stockbroker Chris Gardner all lived in homeless shelters. Haven't you ever seen the movie *The Pursuit of Happyness* with Will Smith and his son? Well, they wrote a book about being homeless. See all the opportunities, Hannah?" He smiles and put his arm around my shoulders.

"Thanks, Hudson, that really makes me feel better." I sarcastically roll my eyes at him.

He tugs me closer and whispers in my ear. "I wish I had the

$400 to loan you. But, I'll loan you one hundred bucks and you can crash on my couch until we figure it out."

"That's really nice, Hudson." I mean it and swallow that stupid lump in the back of my throat. "Do you know any lawyers?"

"What? What are you going to do, sue Adriana and Jamie for kicking you out?"

"No, nothing like that. Isn't it true that whatever you tell a lawyer is confidential?"

"Yes, as long as you hire them, but I don't know if that means anything. I mean, if a guy kills his wife and goes to a lawyer and tells the attorney, 'I just killed my wife,' the attorney can't call the police and tell them the husband did it, but if the wife is dead at the house, I think they have to call the police and say she's dead." Hudson jerks his head in my direction. "Is there something I should know, Hannah?"

Again, Hudson reaches inside of me through my eyes, search-ing for an answer. *I want to say yes, there are so many things you should know, so many things I want to tell you, your head would spin; but I can't tell you.* "No, I'm just asking for someone I know."

"Someone you know. Okay, Miss Mysterious." We walk slowly; Hudson's arm slung around my shoulder.

"I wish you would talk to me. Maybe I can help. Are you in trouble?"

He slows his step and rubs my shoulder as we walk to the park. "Are you going to sleep in your bedroom tonight?"

I freeze. Then back up, moving away from Hudson, my eyes glued to the silhouette of the person sitting on the bench smoking a cigarette.

Hudson slows down and stops, and turns towards me, ques-tioning my sudden stop as if my tension emitted a signal, his brow arches up. "What's wrong?"

Amir stands up, blowing his smoke our way. In the fading light, through a puff of cigarette smoke, he looks older, darker, and sinister. My nerdy, sweet neighbor is gone.

"Good evening, Sunday, who's your friend?"

I put my fake face on, hoping my pounding heart isn't a dead giveaway to my fear. I pray it is not as loud to Hudson as it is to me.

Hudson can't be a part of this. "Hudson, I forgot I was going to meet my friend Amir. I'll catch up with you later. I'll text you." I force myself to move next to Amir, hoping Hudson will walk away.

Hudson stops dead in place, as if he is playing musical chairs and the music suddenly stopped. He exhales with an odd look as he focuses on Amir and then back at me, trying to assess the situation.

"Why is he calling you Sunday?" Hudson stands his ground. He doesn't look a bit intimidated.

Amir has an amused look on his face. But not like a funny ha-ha face, more like a sick twisted amusement. He is a stranger to me.

I force a fake laugh, and say, "It's Sunny, a nickname." I walk over to Amir and, with my back to Hudson, give him a stern look and compel myself to give him a hug. His scent is smokey and sour, unexplainable to my nostrils. And, without turning around, I pray that Hudson will just walk away. "I'll see you at work tomorrow, Hudson. Thanks for the walk home." I use a loud voice, without turning around.

Leave, Hudson. Walk away. I don't turn to say goodbye, which is so awkward. I can't stand being in Amir's space, the fingers on his right hand touch me and slowly dig into my shoulder bone.

Amir leans down and kisses the top of my head and pulls me tight, as I close my eyes, forcing myself not to scream. I count to twenty in my head, hoping against hope that Hudson is walking away. I don't want Hudson to even converse with Amir, and I don't want him to see my fear. I don't want my new friend to be any part of this.

Just let me go, Hudson. Walk away.

"Who's your friend?"

"Just a guy I work with." I study Amir, trying to control the shaking that is overtaking my hands. Amir scares me. It is impossible to see the chubby boy with glasses, the braces, and the dress pants. How did this metamorphosis happen? Amir is a transformer, the worst kind of monster.

I pull my shoulder out of his grasp and lower my body to the bench, still careful not to look at the spot where Hudson stood. I'm focused on the ground, listening. I don't hear anything but the beat of my heart, so I'm guessing Hudson left. Amir sits beside me, his hand on my leg. I study his hand, so I don't have to raise my head. His fingernails are dirty underneath, and long. Even in this dim light I can see the unkempt nails, and it seems odd to me, with his new clothes and overbearing cologne he is wearing.

"I've been thinking, Sunday, about the past—you know, all those times down by the creek; our place." His freakish smile makes me sick.

It was my place, not ours, I want to yell.

He keeps talking. "You talked about your dreams and your plans, but I was never included." He pauses. "So that was then, and this is now. You not including me always pissed me off, and I never said anything, but things are going to change now that we're going to be together."

He sits down. "It's going to be great, just you wait and see."

"I'm not going with you, Amir."

"Of course you are. You don't have anywhere else to go. I'm sorry, Sunday—I mean, Hannah. I'll work on calling you Hannah," he says in a patronizing tone. "Hannah, look at me." He yanks my chin toward him with his dirty fingernails that smell like cigarettes.

I pull back. "I don't know what happened to the Amir I once knew, but you're not him. I'm not going anywhere with you." I slide my backpack on my shoulder, trying to anticipate his next response.

"Hannah." His tone overflows with sarcasm and his fingers grab my wrist. "You're forgetting what will happen if you don't go with me. I'm sure the Maryland police would be extremely interested to know that Sunday Foster is alive and faked her death. Your father... well...."

I hesitate, not sure if I should show my card. I pry his fingers off my wrist and stand up. "You do what you have to, Amir, but I have a great story to tell them if that happens."

"Oh yeah, what story is that?" He stands, his chest an inch from my face. God, he must have grown two inches in the last couple months, or maybe I never noticed how tall he was as he sat behind me down by the creek, hunched over.

My fight or flight instinct is building inside my chest, my hands are shaking, and my heartbeat accelerates into a sprint. "You knew Eric was going to kill all those people, our classmates, and you didn't do anything. You let him do it. I don't even know who you are anymore. How could you let him kill them?"

In a flash he has me by my arms, grabbing them tight and pushing my elbows together. I remember what Hudson said the other night by the lake, to protect myself if anyone like Tyler ever tried to take advantage of me again.

"Eric was angry and wanted to kill something, it's not my fault it only took a little push to set him off. It was so easy. He was just on the edge of doing something. He killed them, not me."

I lift my knee and used all my anger to jerk it into him below his belt as hard as I can. He lets go of my arms and I step back and then I raise my foot and kick him as hard as I possibly can in the same spot. He doubles over.

"But you knew, and you didn't tell anyone. You told him not to shoot me. You knew—you sick creep. What's wrong with you? What happened to you?" I bolt, not sure where I am going, but I run like a track star. I never look back until my chest is about to explode. I stop, a wheezing sound escapes from my lungs, as I try to catch my breath. I survey the street, looking in every direction. Amir is not behind me. I keep running.

Chapter 25

Free The Lion, Truth, and Consequences

The automatic doors continue to open and close as I wait in the lobby of the Cosmopolitan Casino for what seems like hours. Finally, a little breakfast place opens across the street. I scan the crowd from every direction, sipping my coffee and eating my bagel, clutching the wrinkled business card of Devon Perry in my fist. Devon Perry, Attorney at Law. *God, I hope you can help me,* I pray.

His office is only two bus rides away. It will take me an hour to get there.

Something about bumpy, hot bus rides make me queasy; or at least that's what I'm telling myself.

Yes, I even lie to myself. It's the truth that makes me queasy. The naked truth cuts me in half and almost doubles me over. I've been living a lie for so long, I'm not sure if I am ready for the truth or even if I can handle the truth.

The moment I step on the bus, headed to Devon Perry's office, I know that if I do this, go through with this, Hannah will be gone. The end of Hannah. I need to find my strength, pull the tape off my mouth, and let the truth out. The bus pulls up to my stop. I force myself to take a step, move forward, and walk off the bus. *I can do this.*

I spot Devon's office building and drag myself to the entrance. I command myself to push the elevator button. Riding up to the fifth floor, I take in long, deep breaths. Breathe in, breathe out. If someone was in the elevator with me, they might think I was practicing for having a baby. The irony of my thought almost makes me laugh hysterically. *Get a hold of yourself.* The doors open, and there's a long line of name plaques hanging on the glass door. The generic office of Mr. Devon Perry is a rent-an-office space with a general reception area and a variety of companies operating behind the numerous closed doors and cubicles.

He doesn't even have a real law office.

"Mr. Devon Perry is not in," states the receptionist. She has bright cherry-red lips, and heavy black eyeliner circles her eyes and mouth like a bad villain in a Marvel movie. She studies me up and down and both our eyes meet as my trembling hands hold Devon's card. I clasp my hands together.

"I could call him and make an appointment," she says. "Would you like me to see if I can reach him?"

It's a sign. An omen telling me not to go forward. This plan is not well thought out. My emotions are in the driver's seat, my shredding gut instinctively leading the way. I need to flip my actress manners on and make something up—anything—and get the hell out of here.

I lower my body to the cushioned chair with the high back and grip the arms of the chair, so I won't run. My cell phone is dead. Another sign? I'm sick to my stomach and exhausted, my anxiety is off the charts. I lean over and put my head in my hands, taking deep breaths.

"Miss. Miss." I can hear the high-pitched voice of the receptionist and I don't care. Now, I can hear her whispering. *Please let me sit here for a moment before you throw me out. I just need a minute, and...*

"Miss, Miss... Mr. Perry just walked in."

I lift my head. Ward's son is standing in front of me. A sign?

The truth will set me free. I repeat this as I walked toward him, clutching his card in my hand.

I manage to speak. "I'm Hannah Williams. I met you last night with your father at the Magic Hat Casino." I stick out my hand. Ward's son meets my brown contact eyes and ignores my trembling and shakes my hand with a warm and firm handshake, just like last night.

He seems to remember me and then pushes his thick, wavy blonde hair off his face, a series of emotions wrinkle his tiny crow's-feet at his eyes. He is undecided if he should be talking to me. His face reveals time spent basking in the sun, and with his denim button-down shirt, no tie, and khaki slacks, he could have been going to a picnic or a lunch date I interrupted. I can smell his cologne, not overbearing, but barely there and masculine. Compared to the only attorney I unfortunately know personally, HE, Mr. Perry does not appear to be in the same pompous, pretentious, strong-cologne-wearing club. His card said General Practice, and I hope this is not yet another mistake.

He hesitates before he speaks, sizing me up. "I met you last night with my father?"

"Yes, I'm his waitress. He introduced me as Bridget. It's uh... my casino name." My IQ is flying out the window.

He nods as if he understands and cautiously smiles. "Yes, I remember now. You look a little different."

"Yes, they want us to wear a lot of makeup." I'm barely making sentences. Without the heavy makeup, I'm sure he wondered if I was twenty-one. It doesn't help that I sound like a babbling idiot. Right now, I want to crawl out of the room like a toddler. What am I doing here?

"Why are you here, Ms. Williams?" he asks as if he can read my mind.

I open my mouth to reply, but suddenly, instead of my mouth opening, my knees go weak and I have to shuffle in place. I press my hands to my cheeks, trying to hold my head from going backwards, and whisper, "I think I need to hire a lawyer." And in slow-mo the lights get dimmer and everything slowly fades to black.

Mr. Perry was a race car driver and a skier. Pictures of a much younger, athletic man skiing and standing beside a black and yellow race car covered in advertising are plastered in various frames in his office. As I sit on his leather couch, sipping a glass of cold water, he assures me I was only out for seconds, and he'd caught me.

"Is there someone you want me to call? I think you should get checked out to see why you fainted." He is unsure of what to do.

"I'm okay. I know why I fainted." Who would I call anyway?

He sits on the edge of his desk, and his directness reminds me of his father.

"Why?" His blue eyes seem warm with genuine concern; perhaps even caring. I remember what Ward said about his son: "He's one of the good ones." I hope Ward is right.

I take another drink of water and inhale and exhale. "I'm scared to death to tell you the truth, but I need to get it out. If I tell you something illegal, something illegal I've done... do you have to go to the police? Or am I protected by attorney-client privilege?" I fish a twenty out of my pocket and hold it out. We both notice the shaking motion in my unsteady hand. "I know I have to hire you and give some consideration or something to make it legal, so here's some money."

"You seem to know a little about law." He does not take the twenty I am holding, so I place it on my lap and start smoothing it out.

"I do, my..." I must swallow, to spit out the correct word, as I push the creases out of the crumpled twenty, "...father is an attorney and I worked at the courthouse in Baltimore."

He makes a steeple out of his hands and balances his chin on his fingers, studying me before he speaks. "I mostly do family law, bankruptcy, wills and probate, trusts and estates."

"Your card lists criminal law," I respond. I look around his little worn office, my intelligence coming back to life. "Want to get out of this office? Work in a bigger firm? I've got the case to help you."

He moves over to lower his body into the chair beside the couch, the only two pieces of furniture besides his desk and chair in the small office. He looks me squarely in the eyes. It instinctively makes me trust him more.

"Well, that's an interesting statement, but I happen to like my office and I'm not looking for the next big case. I'm a race car driver who never made it to the big leagues and a skier who never made the Olympics. Perhaps I should refer you to someone else who can help you." He pulls his phone out and starts scrolling through his contacts.

I need to talk to someone now. For the first time in forever, the truth is pacing back and forth inside my body and wants to be let out. Like a caged lion gaining speed, ready to charge the gate that keeps him locked in, the lion wants to be free. I think about the MGM lion who stared me down. I give Devon Perry the same unwavering look.

"Please, Mr. Perry, I need help now. I'm afraid later will be too late, and Ward said you were one of the good ones which I could really use right now." A tear slides down my cheek. I let it roll.

Devon Perry leans back and runs his fingers through his thick hair. He hesitates fixated on the air above me. With a deep sigh he takes out two pieces of paper. I read the heading of the one and my heart skips. He lays them down on the desk, a one-page contract of representation and a receipt of payment. He holds out the palm of his hand and I place the flattened twenty in his hand. I sign the page, before he changes his mind.

"Does this mean we now have client-attorney privilege?"

"Yes, unless you're about to tell me you're going to kill someone or do some future criminal act, which is not protected by the attorney-client privilege."

The lion roars inside me. With a burst of adrenaline, I force myself to speak the words. The words I never thought I would utter. "Have you ever heard the name Sunday Foster?"

Devon shakes his head. "No, I don't think so, why should I?"

Why would he? I had forgotten that terrible horrific shootings happen all the time. With so many school shootings, one missing teenager just gets lost in the mix.

"How about the school shooting in Ohiopyle, Pennsylvania?"

"Yes, of course, the one that happened a few months ago back East on the river?"

"Yes, that one." I swallow the thick wad of emotion stuck in my throat. "Sunday Foster was the missing high school student." I look at his kind eyes, and another tear rolls down my face, and then another and another.

He waits.

"I'm Sunday Foster." The lion comes out slowly. But, once outside the cage, the truth roars.

I start from the very beginning, including Tyler, THE PLAN, and Amir's help, which led up to the school shooting. Mr. Perry takes notes and asks a few simple questions here and there, but basically, he listens. He is immersed, as if I am reading a bedtime story.

When I come to the present day and Amir arriving to Las Vegas to blackmail me into going with him to MIT, he stops me.

"How did Amir find you?"

"I took my driver's license exam and the GED as Hannah Williams. I still intended to go to college. Amir is a computer genius: he found me and messaged me on Facebook, threatening that if I didn't meet him, he was going to the police to tell them I was alive. I met him. He is the only one that knows my new identity is Hannah Williams."

"I see." He pauses. "Why would Amir want to do that?"

He waits for me to continue. I take slow, even breaths.

"The thing is, the reason why I'm sitting here, is not just because of what I have done. Amir knew Eric Beck was going to go to the school trip with a gun that day. It's almost as if he dared him and sent him over the edge. He got Eric to look up radical terrorist videos and research ISIS. His mother is a Muslim. Amir is not. But Amir has been bullied his whole life—kids called him terrorist and horrible names. It's like Amir snapped and this whole other person emerged. He looks completely different, his behavior is odd, and he has some weird sense of confidence; a sick power trip inside him. He even told me his parents are afraid of him. They must suspect." I lean back into the couch, my shirt sticking to me with sweat. I take a deep breath. "I think Amir planned the whole thing and Eric did it for him. In fact, I know he knew it was going to happen. Is that enough to question him, investigate him, or arrest him?"

"It depends. If they could prove he was involved, possibly. They would need proof, to charge him with anything."

"Can they throw me in jail?"

Devon Perry leans back in his chair, his eyes never leaving my face. "Yes, identity theft is a crime even if it is ghosting someone who is dead. This is a serious case, Hannah." He pauses and asks, "or should I call you Sunday?"

Chapter 26

Karma, Chapels, and Reality

Scan and check. No one is following me. I twist around, my chest tight as I study each of the diner patrons. Paranoia. I'm full of it. I need to do something to control my anxiety. I peel my fingers off the countertop, focus on my phone, and scroll through the local news of my hometown. I've stopped myself from doing this daily task weeks ago, but in an attempt to kill time, I search the headlines. A post, "Battered Woman Presses Charges Against Abusive Husband in Complicated Case" catches my eye, but the post right below it makes me stand up.

The black coffee cup tumbles on the counter at the diner. The black liquid runs over the edge, dripping on my pants. I can't take my eyes off my phone. The words of Jack's mother, Marcia flash in my head: "Bad things come in threes."

Tyler Glass. His picture fills up the screen along with two other faces of lacrosse players from Towson State. I stop breathing. The headline from a Baltimore news website: *Three Towson State lacrosse players arrested for the rape of an eighteen-year-old freshman.*

A strange series of emotions overwhelm my mind. Fear, sadness, and satisfaction swirl around together. On the one hand, it makes me feel free from self-blame; almost a relief. I did not cause what he did to me. And, it's not my fault that college-boy Tyler is sick. But guilt creeps in behind the respite. Guilt for the innocent freshman. What he did to me was not my fault. But, I carry the burden of silence. I should have gone to the authorities. Maybe if I did, this wouldn't have happened to someone else.

A barrage of questions keeps pounding my mind. The thought of an altered outcome to this mess is overwhelming. Tyler is guilty. That, I am certain. But, I'm not so innocent anymore, but I was then. Now, I, too, was guilty of different crimes. Twisted, lying violent offenders should not be ignored. No matter what package they are wrapped up in. I will make this right. Maybe not today, or tomorrow, but I will step forward. But for this moment, I must focus on the task at hand.

Ward's son Devon (he insists I use his first name) reluctantly let me leave his office with the promise of meeting up tomorrow morning at ten a.m. I need time to think. I purposely skated around the fact that I was only seventeen. Devon would know soon enough, as he researched the case on the internet. I knew what being a minor would mean to the authorities. They would have to contact HE and SHE, and then maybe I would get sent to a juvenile detention center. I have to think this through.

I need proof that Amir was involved. I know he is the master-mind, a stone-cold murderer. I am slowly discovering my gut instinct, which if I only trusted more often, is more right than wrong. Flashes of Amir controlling Eric surface in my mind. He called him a coward more than one time in front of me. Too wrapped up in my own troubles, I hadn't paid more attention to how Amir was speaking to Eric.

This is my one chance to let the truth be told. If I help them get Amir, perhaps the charges against me will not be so harsh. Faking my death is not necessarily a crime, however, all the fraud that comes with it is a criminal act. I've defrauded the Social Security Department, the Motor Vehicle Department, and the State of Nevada, a government agency that processed my new identity. I have been working illegally under the table, underage, at the Magic Hat Casino. Devon also referenced the Search and Rescue efforts for my missing body, which apparently cost thousands and thousands of dollars.

Being sent to prison may not be in my future plans, but a real scary and possible alternative is returning to HE and SHE. Regardless, the families of those poor students deserve to know the truth. Amir should not be walking free. I need to think. Amir is out there somewhere, looking for me, but Las Vegas is a big town. It is also the city of second chances, and I want mine.

I decide to go to the gods.

HE and SHE never took me to church as a child, but it never stopped me from praying to God. Over the years, the few times I went with Jack and his family on the holidays, the safety and serenity of the church wrapped me up like a warm blanket. It felt like a sanctuary away from my cold, evil house. I vowed that when I was on my own, I would find a loving church to join; some non-denominational community full of support.

Amir would not be hanging out in a church or a chapel. He told me once, after kids had called him a Muslim, that he hated all religion and was a self-proclaimed atheist.

Hudson mentioned in our tour that almost all casinos had a chapel. The closest casino was Caesars Palace.

As I ride the moving sidewalk into the hotel lobby, I pray to God to help me. I think if maybe if I could get a little closer to Him in a spiritual place, I will have a better chance of being heard.

Ten minutes later, I walk toward the Forum shopping center, my face flushed, my heart anxious, feeling stupid. The stuffy hotel employee told me chapels are not open to the public; they are for weddings and private guests.

"Do you know someone who's getting married in the chapel?" she asks with an attitude as she sizes me up from head to toe. With the old me, a lie would have rolled off my tongue and I would have fabricated a story of looking at a chapel for my upcoming wedding, but instead a warm flush travels up my neck to my cheeks. "No, I'm just looking for a place to pray." I'm not that knowledgeable about religion, and she's making it worse. I really thought anyone could walk into a church and pray.

Then I hear the roll of the thunder and hear the booming voice of the gods coming alive at the Forum shops. It is a perfect place to think. As their voices rumble, the fire and the water and lights flash and dance, and I realize that Greek mythology is about control. A sister and brother are fighting for the rights of the kingdom of Atlantis. Their jealousy and greed led to its eventual doom.

Today, without Hudson, the show looks old and tired to me as they turn back into their frozen statues, but it sparks an idea. I know what I have to do. First, I need to find Hudson. I owe him the truth before he hears it from the media. He's the one good thing in this mess of the life I created.

I text Hudson and he agrees to meet me at the Bellagio Fountains after his shift. A good place to let it all flow. Then I text Amir. I still have a few more lies to tell, and then I promise myself the lying will end. Forever.

I take a deep breath. I can do this. I text, **Amir, I'm sorry. Would you meet me at the bench in the park and give me a chance to explain?**

As I walk away from the stone statues of the gods, I look at them and then up and whisper, *wish me luck.* With eighteen dollars left to my name and a quick prayer, I walk into a pawn shop hoping it will be enough.

Chapter 27

Last Lies, Control, and Whiskey Courage

Dressed in a white shirt and blue designer jeans, Amir leans back on the bench and glares at me as I walk toward him. Another brown paper bag sits beside him. I catch a whiff of the lingering smoke of a cigarette.

This is it: my final performance of lies. Hopefully, all the years of practice of faking my emotions will assist me in this moment.

I attempt a smile, as I walk up in silence and sit on the bench next to the brown bag, the only thing between us. I turn sideways and pick up the bottle. "Do you mind?" I need some liquid courage and more importantly, I want him to be a little drunk. His expression is rigid, angry, and wary as he stares at me under heavy eyelids of contempt.

"I'm sorry, Amir." I gulp from the bottle and the pungency of whiskey almost makes me gag. I swallow the involuntary retching as warm liquid goes down my throat. "I need you to understand what is going on with me." His expression unflinching. This is going to be harder than I thought. "I panicked. I'm afraid. I have been terrified ever since the shooting and the move here, every second of every day. I have been alone and afraid."

Suspicion clouds his eyes. I hold out the bottle to him, and he takes it. I wait for him to take a sip.

"I've been all alone and just lost everything I had. But now I realize that if we can talk this through, if you will help me, help me understand, maybe we can do this. You're all I have. I have nothing else in this world but you."

Amir places the bottle back to his lips again, takes another long swig, and then hands it to me. I force myself to take another sip. I place the bottle on the bench and push myself to grab his hot and sweaty hand. Mine are hot and sweaty for a different reason.

"Can we do this together?" I say with all the conviction I can muster. "Start all over? You and me. It will take me a while to get adjusted, but if we take it slow, I think we can have the trust we always had."

Amir focuses on my hand on his.

"What are you saying? MIT?" Amir speaks in a softer tone, and when he bites his lip, I can see a reflection of my old Amir.

"Yes, I'm ready to leave this town. Get out of here and begin again. Tonight. I can pack up my clothes and we can catch a bus tomorrow." I swallow and hold onto his hand with just one of mine as I pick up the bottle and take another fake swig. I hold it out to him, and he does the same, not losing eye contact. "I just need to understand one thing, Amir. The lying must stop, at least with you and me. I need one person in my life who truly knows me. One person I can speak the truth to. I'm so tired of all the lies. Let us have some honesty."

Amir leans in to kiss me. I don't know what to do, as his face comes closer, inches from mine. I go with it. My finale, slightly turning my head but half-kissing him on the lips, telling myself I am kissing my old friend goodbye. My sick friend, who is a psychopath. "I don't know how this will work... this thing between us, but we can start slow." I squeeze his hand. "I just need you to help me understand what you meant the other day about Eric. Did you know he was going to the river to shoot at us? If you knew, why didn't you tell me? Save me from being killed. Why would you do that to *me*?" I try to change my tone to make it about me, but I am afraid all the acting in the world can't hide my disgust. I know the truth; I just don't want to believe I'm right.

"How... how did Eric get a gun?"

Amir sighs. "Come on, I'm good with the fake I.D.s, you should know that. I took a drive to West Virginia, same little town where you and I went. That small little shop didn't even question my application. It was so easy."

He bought the gun.

"Sunday, don't you understand? I saved you. That's how I was sure you were alive. I knew you were not missing. You and I, we are so much alike, and we always have been. I knew you would choose that moment for your pseudocide. When the reports came in and you were missing, I knew. I applauded you. You did exactly what I thought you would do. Eric promised me he would not shoot at you. He wasn't even supposed to get so close."

Every ounce of my body wants to run. The bile from my stomach is now in the back of my throat, and it is going to come up, and I know it isn't from the whiskey. A tear runs down my face. I can't control my sadness for this twisted, sick boy. Who did this to him? What makes someone go so off center that they have right and wrong so contorted? The bullies? His father? He has psychological issues. He needs help. Amir wipes the tear off my face and puts his arm around me. I am shaking from head to toe.

"It's going to be okay now, Sunday, we have each other. I've always been here for you and I always will be." He nods as he rubs my arm. "Always."

Amir insists on walking me back to my apartment. I pray my key will work and the locks are not changed. Better yet, the lights are on and I can hear Jamie and Adriana laughing inside.

Amir seems to know my apartment before we reach the door.

Before I tell him which unit is mine, he slows his step and hesitates when he notices the lights are on. His eyes focus on that apartment window, my apartment window, and it only solidifies my theory. He broke into the apartment. I am sure of it. It is too much of a coincidence.

Since my roommates are inside, Amir doesn't try to come in. I promise Amir I will meet him at the Greyhound bus station tomorrow morning at 9:00 a.m.

"I'll buy the tickets," he says. He leans in to kiss me, but I hug him though I'd rather punch him.

When I slip inside, Adriana and Jamie are standing in the kitchen drinking wine. I am never happier to see them. I run past them straight for the bathroom... I can no longer keep my sick insides from coming up. I retch over and over again.

Amir could've saved all those souls. All those students. He could have been a hero. He could have gone to the police. Instead, he let the massacre happen. He bought the gun Eric used.

After I clean myself up, I sit on the toilet lid and calm myself down. *Please, please let it have worked.* As I hit play on the cheap voice recorder, I'd bought at the pawn shop with the last of my money. I pray to God and ask Him to help me get this one thing right. The tears run down my face as I hear Amir's voice clear and strong: "Eric promised me he would not shoot at you. He wasn't even supposed to get so close." I have him. I know I have no choice, but to come forward and reveal the truth. If I don't, I'll be just as bad as him. I will never be able to live with myself, Hannah or Sunday, if I don't stop this sick killer from running around free in the world, just like Tyler. He might convince someone else to kill.

After I clean up the bathroom, I'm ready to leave.

"Well, good luck to you." I say to both Adriana and Jamie—we were never, ever close.

"Good luck to you too, looks like you could use it more than us." Adriana smirks.

"That's all you're taking?" Jamie points to my beat-up brown suitcase once stored in the Baltimore bus station, the suitcase that began Hannah's life.

"The mattress, dresser and mirror are yours or whoever else rents the closet."

Where I am going, I won't need anything.

As I begin walking, I know I'm finishing the last chapter of Hannah Williams and starting a new book of Sunday Foster, whatever the consequences will be.

Life is a lot like books. Sometimes the genre is a dark family drama with no happy endings, or a thriller with twists and turns, or even a mystery where you wonder what is going to happen. Couldn't I have an upbeat story with a happily ever after—just this once?

That's it. I stop in the middle of the street, put my beaten suitcase and backpack down on the sidewalk, and rip my brown contact lenses from my red eyes. Instant relief, both physical and mental. The lenses are in need of replacement, and I can see better. They stick to my fingers and I shake my hand like a bee stung me, and they fall to the ground. I even stomp on the area, trying to crush what was left of the brown eyes. I can see clearly because I am blue-eyed Sunday, once again.

I don't know how I make it to the Bellagio Fountains, because halfway on my trek there, I get paranoid, thinking Amir is following me. I stop several times, searching the throes of people clustering the walkways. In the crowded Las Vegas streets, I cannot find his face. My instinct tells me to take the long way to the Bellagio and cover my tracks. I'm listening to my gut this time. I weave in and out of casinos, using my bus pass to take two different buses for a five-minute trip in the opposite direction. I change my hat twice, and then finally arrive circling the fountain.

There he is. Hudson leans against the wall at the far end of the fountain next to a bench. His face split open with that infectious smile he offers so generously. His forehead crinkles as he studies me.

"What's different, Hannah?" He cocks his head. "I like the hat. Wait, look at me... your eyes are blue."

Of course, he would notice in a split second: that's just Hudson.

The music starts playing loudly, along with the choreographed dancing fountain show, this time to a patriotic song "I'm Proud to Be an American." I sit on the bench beside him and once again, the tears start rolling down my cheeks. I cry through the whole song. Hudson stands there, his hand on my shoulder. I know he doesn't know what to do, but he does what I need, he put his arm around me and lets me cry.

As the fountains settle back under water and the music ends, Hudson removes his hand off my shoulder and scoots next to me on the bench, he puts one hand on each side of my face, and my blue eyes, meet his hazel eyes full of questions. "Hannah, I need to tell you something."

I put my finger up to his lips, unsure what he is going to say. "Can it wait? There's a story you need to hear, and I'm afraid if I don't tell you now, I won't be able to."

I can't look at him while I do this so, I whisper the truth in his ear. Like the fountains pumping tons of water, I spill everything out. I tell him everything. He listens, his eyes now straight ahead, searching the crowds for trouble. He is not interrupting with questions. I pause when the people start lining up for the next show. I realize, I have been talking for almost thirty minutes, without Hudson saying one word.

Finally, when I confess every single detail, I lean back against the bench. Hudson grabs my hand, peers into my blue eyes, and says, "I think your parents are in Las Vegas, searching for you."

Chapter 28

Getting Fired, The Unimaginable, and Passing Notes

Carrying my battered suitcase down the street, I would only be less terrified if I had eyes in the back of my head. I can't shake the feeling that Amir is close, following, watching. Walking down the hot street in Las Vegas, my hair is crammed under a hat, my heart is stuck in my throat and my hands can't stop trembling as I turn my head in every direction.

Hudson is on his way to the Magic Hat to find the note left for me by the woman and man who came into the casino, asking about me yesterday. Hudson didn't get a great look at them, but he noticed as they walked out the door that the woman had blonde hair.

According to Nell, who was cocktailing earlier today, a couple came in and asked to speak to the manager. Nell took them to George, and then she overheard them ask if the cocktail waitress in the video was working. Nell told Hudson that she heard George ask what this was about, and did something happen to her, because Hannah never came in for her shift. All Nell heard them say was they were not with the police; they were from Maryland and just needed to speak to her. They scribbled a name and number on a note, handed it to George, and asked him to pass it on when I came in to work.

Nell went into the kitchen and told Hudson everything. She was worried something had happened to me, since she was covering my shift because I never showed up for work last night or called in sick. Hudson tried to find the couple, but they were far ahead of him in the casino, and he lost them in the casino crowd as they went out the door.

Could it possibly be HE and SHE?

Impossible.

First, there was no way in any universe that they would travel together as a couple, and second, they would never put that much effort into looking for me. It can't be them.

NO WAY.

My life is like dropping a ball of yarn: once it starts rolling, yarn unravels, and before you know it, the whole ball of yarn is unraveled, a mess full of knots. How could anyone know about me? Did Amir turn me in? What other sick game is he playing?

I need to hide out, and Hudson's apartment is my safe place. He gave me the key. All I need to do is make it to his apartment. I'll try to get some sleep. Sleep. I don't know how I can possibly sleep, but exhaustion will lead to stupid mistakes. Just to keep the recording safe, I gave the voice recorder to Hudson and he'd uploaded it to the Cloud. If anything happens to me, Hudson has Devon Perry's number, and if I never show up at his apartment, he will call the lawyer.

I am taking no chances.

A loud noise nudges my subconscious. I try to ignore it, caught in that place between dream and reality. Jack is hugging me and kissing me, saying, "Everything is going to be okay." I watch us in an embrace, as if from above. I have short brown hair and brown eyes. Safe, loved, and comforted, I don't want it to end. The pounding is louder now, and I open my eyes, terrified.

Hammering thumps, as if someone is kicking in the door. Someone trying to get in. I did a full head turn assessment of my space. I'm now awake, in Hudson's bedroom. I listen. I've locked the door and pushed his one chair against the door. Now fully awake, I stand in front of the door and the chair. My heart is about to break through the skin of my chest.

"Who's there?"

"Hannah, it's me, Hudson."

I move the chair and open the door and Hudson walks in. I let out a large sigh. "You scared me."

Hudson hugs me. "I'm sorry. You must have been dead asleep. I was knocking on the door and you didn't answer. You scared ME. Are you all right?"

I nod. What was the definition of 'all right'?

"George is an asshole. I don't know why I'm working there. Well, why I *was* working there." Hudson smirks, and hands me a piece of paper. "But at least I got the note."

I stare at the piece of folded paper. The note my parents left. It can't be from them.

"George fired you? All because of me? Hudson I feel terrible."

"Open it," Hudson says. "It's the least you can do for me getting fired over it."

I rub it in my fingers and then slowly open it up. I gasp and fall back to the bed.

"What?" Hudson asks. "Is it your parents?"

"No, it's Jack. Jack and his parents. They found me."

I read the note again.

Ed and Marcia Grant

410-758-9989

Sunday,

Jack's here, and we want to help you. Please call, we are here for you.

How could they possibly know I was alive? Jack, my Jack, Ed and Marcia here in Vegas.

Did Devon Perry call someone? Did Amir turn me in? Confused, I'm having a hard time believing this is real. "How did they find me?"

Hudson sits beside me on the bed. "Well, they are the good ones, right?"

"Yes, they are the only family I've ever really known."

"See, that's good. Family doesn't have to be biological. They know you're alive and look, they want to help you. Family never gives up."

How could Ed, Marcia, and Jack know where I worked, or, for that matter, that I'm even alive. What if it is Amir trying to set me up?

"What did they look like? Hudson, describe what they looked like."

"I just saw the back of them. The lady had dark blonde shoulder length hair, and the guy wore a baseball cap. I didn't see their faces."

Ed always wears a baseball cap. "But, how? How do they know I'm even alive?"

"I guess you are going to have to call them and ask them. Do you think the lawyer guy called them?"

"I didn't even mention Jack or his parents."

"Well, its four in the morning. Why don't we get a few hours of sleep and we can call the lawyer in the morning and see what he suggests." Hudson tosses a comforter on the floor. "Okay?" Hudson rubs his chin. "You look exhausted, you need to get some sleep."

There is nothing I can do until I speak to Devon. I lean back on the bed and grab a pillow to lay down on the comforter on the floor.

"Hey, what are you doing? You're sleeping in the bed."

"Hudson, you don't have to sleep on the floor."

"Yes, I do." Hudson smiles and give me a cute boyish look as he grabs the pillow from me. "My mother would disown me if you slept on the floor."

"Did you really get fired?"

"Yes, I did, but I knew that note was important to you, and he said he wouldn't give it to me. So, I grabbed it out of his hand and ran. You should have seen his face. Blown up and red. George yelled, 'if you walk out that door you're fired.' I turned around and said 'Okay, have it your way.'"

"That sucks, Hudson."

"No, don't worry about it. Lots of the rich and famous were fired before they made it big. I'm in good company—Steve Jobs, Oprah, Lady Gaga, JK Rowling, Jerry Seinfeld, and even Walt Disney. You don't experience losing a job until you're fired. It has to happen at least once. There's mine. Like my mom says: when one door closes, another one opens."

"I don't know what's going to happen to me, but I'm really going to miss you, Hudson."

Hudson is quiet. He plucks at the cuff of his shirt. "I think it's going to be okay, and I think we will be friends for a long time."

"You think so?"

"I do. I just need you to answer one question."

"What?"

"What should I call you?"

Chapter 29

The Truth Will Set You Free

The phone rings and rings and then goes to voicemail, I hang up and call again. I can't sleep, and I want to get the recording to the authorities.

Every minute counts. After waiting a few more minutes, I try for the third time. I text '**_please call me, urgent_**' about five times. Finally, Devon answers the phone. It's 4:45 a.m.

"What's so important?" Devon shouts into the phone.

I take a deep breath to calm my voice. "Devon, it's me, Hannah. I mean, Sunday Foster. I have a recording of Amir admitting he knew about the school shooting. He admits he had a hand in planning it. He knew, and he didn't stop it. He even bought the gun with a fake ID." I exhale, trying to slow my speech. "I am supposed to meet him at the Greyhound bus station at nine a.m. today, and if we want the authorities to stop him or question him, then I need to meet with you as soon as possible. They can arrest him, right?"

There is a long chunk of silence on the phone. Finally, Devon sighs and clears his throat. "Slow down. Listen, a recording may not be admissible in court if he doesn't identify himself or give his consent. Did you use an app on your phone? Is it a recording or video?"

"No, I have a cheap burner phone. I bought a digital recorder."

"Too bad it is not a video, but it might be enough to bring him in for questioning." I can hear Devon mumbling to himself. "Bus station, something...."

"I'm sorry, what did you ask?"

"You said nine a.m.? You're supposed to meet him at the bus station? Okay, okay, bring the recording with you and let's meet in my office in forty-five minutes." He pauses. "Sunday, can you get here safely?"

"Yes, thank you, Devon, but there's one more thing. My boyfriend's family and my boyfriend Jack are apparently in town, looking for me. I don't know how they know, but they know I'm alive. They left a message at my work. Did you call them?"

"No, I haven't contacted anyone. You and I were supposed to meet this morning. Much later this morning. What boyfriend? Is this a boyfriend from back in Maryland?"

"Yes, he and I were on the school trip together. During the shooting, I pushed him off the raft. He made it." Dead silence. "Devon?"

"Yes, I'm thinking. Something else important is that you forgot to mention to me yesterday was that you're only seventeen. The authorities will want to call your parents immediately."

Oh, my god. "But..."

"I know that's not what you want to hear. There's much to discuss. This is a very serious situation."

If Devon didn't tell Ed and Marcia, how could they possibly know? Calling my parents terrified me as much as Amir, but in a different way. "What about having a parental figure there with me? Jack's mom and dad have been more family than my mother and father have ever been, and they are supposedly here in Las Vegas."

"It's a start. If you can find them, see if they can come to my office. Sunday we're going to have to contact your parents."

I put the phone down. My hands are shaking. How can I call Jack? What would I say? Hey, I'm alive and living in Vegas under another identity. Sorry you thought I was dead.

I can't do it over the phone. I just can't. Hudson, awake now, looks up from the floor leaning on his elbow, concern written all over his face as he notices the phone shaking in my hand.

"Who were you talking to?"

"It's really happening." I manage a half-smile. "I never thought I'd be Sunday Foster ever again. I thought Sunday Foster was dead."

Hudson jumps up, and gently takes the phone out of my hand and extends his right hand, with a goofy smile. "Well, Sunday Foster, it's nice to meet you. I'm Hudson Wagner. I'm sure glad you're alive."

I grab his hand with both of mine and close my eyes. I need his optimistic strength, more than he'll ever know. "Devon Perry, my lawyer, said the authorities are going to call my parents, since I am only seventeen. My parents..."

"Oh damn, that's right, you are seventeen—what can I do to help, Sunday?"

I truly hate buses, and here I am again on a bus, my heart thumping in my chest as if I ran the track. My chest rises and falls in quick succession. Hudson is beside me, both of us scouring the crowds for any sign of Amir. Before we left Hudson's apartment, Hudson called the cell phone listed on the note and Ed answered.

Hudson held the phone, so I could listen.

I knew that voice with the Philly accent: it was Ed Grant, no doubt in my mind. I nodded my head yes and sat down on the bed, so I wouldn't fall over. Hearing his kind voice is something I never thought I'd hear again; I can't imagine how they found me in Vegas. Regardless, I can't talk to them yet. I need to keep myself together until I hand Devon the recorder.

"I'm a friend of Sunday's and she needs your help. Can you meet her at the law office of Devon Perry at 7:00 a.m.?" Hudson reads them the address off the card. "Yes, sir, she is fine, but she needs some support for what she is about to do. She asked me to call you. She'll explain everything."

After a short pause, Hudson relays that Ed was silent a moment on the phone, and then he repeats Ed's words, and my heart swells. "Tell Sunday we will definitely be there, and we love her."

Everything is about to change. My life of making plans is over. I have no idea what is about to transpire.

Will I be arrested?

Will Jack ever forgive me?

A thousand questions swarm around me. I need to move forward and take one step at a time. The first step—getting the recording to Devon and the authorities.

The bus ride feels like an eternity. Hudson rubs my hand, his arm crossed over me protectively.

"Just breathe."

"I'm trying to. I wish I had a video of him saying all those things."

Hudson tucks a lock of hair behind my ear. "I know my mother would say right now is this: the truth will set you free. It's going to be okay, Sunday."

I keep repeating this phrase over and over in my mind. I hope Hudson's mother is right.

Finally, the bus pulls up in front of Devon's office building. We both check the street as we step off the bus. The walk to the front door seems like a long road. Hudson opens the large glass door to the building, and his other arm holds me up. "You're doing a great thing. You can do this. What's the worst that can happen?"

I think to myself, plenty. HE and SHE, prison, Amir getting away, Jack hating me. I take a deep breath, square my shoulders, and push the elevator button.

Hudson takes my hand as we ride up the elevator, not in a romantic sort of way, but like a big brother. I imagine Clark watching over me. Having Hudson beside me gives me strength for what's about to happen.

Chapter 30

Someone Else's Truth Will Set You Free

The door to Devon's office is ajar. The lights are off. An empty chair sits behind the reception desk. It's 5:30 in the morning. We walk through the small lobby area and stop a few feet from Devon's office. It is eerily quiet.

"Devon?" Silence. We push the half open door and walk in. Hudson leads the way.

Lights on, the office is empty. Something is wrong.

Yesterday, Devon's desk was neat and tidy; now huge stacks of papers cover every inch of his desk in a disorganized mess.

Hudson scans the walls and stops at the photo of Devon beside a red race car.

"He's a professional race car driver turned lawyer?" Hudson turns to face me.

From the hallway, a voice says, "That was my first job. I wasn't good enough, never made pro." Devon walks in, his thick blonde hair damp from a shower, and he smells like fresh soap. Today he wears a black suit jacket, white shirt, and an undone tie around his neck.

I breathe a sigh of relief.

"And you are?" He lifts his chin as he fumbles with his tie.

Hudson extends his hand, smiles, and says, "I'm, err, Hannah's, I mean Sunday's, friend Hudson, and can I say: what a great first job, being a race car driver." I can tell Hudson likes Devon immediately. I relax a little now that Devon is here. I trust Hudson's gut.

"Sunday, I have a friend in the Las Vegas police department who works with an FBI investigator. He's doing me a favor. A big favor. He agreed to meet us here this morning. The shooting happened in Fayette County, Pennsylvania, which is out of the Las Vegas jurisdiction, so he is going to get in touch with the department involved in the shooting, and if the evidence is strong enough to bring Amir in for questioning, they can arrange to have someone from Pennsylvania fly in. He wants to hear the recording and take it from there. We need to work fast."

I nod, trembling inside, my heart in my throat, a sharp pain in my stomach.

"They will have to call your parents. I'm not sure about the media, but it's going to be a breaking news story."

The media. Of course, every news outlet and internet blog will try and break the news first. I picture the headline: "Missing teenager from Pennsylvania school shooting found alive in Sin City under a fake identity." Or "Missing student from school shooting exposes the real mastermind behind the massacre." Will the public think I had something to do with it and ran away? Bile rises in my throat. It's hot in this office.

"Sunday, you with us?" Devon asks.

I nod, unable to speak, trying to keep myself together.

"Let's hear the recording."

Hudson pulls the slim voice recorder from his backpack and

hands it to me. My shaky hand tries to push the power on and Hudson puts his hand over mine to turn it on. Amir's voice fills the room. I shudder. Devon listens intently and at the end of the conversation where Amir and I kiss, Hudson squeezes my hand. Amir then talks about the shooting. I twist in my seat, hot and queasy.

Devon replays the conversation again from the beginning as we wait for the officer to show up. My phone dings, and I jump a foot in the air.

A text from Amir. "See you at nine o'clock, inside, by the ticket counter." I hold the phone, my hand, as usual, still shaking, and show Devon.

"Are you up for this Sunday?" Devon asks, I nod. "Text him back. Confirm."

I'm not sure if I should text him back at this hour, but I want to acknowledge his text. I text back: an emoji thumbs up.

Devon hands me a bottle of water.

Jack. My Jack is in Las Vegas with Marcia and Ed, and they are going to walk in this door in about thirty minutes and I don't know what I'm going to do. What can I possibly say to him? Lost in my own torment, my head in my hands, I don't even notice the detective walking in at in first.

From there, everything starts moving at super speed. Devon introduces Detective Harding, who shakes my hand and then runs his hand over his shaved head. His grey eyes possess a depth of seriousness mixed with caring. He shakes Hudson's hand and then asks Hudson to wait outside in the reception area. Hudson meets my gaze, asking for permission to leave me.

"I'll be all right, Hudson, you can go if you want."

Hudson stands up and squeezes my shoulder. "Sunday, I'm not going anywhere. I'll be right outside this door."

After a quick recap, Detective Harding asks if Devon verified my identity. Devon opens a folder from the stacks on his desk and removes three photos. He must have printed the pictures off the internet; they are the same pictures the media plastered all over the news. "Just the hair color's different. She dyed and cut it when she came out West. The blue eyes—there's no mistaking her. This is Sunday Foster, the missing girl from the Ohiopyle school shooting."

Devon pulls out a high school photo of Amir. No resemblance to the new Amir of today, this photo portrays a studious boy with glasses and braces. "This is Amir James Carter, the boy Sunday recorded a conversation with last night. He admits he knew about the shooting and even states he gave instructions for the shooter not to kill Sunday Foster. He bought the weapon. She is supposed to meet him at the Greyhound bus station at nine a.m."

"I also think he broke into my apartment the other night, and stole my money, tablet and jewelry."

"Why do you suspect him?" Detective Harding asked

"I never told him where I lived, and he somehow knew where I lived, and he knew I didn't have an alarm. It would make me need his help, another reason to go away with him. Amir is manipulative, and very smart."

"Did you call the police, was it dusted for fingerprints?"

"No, is it too late?"

"No, but let's start from the beginning." The detective sits down beside me and pulls out a voice recorder. He looks at Devon for approval; Devon nods.

"Sunday, I need your permission to record you," he says in a calm kind voice.

I nod.

"State your name."

The questions begin.

The truth will set you free. I repeat this mantra each time Detective Harding confers with Devon. When I have an extra minute of escape from the barrage of questions, I think about Jack. I can't imagine what's going on in his mind. I still don't know how he found me. Is it 7:00 a.m. yet? Slivers of light peek through the slats of the blinds in Devon's office. I check my phone to make sure Amir hasn't texted again and touch the screen. 7:05. The Grants have to be here. Unlike HE and SHE, they are always punctual, well Marcia is when it mattered. I know this mattered.

The knock on the door startles me. Devon opens the door and Jack's dad holds out his hand to Devon. His eyes dart around to me, recognition lights up his face, and tears fill his eyes. I am unaware my face is wet until Devon hands me a tissue. Ed wraps me in an intense bear hug.

"Sunday, do you want to take a five-minute break?"

I want to say yes, but speechless, I nod, unsure of what to do next. I walk out the door with Ed, and there he is, my Jack, with his mom. Marcia is crying. When Jack's eyes meet mine, my heart does a 360-flip flop or at least it feels like that. Jack flies to my side and embraces me in a hug so tight, I can't breathe. It's as if I'd traveled back in time, the love so strong, just as it always was. Soon all three of us are hugging and crying. My fear disintegrates. This love is what matters, and it is amazing. I understand family; what it means to belong.

"How did you find me?" I finally manage to croak out.

"I never lost you," Jack says as he kisses me in front of everyone. "You were always with me. I knew you had to be alive. But then I saw the video. The casino video: the garbage man who won the jackpot. You laughed. Your tell, Sunday, I knew then that it was you. And I saw your 'live free,' tattoo."

I can't stop looking at him. He grabs my face with both hands and his tender brown eyes penetrate mine to the very depth of my soul. I kiss his scar. I can read the question in his eyes, as he whispers, "Why?"

"I don't know where to begin," I say.

Devon is listening and watching our little family reunion. I wonder if he knows, because of his father, they found me. I think by the look on his face, he understands what transpired.

"I'm sorry to break this up." Devon exhibits beautiful com-passion to Ed, Marcia, and Jack. "You must have a lot to discuss with Sunday, and I know she's eager to answer all your questions. But I'm going to have to take Sunday to Police Headquarters. You are welcome to follow us down there and we can fill you in on the way. But right now, we have to take care of an urgent situation."

The emotion on their faces crushes me. Confusion and concern. I want to start fast-talking and tell them everything as quick as I can, but we have to find Amir. Devon gestures for me to go in front of him, placing a barrier between them and me.

Softly, but with conviction, Devon says, "Sunday, we need to go."

I nod and turn around, looking past Devon at Jack as I am escorted out of the building. He is all I ever wanted, and I let him go and he came back to me. "Will you come to the station with me? I want to tell you everything."

"We will be right behind you, Sunday. Don't worry," Jack says. Ed catches up to us and halts Devon. "We have to speak to you, as well. There are some things that will be important for everyone to know. We have some crucial information about Sunday's parents."

Devon looks at Ed and then at me. "Mr. and Mrs. Grant, Jack, why don't you ride with us to the station."

In the background, I see Hudson standing back from the chaos alone, both hands jammed in his front pockets. Sweet kind Hudson.

"Hudson, you can come to, if you like, or I can call you: what do you want to do?" I say walking back towards him.

Marcia studies Hudson and then my face trying to assess the situation. She says, "I'll bring Hudson with me, we have the rental car. He can make sure I find it. I have no idea where I'm going." Marcia nods her head and Jack's eyes stay on mine as we walk out to the car, his warm hand squeezing mine.

Jack and I climb in the back of the car, my hand in his. I want to hold him, kiss him, and never let him go. The saying that absence makes the heart grow fonder is true. I know right here and now, with all the clarity I have ever had that, I love this boy with all my heart. Jack never gave up on me.

Ed turns around, with a facial expression I've never quite seen. Alarm builds inside me. This can't be good, whatever he is about to say.

"Sunday, we need to tell you about your parents." Ed and Jack exchange eye contact.

"Your father is in jail; your mother is in a rehab facility awaiting trial. Sunday, he is not your biological father. You are not related to that monster," Jack says, his words flying out of his mouth so quick, as if trying to rip a band aid off a wound.

What? I want to hear it again so I can understand what he is saying. My eyes fill up with water for the hundredth time that day. I have no control over my emotions. "What are you saying?

What are you talking about? How?"

Jack holds both my hands, rubbing his finger over the top. "Your mother was pregnant with another man's child. Your father went ballistic. They arrested him for possibly killing Clark. Sunday, I am so sorry... I'm so sorry." Jacks eyes fill up with water.

"HE killed Clark? SHE let him kill my brother?" The trembling starts again, a river runs down my face. I blow out my cheeks to catch my breath. This is too much.

Jack holds me tight; his warmth stops my shaking. "It's going to be okay. I'm here, we're here. We're not going to let anything happen to you."

Chapter 31

Greyhounds Again, The Bus Stops Here, and Shiny Silver Knives

Redemption.

I just hope Amir doesn't suspect my lies. I know I'm a good liar—I practiced lying all my life—but somehow this lie is different. This lie is important to get right. I need to do this for all the families and all the students from school. I need Amir to be questioned and taken in by the police.

I step on to the bus headed to the Greyhound station. Can I possibly do one good thing to make up for my lies and deceit?

All I need to do is meet Amir and identify him for the police. I want to do this, I need to do this, and thanks to Devon, here I am.

Detective Harding believes me, I know it. My gut is right. My stomach might be doing flips right now but my instinct is spot on. Amir is the orchestrator of the school shooting. I'm certain he was the mastermind and although he didn't pull the trigger he might as well have. He used Eric. I mean Eric pulled the trigger, he is a killer, but Amir set it all up, every bit of it and pushed Eric to take the leap.

Surveillance cameras are live at the bus terminal, I remind myself I'm not alone as I push through the passengers and exit the bus.

One block away.

My phone's microphone can be remotely activated by the police. Didn't know that until I asked if I needed to wear a wire. I hear Detective Harding commanding voice in my head, "No wired needed, not in today's world, all you need is a phone. We'll be right with you.'" I hope he is right.

I keep walking, trying not to walk too fast or too slow. I need to do this, to make up for my mistakes. I spent hours with Amir and never saw that he was sick. I mean how did I miss it?

There are supposedly undercover officers at the terminal; I quick scan everyone wondering if they are there to assist me if I need it.

I slow down. My breath is abnormally fast. The authorities had a long debate over whether or not Amir might have a weapon and create another possible shooting spree. They're wondering if he figured out I had gone to the authorities.

Amir is smart. But, I'm a great liar, and I hope he believes me and shows up.

Amir with a gun. I can't picture it. I've never seen Amir touch a weapon, knife or gun, and his father had plenty of guns in the house.

I know now Amir can change and learn anything. My noisy head is affecting my breath. My inner voice is shouting. *He bought the gun. He went to West Virginia and bought the gun. Did he have another one?*

Inhale. Exhale. Focus.

I will not let Amir win and frighten me away.

Where are the two undercover officers? They are here some-where to arrest him for a firearm purchase under a fake ID. When I left this morning, they were waiting for confirmation from the gun shop in West Virginia.

My brown suitcase in hand, my backpack on my back, I scan the crowd. The Las Vegas Greyhound bus station may be newly renovated, but all the modernization can't rid the typical shadiness of a bus environment. Homeless people are sitting on the ground, and a few unfortunate others are sitting on their luggage, waiting. After traveling across the country on a Greyhound, I remember the fumes, urine scent and moldy odor. The beggars, the smells, and the intoxicated people are the same in every city.

I place my backpack and my battered old suitcase on the floor and I set the trap. Perched on my suitcase, forcing my leg to stop twitching. It doesn't. I move to the floor, checking my phone, and I wait. I grasp my phone with two hands to calm the trembling. I want Amir to be caught. I need him to be accountable. My motive gives me strength. Twenty-eight victims, the ones Amir could have saved. Brothers, sisters, daughters, sons, girlfriends, boyfriends, mothers and fathers, gone from this world forever. Amir did this. My fury ignites the fuel of courage.

I'm ready.

I wait and wait and keep checking my phone, no text, nothing.

I text Amir.

Where are you? I'm here waiting at the bus station.

My heart drops when it buzzes

The customer you are trying to text is temporarily out of service.

Last call for the 10:05 am bus to Massachusetts is announced.

Amir and I are supposed to be leaving on this bus. A curdling high-pitched scream follows the announcement. A woman with three unruly children is trying to gather her belongings. The dark-haired toddler, a girl with a tear stained face emits a high pitch squeal at an octave that hurts the ears. She doesn't want to board. I know her pain.

I walk over, examining every passenger.

He's not here.

I'm not sure what to do, so I sit down and wait.

If he's not here, then where is he? Watching me?

Maybe the police already arrested him.

Will someone text me? I check my phone again.

It's possible he bought a new burner or untraceable phone. No, deep down, I know the truth.

Amir figured it out. I guess I'm not such a good liar.

I wait another hour.

Now another 30 minutes pass.

My phone buzzes.

Leave and get on another bus toward the Strip.

A text from the police not Amir, unless Amir is acting like he is the police. He could probably do that. I don't know how to respond.

I scan the crowd. Where are the undercover police?

I stand and start walking away from the terminal, certain Amir is going to pop out at any moment.

In the distance, I see a city bus. *Should I get on?*

Walk and get on.

Moving forward like a robot in slow motion, I step on the bus and analyze every face. I am never getting on another bus again. I'm making myself a promise right now. No more buses.

At the next stop I can barely swallow, my heartbeat accelerates. I imagine Amir walking on this bus with a gun.

I'm wrong.

Finally, I'm approaching the Las Vegas Strip. I pull myself up, gripping the back of the seat in front of me to steady myself. Out the window I see the meeting point up ahead, I walk toward the exit and try not to run into the restaurant.

Devon is waiting in the first booth.

"Did they find him?" I whisper.

He shakes his head as he hugs me and gently guides me to the back exit. I'm shaking.

Amir figured it out.

Somehow, he knew I was lying. How? What tipped him off.

Devon takes me to the police station and escorts me through booking. Dazed and in denial, I just follow Devon's direction and kind voice through processing.

Like a trained dog, I move on command. In a sterile white room, with four chairs and a table, I sign paper after paper. Devon explains since I cooperated and voluntarily turned myself in for identity theft and defrauding a government organization, a special court would be fast tracked and assembled due to the extraordinary circumstances. By the week's end, I will appear in front of a judge.

And now, here I am, staring at the ceiling of the hotel room. Dead bugs are trapped under the overhead light.

I try to fit the pieces of the puzzle of my life together. My puzzle must be a million-count jigsaw puzzle that is now missing pieces. A faint light shines from the window, illuminating Jack's beautiful features. My sunshine. He's always been my sun. Asleep next to me, on top of the covers, his jagged pink scar is barely visible on his cheek. I know now that saving a dog on the cracking ice of Briar's Lake was nothing compared to what he is capable of—saving me.

Jack saved me.

If he can do that, he can do anything.

It doesn't matter to Jack why I left.

I told him everything. The hardest part was telling Jack about Tyler. Jack didn't question me. He listened. I was ready for questions about the pregnancy, or questions of why I didn't tell him. I was ready.

No inquisition. Jack wrapped his arms around me and whispered in my ear, "I'm so sorry, Sunday. What matters now is you're safe and with us. We can't change the past, but we can decide what happens next." His love for me is unconditional. He held me tight and then he drifted off to sleep with his arms around me.

My hand touches his cheek, and I brush my fingers over the scar. His eyes open, and he sees me, and a slow smile spreads across his face.

"I love you, Jackson Grant."

"I love you, Sunday Foster."

"Still?" I ask.

"Forever and always." He kisses me, and for the hundredth time in a span of 48 hours, tears run down my face. I nestle closer to him. It's not hard telling him I love him, because now I understand what love is.

"He's still out there." I use the back of my hand to wipe the tears.

"You tried, Sunday, you did your best. They will find him."

I'm not so sure. Amir is smart. He knows how to disappear.

Another day and Amir is still out there.

Jack's parents have already started the paperwork to gain temporary custody until I turn eighteen. Devon helped me with an emancipation request as a backup. I do not want to spend time in jail, but if I have to, I am prepared to accept my consequences. I've known worse.

It confirms what I always knew: I had been living with the devil and his sidekick.

Yes, in light of several news reports, the media paint SHE as an unwilling sidekick, but it doesn't really matter to me. Isn't there something, anything SHE could have done years ago? The answer always comes back loud and clear: SHE had choices.

We all do.

I don't know how to process this new reality, this new supposed truth. I need time.

Devon contacted the rehab facility where SHE had been admitted. When the detox period is completed, the doctors will tell her I am alive. I can't imagine SHE would care—well, at least the old SHE—and people that old don't change. Do they?

When I was presumed dead, old remnants of morality bubbled to the surface. Apparently, SHE went ballistic after the shooting. Jack showed me the media reports. I read half a dozen articles.

Abused woman walks into the Owning Mills Police station and accuses her spouse of killing her son.

Cindy Foster of Ownings Mills, also the mother of Sunday Foster, a victim of the Ohiopyle Shooting walked into the police department yesterday bruised and battered, to press charges against her husband Charles Foster, of Ownings Mills. The mother told the police her husband, Charles Foster drowned her son, Clark Foster, in a violent rage, seventeen years ago in Fenwick Island, when he found out she was pregnant with a daughter from another man. Foster stated he threatened to kill her newborn daughter if she went to the authorities and has been threatening her ever since. The woman was quoted as saying: "My daughter Sunday is now dead, so I don't care if he kills me; my life was over a long time ago when he murdered my son."

Little flashes fill my mind: vivid images of HE screaming at SHE in the kitchen. HE holding a shiny silver knife and SHE pushing me behind her, screaming, "I won't ever tell! I won't ever tell!" I never remembered her protecting me until now. Somehow, that image knocked on my memory door. Was I five? Maybe even four. Had SHE actually cared about me at one time, or was I reinventing these memories?

I am not HE's biological daughter. HE is not my father.

So, who is my father?

My body is limp with exhaustion from the trauma of the last 48 hours, but my mind is a raging fire that has a long time to burn before it can go out. Embers can stay hot for days. Jack has fallen asleep again, his head against my arm. Oh, how I love this boy. His love gives me courage to work through this mess of a life. And, oh what a mess.

I remember the quote the kind woman had repeated at the bus station in St. Louis: "If you love something, set it free. If it comes back to you, it's yours; if it doesn't, it was never meant to be."

Jack came back.

Chapter 32

Silver Stars, Fallen Angels, and YOLO

The TSA agent appears irritated when Ed hands him the letter from the courts in Nevada. He opens it and turns to me. His stare is unflinching.

"What is your home address?"

I stumble, stutter, and cower from his gaze. What is my home address? It's an easy question I can't answer. The cold stone house I grew up in—never a home—was seized when HE was also arrested for tax evasion. Ed supplies the agent with his address, his arm tight around me, as I just stand there. Typing in his database, the agent pulls up my Maryland driver's license. Technically, being seventeen, I do not need an I.D. to travel. He made his little squiggle on my boarding pass and I breathe a sigh of relief. I am through security and on my way back to Maryland.

"Your home is our home," Jack says as we walk toward the gate. "And, we are so glad to have you home, Sunday."

Home. All I ever wanted. And the Grants are all I ever envisioned a family to be. How many high school seniors are lucky enough live to with their boyfriend?

Today is the last day before Christmas vacation begins at Sunset Park High School. A light dusting of snow covers the ground, not yet sticking to the spindly branches of the trees. White fairy lights twinkle in the trees and bushes.

Jack's arm is around my shoulder as we walk into the ballroom to attend the Christmas Dance. Our Senior Christmas Dance. Jack looks beautiful in his black jacket and grey shirt. My short black velvet dress makes me feel sophisticated unlike the clothes I wore in Vegas. I study the picture on my iPhone, that we took before we left. My hair, back to blonde, is still short, but wavy. Marcia helped me put it in an up-do with little curls around my face. Jack calls it my sassy look. To be honest, I am sassy. And happy. All things considered, I am extremely grateful to the Grants and how everything turned out. I am alive, with my own identity and with a family I love. Love. I must've been born under a lucky star, not just Jack.

The media reports have finally died down on my reappearance and the information I shared regarding Amir and the shooting. I wanted to meet with Amir's parents, but they refused to see me. Jack told me he heard they'd moved out of town last week. They cooperated with the police, handing over everything of Amir's. The police scrubbed Amir's computer. Nothing was found. His lack of contact with his parents, his forfeiture of his MIT scholarship, and my recording of our conversation made him a person of interest in the Ohiopyle shootings. I tried to locate the mom-and-pop gun store in West Virginia where he had used a fake I.D. to buy the gun, but no one ever confessed to ever seeing anyone that looked like him buying a gun. The gun Eric used didn't have any serial numbers on it.

Besides the recording and my testimony, I am certain they will never find tangible evidence to link Amir to the shooting.

He is too smart for that.

Things worked out for me.

The courts were extremely compassionate regarding my case, and I'm on probation until I graduate from high school. Devon has stayed in touch with me, and assisted me on putting closure on Tyler. He set up the meeting with the Towson police regarding my statement. Ward surprised me, he sent me a large black top hat, inside a hand written note stating 'maybe this hat will be YOUR magic hat' and included a large check labeled 'college fund'. I have now logged 100 hours of community service with runaway teens. I will not have to spend time in jail or juvenile detention, and the teens I've been working with in the Baltimore youth shelter have taught me more about redemption than any prison cell ever could.

I know now what I want to do with the rest of my life. I want to help teens in trouble. Teach them, counsel them, and be there for them. I'm not sure exactly in what capacity, but I'm thinking guidance counselor or mental health counselor. Who knows? The teens I speak to and meet with one-on-one find it hard to imagine I lived in Sin City on my own.

Of course, I leave the whole pseudocide element out of it. We don't want anyone getting any crazy ideas about faking their deaths, note my mentors, Mitchell and Mildred Alexander, an absolutely wonderful couple who run the center. They have taught me how to be there for teens.

I'm really just there to listen. Listen and observe.

Because if you listen, every once in a while, you hear the cries for help behind their tough exterior. Troubled youth: what to do with them? Mental health, how do you fix it? You fix it by paying attention and working with kids, taking notice when their parents don't, or can't. All I know is, you can't just push it off on the parents. Even great parents like Amir's will ignore the truth, push it under the carpet, attribute it to video games. Everyone needs to stop making excuses and pay attention. The signs are there.

I've lived the lie and acted the parts I thought everyone wanted me to be. My experience in 'playing the part' help me identify the façades. When you act like different characters, you can usually identify them, in a second.

I'm getting used to living with the Grants, Ed, Marcia, and Jack. It's the sitcom family I have always dreamed of, and I now know love and respect among family members actually exist. We are like a real family: we discuss issues and opinions and ask for advice. We ask permission and we respect each other. Tara is at college and so I have camped out in her room. It is a little odd with Jack and me being boyfriend and girlfriend, but after everything we have been through, the trust is there. Everyone is thankful for the happy ending. Jack and I are both so grateful; we would never take advantage of the situation.

Jack and I are applying to colleges together, and ironically, they are all back East. We want to stay close to Jack's parents. I finally have a reason to be around family. Good family and good people.

And speaking of good people, my mind pictures handsome, one-of-a- kind Hudson. He waited in the restaurant with Devon and the Grant family the whole time, while I waited for Amir to show up. I will always remember the last time I saw him in Vegas.

Hudson hugged me and told me, "The police will catch him. You're going to be okay. I know because you have a great family right here," he motioned to the Grants, and gave me a hug. When I thought I was going to cry again, of course he had to add, "And did you know Shaquille O'Neal was not only one tough dude on the basketball court, but the 7-foot Hall of Famer was a police officer as well? Yeah, besides basketball it was one of his first real jobs. Dennis Farina from Law and Order, same thing, first job was a Chicago police officer."

Hudson attends UNLV full time and is coming out for a visit to Ocean City, Maryland to see his mother. We are all going to Ocean City to visit him and spend a weekend at the beach during spring break.

HE (who is not my real father) has been sentenced to life without parole. I was indifferent when I heard the news of his conviction. HE confessed, so he wouldn't stand trial for a death penalty conviction. HE is nothing to me but the monster of my youth and the murderer of Clark.

I can't erase the nightmares, but they are put away, although I now know, I am going to have to take them out of the closet and deal with them in counseling sessions.

SHE is awaiting trail and her attorney wants me to meet with her. Ed, Marcia, and Jack have told me they will support me in whatever decision I make. Jack thinks I should at least meet with her one time, hear what she has to say, and then decide.

I'm undecided.

Hudson's mother's quote sticks with me: the truth will set you free. I just might give her a minute, one day, to see if her truth sets her free.

The students at Sunset Park are gentler and kinder since the school shooting. I hate to admit that Amir was right about anything, but the horrific devastation formed a closer community. In his sick, twisted mind, he took credit for the transformation. Maybe that's what tragedy does to you: it wakes you up and gives you a second chance at life.

When you're faced with death and you survive, you try and dissect a reason why you made it and the others didn't. The students who decided not to go on the whitewater rafting trip that day realized that one small decision changed their life. Take one of the Dream Team members who survived because she ate bad shrimp the night before and couldn't go on the trip. Bad shrimp saved her life.

You only live once.

It's that same message written in the words of a poem or the lyrics of a song, "If you knew this was your last day on earth, wouldn't you live it a little bit sweeter?"

Holidays have always been difficult for me, and this year, it is a holiday of healing and remembering. The gym's twinkling white and silver lights metamorphosized the sweaty space into a Christmas wonderland. A 12-foot tree stretches high to the ceiling, decorated with twenty-eight shiny silver star ornaments, each star inscribed with the name of one of the fallen angels from the shooting. The stars sparkle as they slowly turn. I'm elated there is not twenty-nine.

It is a Christmas miracle there is no star with my name or Jack's.

My eyes scan the crowd. This new habit is ground in deeply, I just need to make sure Amir is not here or close by or watching. They have not caught up with him and it's been months. I can't imagine where he's hiding. I close my eyes and swallow the fear away.

"Where did you go right now?" Jack asks.

"I'm taking it all in. I'm right here, happy." I nuzzle my head in his neck.

No more lies. "I'm just making sure he is not here." I whisper, "I can't help it, bad habit."

"It's okay Sunday. Wherever he is, I'm sure it is far away from here. They'll find Amir, he can't hide out forever."

I'm not sure I believe that. I wrap my arms tighter.

The magic of Christmas swirls around us as we dance and hold each other close. The smell of Jack hasn't changed. Underneath the new cologne he's wearing, I still smell dryer sheets and cookies.

He kisses the top of my hair. I lift my head; Jack's smiling brown eyes melt my heart. He whispers in my ear, "I love you, Sunday Foster."

"Still?" I whisper.

"Always and forever."

The computer screen is blank as my fingers rest on the keyboard. Time to write my college essay. The three most challenging questions in front of me invoke a book of complicated answers.

1. What does #YOLO mean to you?
2. How has your family background affected the way you see the world?
3. Write about one decision you made, that you have changed your mind about in the last three years?

Wow, where do I begin?

I could write a book.

Epilogue: A college campus, somewhere in the northwest

A classic fall day greets me. I roll my bike into a small motorcycle area in the heart of one of the most prestigious college campuses in the Mid-West. The heat of the yellow ball in the sky is a welcome distraction from the activity on the ground. Leaves on the towering trees are turning to the warmth of the sun, transitioning to their final effort: brilliant reds. I like the red leaves. Red is power. Red is death.

Soon they will turn to their last vibrant moment and with a gust of wind will fall to the ground. They will shrivel up, crumble and die.

Dead.

The towering green pines are swaying in a silent dance, melodic and mesmerizing in the breeze, while falling leaves create the illusion of chaos being thrown from above, signaling an occurrence, a great event is about to begin.

Even nature is celebrating my arrival. I lean back on the seat of my bike and I glance in the rearview mirror, checking out my left side profile, then my right. Who is this handsome guy? I pull my long hair back into a ponytail. I'm even unrecognizable to myself, with my own blue-colored-contact eyes.

That's okay: this is a college land of opportunity. Students unload their beat-up cars filled to the top with their belongings, hoisting packed boxes that won't close and pulling suitcases across the cobblestone paths and green lawns of a postcard perfect oak grove.

Guys are helping beautiful girls carry their heavy luggage up the winding stairs and they are exchanging names. Exaggerated laughter, shoulders puffed back and low-cut shirts.

I study the bookworms, the chubby, heavier-built girls sweating as they make the tenth trip up the same set of wicked steps with no help. Just wait until they gain the freshman fifteen. A few may change, get in shape, modify their appearance, and discover who they really are. It's unlikely but possible. Depends on how much strength they have, determination, and grit.

It can happen, I know. I'll watch out for those.

They are the special ones.

The fall semester is about to begin. The freshman class is moving in. The triumph of being alive to participate in the dawning of a new year is invigorating. It is contagious. On these hallowed grounds, future leaders will be born, created from diversity, determination, and hard work. Others will slide by with a fistful of dollars and Daddy's good name.

I'll spot those slick trust fund babies easily. Oh yeah, I'll find them.

Students are full of laughter, anxious to start what they believe will be the best times of their lives. The mystery of what lies before them is enticing.

Some looking for the easy road, while others are looking for all the answers.

I can't relate.

I know the answers. I've been down this road before.

Heartaches will happen. A fraternity brother will sweep a young freshman off her feet and break her heart less than twenty-four hours after he takes her virginity. A perky blonde will smile at a nerdy loser in class, ask for his help, and then not acknowledge him in a group of her peers. Cliques will form, friends will be made, and enemies will be chosen.

The bullying has already started.

Even on this beautiful day, right now, there's a group of freshman jerks who will laugh a little too loud with a cocky city boy, taunting the farm boy with his broken-down suitcase and short pants. Others wanting to belong will look down at their clothes, wondering where they match up, and then will laugh with the bullies, trying to pick their sides before they don't have a choice.

And every day the sun will rise again. But, it's time for a new change.

I know this to be true.

I know what lies ahead for these cliques.

I'm watching, deciding what side I'm going to pick; for on this day, I have choices. I can fit in where I choose.

I've done my homework. I've watched and listened to the most popular frat boys, bought the right clothes, and created my door into the cool. I'm into studying the human mind, excited to analyze the actions of freshmen and unravel the puzzle of their brains. No one will know who I truly am... until one day, when it's too late.

I'll shock them all.

When the moment is perfect.

Amir James Carter is dead. I know this to be true because I am Amir James Carter. Did he kill himself?

No, not suicide: pseudocide. Amir no longer exists.

No one can find him.
I made sure of that.

Resources

If you have experienced bullying, a school shooting, date rape, sexual assault, verbal or physical abuse you are not alone. Try talking to someone.

International
  https://teencentral.com/

USA
  National Safe Place has created TXT 4 HELP Interactive, which allows youth to text live with a mental health professional.
  Go To URL: http://nationalsafeplace.org/text-4-help/(link is external)
  Agency: Dept. of Health and Human Services
  Audience:
  High School/Young Adult: 14 to 24 years
  Middle School: 11 to 13 years
  Youth - All Ages

loveisrespect.org
  Highly-trained advocates offer support, information and advocacy to young people who have questions or concerns

about their dating relationships.

Peer Advocate Line: 1-866-331-9474.

https://www.saysomething.net/

Say Something is a youth violence prevention program from Sandy Hook Promise (SHP). SHP is a national, nonprofit organization led by several family members whose loved ones were killed in the tragic mass shooting at Sandy Hook School on December 14, 2012. SHP is focused on preventing gun violence (and other forms of violence and victimization) BEFORE it happens. Call the hotline or text all anonymously.

Conclusion

Dear Cherished Reader,
I'm absolutely thrilled that you've journeyed through the pages of "Her Perfect Disappearance"! Your choice to spend time with my characters means the world to me, and I hope their story captivated you as much as it did me while writing it.
If the book resonated with you, I'd be over the moon if you could share your thoughts in a review. Your words have the power to guide other readers to this story, creating a wonderful ripple effect in our reading community. You can easily leave your review HERE

I read and treasure each and every review, savoring the unique perspectives they offer. They're like little windows into how the story touched different hearts – and if you loved this book, know that you're the very reader I had in mind while crafting it. As a small press author, your support through reviews and recommendations is incredibly precious.
Here's an exciting opportunity: if you're intrigued about Hudson's fate and would love to shape future stories, I invite you to join my Seaside Readers Facebook group www.facebook.com/groups/seasidereaders/. If you're interested, you might even be chosen as a beta reader for my

upcoming book!
I absolutely love connecting with readers like you. Feel free to reach out through the Seaside Readers group or visit my website at www.AKSmithAuthor.com for more bookish adventures.
Thank you again for choosing to read "Her Perfect Disappearance." I'm honored to have you as a reader.

Warmest wishes,
AK Smith

P.S. If you'd like to stay updated on new releases and exclusive content, you can sign up for my newsletter www.aksmithauthor.com I promise to keep your inbox filled with only the most exciting bookish news!

Acknowledgments

There are so many wonderful people to thank for the final edition of Her Perfect Disappearance. First, I have to thank my husband, Darrell(aka Diego). As you might imagine, being married to a writer isn't always the easiest partnership. Writing is a solitary job, and I write from wherever home is. I'm blessed to have a partner who understands and supports my passion. Thank you for never freaking out as I researched "how to fake your own death". Your enthusiasm and love are amazing.

I'm blessed to be the youngest of six children and have an incredible mother. Thank you Mom, Coleen, Iris, Lisa and my brother Pete for your support and advice. Coleen, you're awesome for constantly re-reading various drafts, and believing in this story! I can't thank you enough.

As for my wonderful friends who read the first draft and gave advice, thank you. Judy Brinkhurst, Susan Ciardullo, Janine and Michael Wehner, Karla Engel, Cheri Jones, Marcia Brockmeyer, Shonna Andrews and teacher Stephanie Cook. Thank you goes out to my teen (at the time) beta readers, Mckenna Rafferty, Avalon Andrews and Ashley Kennedy. Special thanks to my awesome supporters and friends, Tracy Grandas, Jill Dumin, Nell Tosetto, Corb Harding, Jan Powell and Pam Lindley, I thank you for always being excited and spreading the word about my books.

A very special thank you goes out to Amanda Gin (and Sophia & Durwin). Amanda you are amazing, and I can't thank you enough for all your input! I can't wait to see your future after high school. I'm certain you can and will do something awesome in this world!

Jessica Lee Anderson, we may have only met over Zoom during the pandemic, but I feel so lucky to have found you as an editor. You are wonderful— your input is invaluable. I can't wait to keep working together. Thank you for loving my book.

And, for all aspiring writers, *keep writing.* Need help getting started? Create a goal to set a timer each day, and write for 30 minutes a day, write and write, and don't give up. Your story will come alive. Subscribe to my writers help newsletter at seasidewriter.com.

A note from the author

Thoughts of writing *Her Perfect Disappearance* began in 2015. I read an article about a man who faked his death, and then got caught. I reasoned, if I was ever going to fake my own death, I would never get caught.

Why would one want to fake their death? Typically to start over, to escape something terrible, and in my personal opinion, a much better choice than suicide. When I was younger I had the mindset—before I would ever think about killing myself— I would reinvent myself. Unfortunately, I've had people in my life, who thought of, gestured, or attempted suicide. I prayed then, and still do with all my heart, that they would change their life instead. Okay, not to the extreme of faking your death, but to reach out and get help, and reinvent yourself. There are resources in the back of this book for anyone who has these thoughts. Talk to someone, seek help and stick around. The world needs you. Reinventing yourself is a much better choice than leaving this planet.

There are numerous stories in history of men and women faking their death and starting over again. As technology progresses, and humans create more and more digital footprints, it will become difficult to accomplish this. We are tracked by our digital footprint.

Because of technology, and for the integrity of the story, my main character had to be young. Digital footprint of an adult is much harder to erase. The first few drafts were written before the pandemic, and as the pandemic of 2020 exploded, I tried to rewrite the manuscript and set it during pandemic times. It didn't work. In the year of the pandemic, we are all more connected by technology than ever before; even children with online learning.

As I googled 'how to fake your death', 'school shooting' and 'radical and domestic terrorism' theories, I was concerned what my digital footprint must look like! My wish is to take my readers on a journey from Sunday's point of view. I hope this book makes you realize all the tough situations teenagers face. There are strong social issues such as bullying, racism, sexual assault, domestic abuse and gun violence, which unfortunately are all too real in today's world. For anyone who has experienced any of those issues, please know you are not alone. **Talk to someone**.

Book Club Discussion

Thank you wonderful readers. I know there are millions of books out there, and I am honored you read mine. If you have chosen to read *Pseudocide* as your next book club selection, or book discussion, invite me to attend your event.

If you are interested, I have committed (free of charge) to attend 10 book club Zoom calls, Facetime meetings, or phone calls each month. If you would like to have me virtually attend 30 minutes of your next book club, writers group meeting or school event, please email me at aksmithbook@gmail.com to get scheduled.

I love themed book club discussions. For *Pseudocide,* you could try to recreate one of the menus Sunday experienced. Of course there's always road trip food, chips, pretzels, protein bars and candy. But, if you want to recrcate the Gamblers Special, go to my website aksmithauthor.com for the recipes. You could also ask all attendee's to wear a disguise. How you would recreate yourself, if you were going to fake your death.

To help your book club discussion, below are some questions you might want to ask:

1. If you decided to fake your own death, where would you

escape to?

2. If you decided to fake your own death, how would you do it?
3. Describe Sunday. In what way does her family environment impact her life choices?
4. Describe Hudson. What five words would you use to describe him?
5. Do you think Hudson falls in love with Sunday/Hannah?
6. To what extent does the family dynamics influence each character?
7. Were you surprised about how Sunday faked her death?
8. What do you think Sunday learns at the end of the novel?
9. What do you think about Sunday's parents? Jack parents? Hudson's parents? Amir's parents?
10. What do you think happens to Amir?
11. Do *you* have a *tell*?

About the Author

Full of wanderlust and a professional sunset watcher, A.K. Smith writes books that will keep you up late. An avid traveler, she travels to find new settings to feature in her novels. If she's not on the water or in the water, she is looking at the water. She spends her days working remotely online in either Mexico or Arizona. Her big loves are her husband, family, friends, and kindness. Her goal is to step foot on every continent on Planet Earth—she's slowly getting there

Follow her on social media (www.facebook.com/groups/seasidereaders/) or join her newsletter at aksmithauthor.com

For fans of suspense and adventure lovers of all types. Check out A. K. Smith's debut award winning novel, "A Deep Thing" Readers Favorite Gold Medal Winner.

You can connect with me on:

- https://www.aksmithauthor.com
- https://www.twitter.com/aksmithbook
- https://www.facebook.com/aksmithauthor
- https://www.pinterest.com/aksmithbook
- https://www.instagram.com/aksmithbook

Also by A.K. Smith

Please check out my website AKSmithauthor.com for updates and giveaways. If you took the chance to write a review, Thank YOU, authors really appreciate every review!

A Deep Thing

Readers Favorite Award- Gold Medal Winner

Dive into A Deep Thing

A suspense conspiracy adventure novel full of twists and turns.

Love - Lies- Secrets and the possibilities of the What if's?

5 stars "Such an intriguing story that I couldn't put it down. If you are looking for a great summer read, you have found it". -**Amazon Customer**

What WAS her husband hiding in the jungles of Mexico?

From the campus of Western Maryland College to the woods of Camp David and the caves of the Yucatán, a widow and her step-son take a journey to discover what her husband worked so hard to hide, and to protect his treasured secrets from falling into the wrong hands. The choices they make will decide their fate and the future of others. Will they risk everything for the truth?

Available on **Amazon and other fine booksellers**